Kiss and Cry

Also by Keira Andrews

Gay Amish Romance Series
A Forbidden Rumspringa
A Clean Break
A Way Home
A Very English Christmas

Contemporary
Kiss and Cry
Only One Bed
Merry Cherry Christmas
The Christmas Deal
Ends of the Earth
Flash Rip
Swept Away (free read!)
Santa Daddy
Honeymoon for One
Valor on the Move
Test of Valor
Cold War
In Case of Emergency
Eight Nights in December
The Next Competitor
Arctic Fire
Reading the Signs
Beyond the Sea
If Only in My Dreams
Where the Lovelight Gleams
The Chimera Affair
Love Match
Synchronicity (free read!)

Historical
Kidnapped by the Pirate
The Station
Semper Fi
Voyageurs (free read!)

Paranormal
Kick at the Darkness
Fight the Tide
Taste of Midnight (free read!)

Fantasy
Wed to the Barbarian
The Barbarian's Vow
Levity
Rise
Flight

Box Sets
Complete Valor Duology
Gay Romance Holiday Collection

Kiss and Cry

KEIRA ANDREWS

Kiss and Cry
Written and published by Keira Andrews
Cover by Dar Albert
Formatting by BB eBooks

Copyright © 2022 by Keira Andrews
Print Edition

ISBN: 978-1-988260-66-2

This is a work of fiction. Names, characters, businesses, places, events and incidents are either the products of the author's imagination or used in a fictitious manner. No persons, living or dead, were harmed by the writing of this book. Any resemblance to any actual persons, living or dead, or actual events is purely coincidental.

Acknowledgments

Many thanks to Leta Blake, Anara, Mary, and Rai for their cheerleading and help in making this book its best.

Special thanks to Elizabeth for her insights on growing up Japanese Canadian.

I've been a skating fan for decades, and it's always a joy to write about the sport. Any similarities to real skaters and coaches is entirely unintentional and coincidental.

Chapter One

Henry

THAT SAYING ABOUT the exception proving the rule was true. As a rule, I didn't hate my competitors. Like most athletes, I hated losing, especially when my performance should have been better. But sometimes, I admired my rivals. Sometimes, I was jealous of them. Sometimes, I would have liked to be friends if I had time for friendship.

Not Theodore Sullivan.

I hated him. Loathed. Despised. Detested. Abhorred. I could have gone on—I had an excellent vocabulary. When I was a child, people said it was ironic I loved words since I spoke so little. (I'd quickly given up trying to correct the rampant misuse of the word "ironic.") What they didn't understand was that the less you spoke, the safer you were from saying the wrong thing.

Manon was still talking, and I tried to focus through the red haze of resentment. I must not have heard her correctly over the rush of blood in my ears.

I blurted, "Pardon?"

Sitting shoulder-to-shoulder on the love seat in the corner of their office, Manon and Bill shared a glance. Even for married people, my coaches had impressive silent communication. I didn't always know what they were thinking, but I recognized the wary expression that meant: *Henry isn't going to like this.*

The knot in my stomach tightened. I sat frozen on the mismatched couch across from them, my socked feet gripping the shaggy throw rug I liked to use for strengthening toe scrunches. My throat had gone dry, but I couldn't even move enough to grab my water bottle off the ring-stained coffee table between us. The lack of coasters had always baffled me, but the wood was too far gone now anyway.

"Theo wants to join our training center." In Manon's Quebecois accent, the name sounded like "Teo," and for a moment I let myself dream that perhaps she was talking about another figure skater. *Any* other skater.

But it could only be Theodore Sullivan, especially judging by the little grimace creasing Manon's face. She seemed to be waiting for me to react badly.

She said, "We know it's last minute and probably a bit of a shock, and of course we're having this sit-down with you before we give him an answer."

"Sit-downs" always happened in this corner of the cramped office in the arena basement. Manon sounded calm and measured, her hands clasped loosely in her lap. Her nails were glossy with a deep purple polish that matched the big hoops in her ears.

She had dark brown skin and kept her afro short, and she must have owned hundreds of pairs of earrings. Even in her usual black leggings and hoodie, she looked far too glamorous for the saggy leather love seat and ugly red rug.

And too glamorous for Bill, if I were being honest, but they worked somehow. His blond hair was almost gray and in need of a cut. While Manon made workout gear look elegant, Bill reminded me of my dad puttering in the garage on weekends. He'd gotten too much sun; his nose was burned a distracting red. He really needed to use sunscreen.

Bill smiled in the encouraging way he did when I was about to try my shaky quad Lutz. "It could be the best thing for you to train with one of your biggest competitors."

Incorrect. The best thing for me was Theodore Sullivan on the other side of the continent. "But he trains in California. It's too late for such a big change."

"Making this move at the end of September isn't ideal," Bill said, holding his meaty hands out wide. "But we have more than four months until the Olympics."

"A hundred and twenty-nine days," I said automatically. "He can't change coaches now."

I swiped at my bangs impatiently. My hair was sweaty from my morning jump drills, and it flopped into my face. When I styled it, my bangs made a neat swoop, but I was due for a cut.

I was fortunate to have thick hair, and my grandma still mentioned how naturally black it was. Obaachan grew up in Japan and had always dyed her brown hair jet black.

"We wouldn't even consider taking on Theo if we thought this would harm your training. It's going to fuel you." Manon's brown eyes lit up as she leaned forward. "This is the final key in your Olympic preparation. It won't be easy, but this will make you stronger."

"You know how many recent world and Olympic champions trained with their fiercest rivals," Bill said. "Look at the Russians. That daily motivation and competition is powerful stuff. I wish like hell I'd had it back in my day."

Bill had once been Canadian men's champion, although he'd be the first to admit he only won that year because the favorites messed up. Still, he'd gone to Worlds a few times and had made an Olympic team. He'd become known as one of the best jump technicians in coaching, second perhaps only to the legendary Walter Webber, who'd been his coach.

"I have competition here. Ivan is almost landing his quad Sal. He's a national champion."

Manon raised a narrow eyebrow. "You know as well as we do that Ivan represents Ukraine because he's not strong enough to make the Russian team. We're very proud of how far he's come, but he's not a medal contender."

"If Julien was old enough to compete as a senior, he could be." My heart thumped. This wasn't part of the plan. Theodore Sullivan coming to Toronto to train was *not the plan*.

Bill said, "True, but he's not, and Theo is currently ranked number one in the world."

I was very, very aware of that fact. "But you're *my* coaches." I cringed at my plaintive tone. I was an adult. I shouldn't have an emotional reaction to this news. Skating and coaching were a business.

Their faces softened, and Manon reached across the ring-stained table to briefly squeeze my hand. "We are. And we're committed to helping you be your very best. You know we love you, Henry."

The saggy love seat springs creaked as I squirmed, dropping my gaze and nodding. Manon spoke so openly about *love* and feelings, but it made me want to be anywhere else. Not that I didn't appreciate it and reciprocate her affection, but did it really have to be said aloud?

"He's been taking from Mr. Webber for a long time." I thought back and calculated. "Four years. He won Worlds in March. There's no reason to switch coaches."

You didn't change the formula when you were winning, and I could bitterly confirm that Theodore Sullivan had been undefeated the past two seasons.

They shared another look, this one serious and sad. Bill blew out a long breath. For a terrible moment, his perpetually chapped lips quivered, and I thought he might cry. "This isn't public knowledge yet, but Mr. Webber's been diagnosed with pancreatic cancer. He needs to start aggressive treatment immediately."

My heart sank. "Oh."

Even though Bill was in his late forties, he still called his old coach "Mr. Webber" like he had as a pupil and as most everyone in the skating world did. Many coaches were known by their first names, but Mr. Webber was a legend. He was almost eighty now and had always seemed indestructible.

When I was younger, I'd dreamed of being coached by him, but when I had to leave Vancouver three years ago, Theodore Sullivan was Mr. Webber's star pupil. I hadn't even considered training with my archrival. Having to see him and his careless smile and natural jumping ability daily? No.

"You can imagine how upset Theo is." Manon shook her head. "It's a shock for everyone. Mr. Webber sounds in good spirits, though. He's going to fight this."

"You talked to him?"

Bill nodded. "He called us yesterday to ask personally if we'd take on Theo."

My heart sank all the way down through the ugly shag rug. How could I say no?

Manon seemed to read my mind. "We realize we're putting you in a tough spot. But we truly believe this is the extra training push you need."

"I'm going to beat him."

I'd imagined seeing my name in first place over Theodore Sullivan for years. Gold: Henry Sakaguchi, Canada. Silver: Theodore Sullivan, USA. Or sometimes he didn't even make the podium. I imagined wiping that infuriating smirk off his perfectly symmetrical face.

Manon grinned. "That's the confidence we love to see. Our job is to train you both to be your best, and then it's up to the judges. It's a win-win if you two can push each other to new heights."

I wanted very badly to argue, but they were right. I'd been the top skater at the Ice Chalet the three years I'd trained here. I knew I couldn't be childish about the idea of *my* coaches helping the competition. It was the norm in skating these days.

"What's the verdict?" Bill asked. "Of course we understand if you want to sleep on it."

It was selfish to deny Manon and Bill the prestige and potential income that would accompany coaching another world champion. Even if it plagued me that while we were tied at two titles apiece, he'd beaten me the last two years running. He had the momentum and was the favorite going into these Olympics.

It was selfish to deny them even if I hated Theodore Sullivan.

I thought of Mr. Webber being sick, and my skin prickled with a hot rush of guilt. Manon and Bill waited for me to respond, though Bill's foot tapped on the rug, jiggling his knee.

They were good about giving me time to find the right words, but I could see the tension in their bodies. They wanted this opportunity. Really, they didn't have to ask me at all—they were the coaches and this was their business. If I didn't like it, I could hire someone else.

But I didn't want anyone else. Where could I even go at this point? My old coach in Vancouver would probably take me back, but… I quickly shut down thoughts of returning to that particular arena.

What if I ran into *him* in the locker room? My stomach lurched. It was bad enough to be dealing with Theodore Sullivan—I didn't need to think about my humiliation in Vancouver too.

I nodded, and they exhaled in a rush.

"You won't regret this." Manon's grin gleamed.

"But he's not disciplined."

They shared another glance before Manon said, "It's true that Theo is blessed with an abundance of natural talent and perhaps not such a strong work ethic. You'll be an excellent influence in that regard. And he'll get under your skin with his ability to toss off quads at the drop of a hat."

That I could certainly agree with.

"It's going to be great," Bill said. "This is the Olympic season, and we're turning it up to eleven!"

That was one of Bill's favorite references, from an old movie I'd never seen. I nodded miserably.

Manon frowned. "There's no issue with Theo we should know about, is there? Aside from beating you sometimes. He hasn't been unkind, has he?"

I shook my head. Though we'd never been *friends*, he was unfailingly friendly, which was honestly infuriating because it made it more difficult to resent him. I still managed.

We were rivals, and I'd prefer it greatly if he'd ignore me the way I tried to ignore him. Win or lose, he was the same, smiling and cracking jokes. All the way back to our junior days, I couldn't recall him ever being upset about anything.

I said, "It's time for cardio."

"So it is." Bill patted his stomach under his worn T-shirt. "I should race you and burn off those Timbits."

He said that often but never did. I was relieved as I escaped upstairs and laced my running shoes so tightly I had to redo them or risk the blood flow to my toes. I jumped over a pothole in the Ice Chalet's parking lot as I jogged out.

The arena's brick had been decorated with mountains in the eighties, and I could still make out the edges of a snowy peak in the corner where it hadn't been painted over properly.

Cars whizzed by on the road, some turning into the plaza across the street. The Shoppers pharmacy drew most people, though I heard from other skaters the tiny roti restaurant had excellent food. I'd try it if I ever allowed a cheat day.

A few of the storefronts were up for rent, and the wholesale flooring warehouse was going out of business. The grassy field next to the plaza had a big sign saying another subdivision of identical houses was coming.

Past the field was a trail that led down into a woodland valley I hoped would never be sold for tract housing. I counted my inhalations and exhalations as I descended, leaping over roots, a few dry leaves crunching beneath my feet.

It was still mostly green, and birds chirped in the mid-morning sunlight. I usually only listened to music while running when there were other people around who might want to talk to me.

Today, Theodore Sullivan barged into my meditative focus of breath and footsteps and forest sounds.

"There's no issue with Theo we should know about, is there?"

I could have told them he was a distraction. It was the truth— I stumbled as the path twisted toward the tall maples crowding the valley floor and wanted to shout, *"See?!"* as I caught my balance and increased my stride, my footsteps thudding on the earth.

But I couldn't tell them all the reasons Theodore was an issue. I couldn't confess that on the eve of the free skate at the junior world championships when I was fourteen, I'd seen Theodore Sullivan and his new body hair naked in the communal shower room in a concrete Croatian arena.

I'd still been small for my age, but he was sixteen and had had a growth spurt in…every way imaginable. Our eyes had met after he caught me gaping. After he'd spotted my erection.

And he'd smirked.

He'd *laughed*. Carelessly. Light and airy as though nothing mattered. When *everything* mattered.

I'd run, shampoo still lathered in my hair, and yanked on a winter hat and sweats over my wet body. I'd always been focused on skating and school, and I was so confused by the new desires that were inconvenient at best.

I'd had an extremely explicit and detailed dream that night of

Theodore. The next day, I'd blown my lead from the short program and missed both my triple Axels. I'd ended up with bronze—barely—while he took gold, and the worst part was that I couldn't stop thinking about him.

Couldn't stop thinking about kissing him. Doing…more. I wasn't even sure what, but doing *everything* with him. I'd been reluctantly attracted to boys before that moment in the shower room, but actors on TV weren't *real*.

Wet, naked Theodore had been very, very real.

I'd apparently imprinted on him like an infant duck, much to my horror and humiliation. Other people seemed to shrug off embarrassing incidents and blithely forget them, but I couldn't fathom how.

Even now, my heart pounding as I raced through the trees in an outlying Toronto suburb nine years later—*nine years*—I imagined what grown-up Theodore would look like wet and naked.

Light brown hair, thick lips, dimples, lean muscles, and dark hair scattered over his pale chest, accentuating pink nipples. A trail of hair below his navel leading down to…

I roared in frustration, sending a flock of birds flapping out of a birch tree. I shouldn't have been thinking about this. Normally I could quell this sort of distraction. Though occasionally, I'd been tempted to finally shrug off what had happened the first time I let down my guard and trusted a guy…

Acid flooded my stomach with the surge of familiar anxiety. I wanted to crawl into a hole with the shame of it, which was pitiful all on its own. It'd been three years and eight-point-five months.

I'd left Vancouver. I was an adult now—twenty-four. I should have been able to put that incident behind me. I shouldn't have felt like I was still a gullible teenage virgin.

The ground was soft in a shady gully with a few lingering puddles from rain the day before. My shoes squelched as I ran and ran, my head a jumbled mess. Theodore Sullivan had nothing to do with my humiliation in Vancouver. I had to focus.

My stubborn, pathetic attraction to Theodore didn't top the list of why I hated him. No, the worst thing was that it all came so easily for him.

He didn't follow the unwritten rules. He was famous for skipping practice. For partying. For making a joke out of hard work by winning anyway with undeniable natural talent. He made a joke of the blood, sweat, and tears I'd dedicated to skating my whole life.

It wasn't *fair*.

And I knew my resentment was petty and beneath me, but he seemed to have this way of charming everyone, including the judges. It was natural to be jealous of other skaters once in a while. But they worked hard. They didn't get PCS handed to them on a silver platter like Theodore. Our program component scores were supposed to reflect artistry and skating skills.

My component scores should have been higher due to the quality of my musicality, deep edges, and transitions between elements—but with every quad he landed, his PCS went up. The two scores shouldn't really be related, but the better you were at jumping, suddenly your artistry improved in the judges' eyes too.

It had taken a lot of work with my sports psychologist not to obsess about how the judges scored me. So much of it was politics and which federation had which judges in its pocket. Still, it was a challenge not to examine Theodore's scores with gritted teeth.

Every tenth of a point had grated. For years.

I was an excellent jumper, but that was because I worked at it constantly. He'd seemed to learn new quads overnight and started reeling off quad-triple combinations like they were nothing. He'd stopped losing concentration and rushing takeoffs.

Now I'd be stuck with him in my face every day being charming and perfect and lazy and gorgeous and infuriating.

Taking a deep breath, I raced up the other side of the ravine, legs burning and sweat sticking my T-shirt to my back. Manon and Bill were right. This was the final push I needed. I hated Theodore Sullivan, and I was going to use every ounce of that loathing to fuel me straight to the top of the podium.

Chapter Two

Theo

THE HAIR OF the dog theory was bullshit.

I nursed my pint of some local IPA the airport bar was pushing, ordering myself not to puke. LAX was crowded—shocker—but at least I'd snagged a stool, squeezed between a man in a cheap suit and a bleached-blonde woman wearing too much flowery perfume. I should have known better when Emily suggested we all go out for "just one drink" as a bon voyage.

I figured I deserved one last night out with my training mates, especially since Toronto was going to be all business. If it wasn't the Olympic season, there was no way I'd voluntarily spend every day with Henry Sakaguchi, but Mr. Webber really wanted me to go.

My fingers slid on the condensation as I took a gulp of beer, and I almost dropped the glass. My throat was too tight, and I coughed, pretending that's why my eyes were watering. Cheap Suit shot me a glare, and I pretended he was a Ukrainian judge and gave him my most charming smile.

It was a game I played when I was traveling—deciding which strangers were the judges from various countries. The woman who reeked of roses could have been an Australian judge who randomly showed up on panels sometimes. The bartender with a man bun was too young to be a judge, but he did have nice forearms displayed as he poured a pint.

There. I wasn't going to cry. Mr. Webber was going to be okay. He wasn't giving up and neither were the doctors. I felt like an asshole abandoning him—if I stayed, maybe I could do something to help, though I had no clue what.

But he wanted me to go train with the Richardsons, so I'd do it. And he was going to beat the odds. And I wasn't going to cry every time I thought about not having him by the boards giving me that impatient-but-fond glare.

My phone buzzed in my pocket. I knew who it was before I looked, and I guessed it was time to bite the bullet. The bar was so noisy with people talking and *Sports Center* on the TVs that I didn't walk away to answer.

"Hey, Mom."

"Where are you?"

"Waiting for my boarding call."

She exhaled noisily. "I don't like this."

"I know, but it's not up to you." How many times could we have the same conversation? A zillion, apparently.

"I'm still your mother." If she were next to me instead of Cheap Suit and Blonde Perfume, she would have jabbed my arm as she said it.

"Of course you are. But this is my career. I pay for my training now. I make the decisions." It had been the only way Mr. Webber would take me on four years ago after I stupidly failed to make the Olympic team. No skating mothers allowed at his rink second-guessing and butting in. "It'll be fine."

"*Fine?*" She sighed dramatically. "Sometimes I think you don't even want to win."

I gulped my beer, drowning my first response to tell her: *no shit.* "Of course I want to win," I said dutifully. And I did.

I mean, why wouldn't I? I had the talent to win. Winning was fun. Winning was good for endorsements and my future income doing tours. But I'd never wanted it as much as my mother. I'd never wanted it at all costs.

"Why would you train with the one person who can take the gold away from you?"

"Because that's what Mr. Webber wants. And you know how successful it's been for other skaters. Look at the past decade or more in ice dancing. Practically the whole top ten train together. And look at the Russian pairs."

She grunted. Even my mother couldn't argue with the Russian pairs' sweep of the podium at the last Worlds. The three teams had the same coach and pretty much hated each other, but boy did the tension push them to new heights.

"I don't want you distracted by Sakaguchi. He can beat you."

"Henry's, like, the least fun person on the planet. No passion. He's like an alien but the most boring extra-terrestrial imaginable."

"You can't let down your guard. No making friends this time."

I rolled my eyes. She'd always hated that I was friendly with everyone. She was going to criticize my lack of "killer instinct" any minute. "Henry can't stand me. I'm the last person on Earth he's going to hang out with."

"He works harder than you." She muttered reluctantly, "Maybe he'll be a good influence."

I shrugged, though she couldn't see me. "Maybe. Mom, Henry Sakaguchi is irrelevant. I know I can beat him. I beat him in March at Worlds, and I'll beat him again. I'm going to win gold in Calgary."

She made a humming noise that sounded dubious. "You don't have the killer instinct. He does."

There it was. "And I'm still beating him because I have more quads." How many times could we have this debate?

"And he keeps himself to himself."

I gritted my teeth. This was her code for "*Henry doesn't talk about being gay on Instagram.*" She honestly didn't have a problem with me being queer, but she'd been dead set against me coming out since the skating establishment could still be stupidly homophobic.

But I was out, I wasn't going back in, and it hadn't been an issue. I was currently the best jumper in the world, and even the most bigoted judge couldn't argue with my quads. The judges had been firmly behind me the past couple of seasons.

"That's because no one's interested in Henry's love life. He doesn't have one from what I've heard." Yeah, he was good-looking, but too cold to be hot.

It was widely known in the skating world that Henry was gay—he'd informed people at his old training center some years ago—but it was never mentioned in the media or whatever. It wasn't a secret, but it also wasn't *official*.

I added, "Besides, I'm not the only out person in skating. Alex Grady, Matt Savelli. It's changing every day. Especially after Dev Avira and Misha Reznikov went public."

"They weren't competing anymore when they came out."

"Yeah, well, the times have changed."

She grudgingly admitted, "It seems so. Which I'm happy about, of course!"

"Uh-huh."

"You know the facilities won't compare to what you have in LA."

"It's cheaper for ice time and there's a new hockey arena close by, so there's more time available."

As if she didn't hear me, she said, "Or you know there's a new arena here in Chicago. I ran into Pavel the other day in the deli section, and he said he'd love to take you back."

I bit back a laugh at the thought of my mom stalking my old

coach through Mariano's, peeking out from behind a rack of flatbreads, ready to pounce. Never let it be said that Patricia Sullivan wasn't dedicated to her son's career. "That's so sweet of him, but I left Pavel for a reason."

She huffed. "It wasn't his fault you didn't make the team."

Yes, I knew damn well that I'd lost focus at Nationals that year and fell on two of my jumping passes in the short program. After a mediocre Grand Prix season that fall, I'd needed to nail Nationals. "I didn't say it was his fault!"

Breathe.

Blonde Perfume was side-eyeing me, and I took another breath, watching a basketball replay on the TV. "Pavel's great, but I'm going to Bill and Manon."

"If you have to go to Toronto instead of coming home to your family, why don't you ask Elena Cheremisinova?"

"Because she's focusing on ice dancing these days. She hasn't had a male contender since Alex Grady won Worlds. Most importantly, Mr. Webber wants me to go to Bill and Manon. It might be the last thing—" My throat closed again. Fuck, I refused to cry. "I trust his judgment."

"Did Melody tell you she was in the ninety-ninth percentile in the mock SAT?"

I was used to her abrupt changes in topic now. She used to argue with me for hours, but since I'd packed up and moved to LA to train with Mr. Webber, forbidding her from coming along, she'd eventually learned when to give up. Well, once she'd started talking to me again, which had taken almost a year.

"Yeah, she did amazing. She'll crush the real thing, don't worry."

"I'm not worried. Veronica and Melody are very focused. Your sisters have never disappointed me."

Gritting my teeth, I kept my voice light. "I'm so proud of them."

She couldn't argue with that. "Where are you going to be living in Toronto?"

"In a basement apartment with a meth lab upstairs."

"So cruel to your mother."

Before she could launch into all the ways I'd disappointed her or made her worry, I said, "They're calling my flight. I love you, Mom. I'll text when I get to Toronto. Say hi to Dad and the girls."

"Count the rows to the nearest exit. If the cabin fills with smoke, you'll thank me." She hung up.

I drained my glass and motioned to Man Bun Bartender for another.

THE ICE CHALET really was like something out of the eighties with the purple and orange racing stripes painted along the walls surrounding the rink. There were no boards, just a step down onto the ice, and all heads swiveled my way as I took off my guards and tossed them on a bench.

Crap. I was later than I realized. I shook off the thought of Mr. Webber's disapproving frown and gave the assembled skaters on the ice my biggest smile as I glided over to join the group.

Bill and Manon stood before the skaters with a couple of assistants I recognized vaguely. The ten or so students ranged in age from about twelve to early twenties. Most of them smiled back at me, one little girl clearly starstruck. I gave her a wink.

Bill said, "There you are. Remember we start and finish every week with an early team session."

"Right, right. Sorry—still jet-lagged." Which was the truth! Although I also hadn't practiced at seven in the morning for years. Mr. Webber had accepted that I wasn't a morning person. Manon had emailed me a weekly schedule, but I hadn't looked closely at it. Or at all aside from noting I had to be here way too early on Monday.

As Bill introduced me to the other skaters, I was aware of Henry Sakaguchi's disapproving stare boring into me. He and my mother could exchange notes on their techniques. Naturally, I gave him my best smile as Bill came to him last.

"And you know Henry, of course."

"Hey, man!" I held up my hand for a high five because it would probably piss him off.

Wearing a typical practice outfit very similar to mine—black skating pants and a long-sleeved black athletic shirt—Henry stared at me, his arms still crossed over his chest. Not breaking even a hint of a smile, he barely slapped my palm since apparently even Henry's alien leaders had taught him you couldn't leave someone hanging.

Manon announced, "All right, let's start with bubbles."

I blinked in surprise as everyone—including Henry—fell into line along the ice, moving their feet in and out rhythmically to form big circles. This was something we'd learned as little kids.

Manon said to me, "We always start with the basics. Knee action and balance for a strong foundation. Skate *in* the ice, not on it."

I wanted to argue that I'd learned the basics many years ago, but it was my first day, so I joined in, feeling a little ridiculous. Manon had been an ice dancer back in the day, so it made sense that she focused on edges and fundamentals. But I could have slept in and skipped this.

After a ton of bubbles, we moved on to edges. Again, this was basic stuff. I peered at Henry tracing an old-fashioned figure eight. They'd abolished compulsory figures at competitions before we were born—thank God—but I bet Henry would have crushed them. I couldn't imagine how boring it would be to practice these for hours on end.

I forced myself to concentrate and carved out my figure eight, my blades curving and gliding. I wasn't known for my finesse, but that was because jumps were way more important and fun to practice. This was dull.

Manon nodded. "*Très bon*, Theo. You're such a natural."

It was true—I'd taken to the ice like a duck to water as a kid tagging along to my sister Veronica's skating lessons. She was two years younger than me, and I was supposed to have been playing hockey in the rink next door, but I'd kept sneaking into the back of the figure skating class.

Even in hockey skates, I'd been able to spin and jump. The instructor had told my mom I could be great, and that was that. Sometimes, I wondered what my life would be like now if I'd never put on skates, but I did love it. Kind of. Most of the time.

Henry stared at my perfect tracing with his usual blank expression. He was such a freak, going back to do three more figures in a row with precision. I'd competed against him since we were kids, and I wasn't sure I'd ever heard him string together more than three words outside press conferences.

The session ended with each of us performing the element we were going to especially focus on that week. Manon called it "setting our intentions."

The junior skaters went first, the girl skating down the rink on her spindly legs and launching into a triple Lutz-triple toe. With the top women—who were all teenagers these days—doing quads and triple Axels, I wasn't surprised to see a kid doing what used to be the hardest jumping combo for women.

Everyone applauded her, and I joined in. The younger Canadian man, Julien, fell on his quad toe, but we all clapped anyway and Bill told him how close it had been.

It went on like this until Henry stormed down the rink and launched off his toe pick into a quad Lutz, which he'd struggled with last season. This was the hardest jump for men these days, and he squeaked it out, the rotation questionable.

I couldn't lie—I was relieved he hadn't nailed it over the summer. My arsenal of quads—loop, flip, Lutz, toe, and Salchow—were my ticket to Olympic gold. I'd tried the quad Axel, which was four and a half revolutions since the Axel was the only jump that took off going forward.

I'd managed a few in practice, but the risk of hurting myself wasn't worth it. Landing a jump on practice ice was still miles away from landing it in a program in competition. Unless I had eighty percent consistency in practice with a jump, it wasn't going in.

Before I'd moved to Mr. Webber, I'd had a tendency to rush into jumps. Mr. Webber said it was because I wasn't focusing and concentrating through every moment of the program, and he wasn't wrong. I'd needed patience. He'd beat it out of me— metaphorically—and my quads had launched me to the top of the podium.

After applauding Henry's attempt, it was my turn. I hadn't given any thought to working on a particular element—I figured Manon and Bill would tell me what they wanted me to do. But I couldn't resist tossing off my own quad Lutz, snapping up into the jump with plenty of flow for a triple on the end for good measure. I held my running edge as applause rang out.

"Don't think you have much to work on with that combo," Julien said, shaking his head. "Wow."

Henry turned away, but not before I could see the clench of his jaw and flash of stink eye. He'd always hated me, but I didn't let myself get riled by my competitors.

Really, the only person who could beat me was *me*. And Henry would be waiting to pounce, sure. But being rivals on the ice didn't mean we had to hate each other, at least not in my book.

I was pretty sure Henry disagreed. *Strongly.*

The younger kids left for a morning of school before coming

back in the afternoon. I was ready for a nap, but apparently Henry, Julien, Ivan, and I were doing another session.

While Manon and I discussed the straight-line footwork element in my short program, Henry worked on his quad Lutz with Bill with varying degrees of success.

Though neither of us were tall—he was about five-six to my five-seven—he had long legs that looked great when he held the extension on his landings. After a hard fall that made me wince, he leapt back up, and our eyes met.

"Theo?"

I snapped my attention back to Manon. "Sorry! Jet lag."

She laughed, dangly gold earrings clinking as she shook her head. "Why do I feel like you'll be saying that for a month?"

I laughed too. "Because Mr. Webber warned you about me?"

"He did indeed." Her smile faded. "Did you speak to him on the weekend?"

"Yeah, I called yesterday. He still refuses to text. He sounded good! The same." He was starting chemo this week, so that would probably change, and I hated it so fucking much.

"Good, good. I know you only arrived Friday night, but are you settling into the condo all right? Giselle got you all set up with your rental car and everything you need?"

"Yep, everything's great! Thanks." It was honestly too embarrassing to admit the truth, and I'd figure out the car situation later. I watched Henry's flying sit spin. Level four for sure.

I said to Manon, "I'm surprised he agreed to let me train here."

She watched Henry, smiling fondly. "He's too honorable to refuse." Her gaze turned to me, sharpening. "Most people think Henry's cold and that nothing bothers him. That's not true. Just so you know."

"Right. Noted. We've never had a problem. He's so quiet I hardly notice he's there."

She frowned. "You shouldn't underestimate him either. All right, time to focus. Jet lag or not."

At some point, Henry moved on to his long program, which the ISU officially called "free skating." His short program was to "The Blower's Daughter." The long was "Moonlight Sonata," which was historically a bit cliché and overused in skating, but honestly sounded refreshing these days.

After they allowed lyrics in competition music, there'd been a steady stream of emo ballads like you'd hear during one of those mom shows like *Grey's Anatomy* or something. Or sometimes edgier music, but not a lot of true classical. This piece suited Henry's quiet intensity perfectly.

The gentle piano of "Moonlight Sonata" had a meditative quality, and at least if I'd be hearing this music over and over and over all season, it was a beautiful piece.

It filled the rink despite a tinny edge via the sound system that was probably getting old. Manon and I were sure to stay out of Henry's way as he did his run-through. I couldn't help but notice when he missed his quad Lutz, but the rest was good.

Frighteningly good. It was still early in the season, and Henry was competition-ready. My stomach flip-flopped uneasily, and I tried to focus on my camel spin position as Manon encouraged me to point my toe. Which I already *was*, but I grudgingly pointed it harder even though spins weren't worth enough points to spend too much time on them.

Meanwhile, I realized "Moonlight Sonata" was playing again. And again. Bill was working with Ivan at this point. When it started *again*, for a split second, Manon's mouth tightened before smoothing out into a smile as she called across the ice, "Okay, Henry. That's enough. It's time for your Pilates session." She raised a hand to whoever was in the booth, and the music stopped.

Henry was breathing hard, but I realized as he passed that he was still doing his program, gliding into a tough spread-eagle transition into his triple Axel-triple toe, which he landed perfectly with flow and glide. Then he picked up speed and went for the quad Lutz again, squeaking it out and putting a hand down. But it looked fully rotated. I applauded, and he shot me an acid glare that could have stripped the ugly orange paint off the walls.

"Geez," I muttered. "I thought this was a clapping rink too? Mr. Webber always taught us to be supportive when someone lands a tough element they're struggling with."

One summer when a top Russian skater had come to train, I'd applauded his quad Sal after he'd missed a bunch. He had *not* appreciated it.

Manon winced. "I'm sorry. Henry's a perfectionist, and he can be…"

A humorless tightass? "A perfectionist?"

"Indeed."

"Yeah, but…geez. He just did three full run-throughs in a row that were practically perfect."

"If we let him, he'll keep going until he does it absolutely clean."

My eyes were probably bugging out. "Why doesn't he just stop if he makes a mistake and start again?"

"Because that's not good enough for Henry. Anyway, it's your turn. Short or long? We'd love to see both since we weren't involved in the choreography."

"Now? I don't do a lot of run-throughs. Especially on Mondays. With jet lag."

She laughed. "All right, we'll let you get away with the jet-lag excuse today. But not tomorrow."

After my session, I shoved my feet into my sneakers and followed an arrow into the basement, untied laces flapping. I wandered through the bowels of the Ice Chalet until I reached the gym.

It was a rectangular cinder-brick room painted purple with

harsh overhead lighting. At least the equipment looked newish, including two Pilates Reformer machines.

Henry was in the stretching area of thick mats in the corner working on his left quad. I kicked off my shoes and plopped down, spreading my legs into a wide side split. Leaning forward on my elbows, I scrolled Instagram.

I swear I could feel the weight of Henry's disapproval, and sure enough, when I glanced up, he was staring at me. His brown eyes were *intense*. His lashes were really thick, and he had this way of glaring while otherwise seeming impassive, his face like a mask of placid tension.

I gave him a cheery smile because it would probably annoy him. Which I admit was immature, but if I was going to be stuck with him all season, I was compelled to push Henry's buttons. It would be boring as hell otherwise.

Ignoring me, he shifted into a single-leg hamstring stretch, leaning low over his knee. Grimacing, he grunted, his hair flopping over, his hands gripping his flexed foot.

"Don't pull so hard. Just let the stretch happen."

"We're not all naturally flexible." His tone was stony.

I think if he did one of those aura photographs, his would be solid gray. I'd done it at a disastrous new-age yoga retreat in Mexico one summer, and my aura was a mix of red, orange, and purple. Joyful, creative, relaxed.

My ex, who was the one into crystals, boring-ass meditation, and endless yoga classes, had come up almost all white for spiritual. We still followed each other on Insta, and last I saw, he was living his best *ommmm* life in Thailand.

"I guess I'm hashtag-blessed." I smiled again. I *was* naturally flexible, so I supposed I was lucky. I hadn't thought much about it. "By the way, thanks for agreeing to me training here this season."

He opened and closed his mouth, his lips a full reddish pink.

Usual blank mask in place, he switched legs and lowered his head to his knee. This near, I could see a nerve in his jaw jump where he was clenching. I seemed to make him furious with my presence alone.

It was stupidly immature, but I wanted to poke him and get a reaction. Break through that mask and get him pissed off. Henry had clearly hated me for years, and it did bother me a bit—my inner kid wondering: *Why don't you like me?*

I was friendly with everyone, but I didn't really have *close* friends. My mom had made it hard getting to know other kids when I was growing up. I wasn't allowed to go to anyone else's house in case I ate junk food, and she'd homeschooled me once I won the novice US championship.

When I moved to LA, I was friendly with a lot of people even if we didn't get super close. But Henry was like a brick wall. Really, I should have left him alone and been grateful. I could understand he wasn't thrilled I was suddenly training with him.

And I *was* grateful, so I said, "Seriously, thanks."

He ignored me.

"It's cool of you to do me such a big favor." It was true after all. "I really do appreciate it. Thank you."

With a barely audible sigh, he lifted his head enough to glance up at me and nod before lowering his face to his knee.

Ah, his Canadian politeness was a weak point. I wondered what I could do to actually get him to smile at me. Not a fake-ass smile while we shook hands on the podium, but something genuine. Warm, even. Something just for me—even though I was very likely his least fave person on the planet.

With Mr. Webber being sick and the Olympics looming, I needed a distraction. This game could make Henry slightly less boring. I grinned to myself as I scrolled.

There was no way he'd be able to resist me.

Chapter Three

Henry

AS THE DOOR thudded shut, I punched in the code to silence the mildly beeping alarm. Esmeralda's soft meows welcomed me as she raced over from the dark living area, probably from where she was napping under my bed by the window. Or directly on my pillow.

I crouched to pet her in the ambient red light of the rice cooker in the kitchen. "Did you miss me?" I asked as she rubbed against my legs. "I missed you too." Honestly, I preferred cats to people much of the time.

She meowed for her dinner as though absolutely starving. After I took off my running shoes and stowed them on the rack inside the hall closet, I flicked on the kitchen light to my left and opened the cupboard. Esmeralda excitedly wove in and out around my ankles.

I carefully portioned out her wet food, then after a moment's deliberation added an extra teaspoon. The vet said she needed to lose weight, but she'd been so thin and small when I'd found her in the woods near the Ice Chalet—when she'd found *me*—that I struggled to deny her anything. I scooped half a teaspoon back out. There. I wasn't breaking the rules as much.

I turned on the TV. Esmeralda gobbled down her dinner, and

I pulled out leftover chicken cauliflower curry. The brown-toned galley kitchen was partly open to the living room/bedroom via a dated pass-through. If the condo was built now, it would likely be completely open concept, but it was an older building.

Since Bill's cousin was the property manager, I rented the suite for a good price, so I couldn't complain even if I'd have preferred sleek white counters and cabinets to the reddish brown and black, and hardwood floors to the synthetic tiles and gray carpeting.

Half watching HGTV, I spooned fresh rice out of the electric cooker while waiting for the chicken in the microwave. Growing up in a Japanese-Canadian household, we'd eaten a variety of Western and Asian food, but the rice cooker had been on at all times.

There was something strangely soothing about the omnipresent red light. Even though my family still lived in Vancouver, it made me feel closer to them somehow. I didn't need nearly as much rice living on my own, but it felt wrong not to keep it on all the time.

I'd just settled at the small round bistro table beside the love seat when my phone buzzed with a video call. I propped it on its little stand and tapped the screen before muting the TV. My younger brother grimaced.

"Dude, why are you giving me a nostril view? Hold up your phone like a normal person!"

I sliced a chunk of chicken breast baked in a red coconut milk curry. "It's dinnertime."

Sam rolled his eyes. "Fine, fine. We need to get something for Dad's birthday. Want to go in on it together like usual?"

I nodded. "And I'll pay for most of it like usual?"

He grinned. "If you insist. I'm still a student, after all."

"You pick something, and I'll send money."

"Cool. But we're not getting something *practical*."

"I'm confident you wouldn't recognize a practical gift if you tried."

He grinned, tossing back his bangs. He'd dyed a purplish-gray streak in the black. "I'll take that as a compliment."

"How are Etienne and Brianna doing with training?"

"Good! They're so glad they left Hackensack and came back. Their coach here in Vancouver might not have clout with the judges, but they don't hate going to the rink every day. And Bree loves living with Tim."

"Mm. Does Etienne love living with you?"

He blushed. It was still odd to see my brother so smitten. Etienne had been his best friend for years, and it had been quite obvious even to me that he'd had feelings for Sam. Last Christmas, they'd discovered Sam felt the same way.

"It's been, like, six months now. Of course he loves living with me."

"He's not tired of you yet?"

Sam gave me the finger.

I said, "I hear Anita Patel is off the ice with a broken foot. She and Christopher might not be ready in time for Nationals. Etienne and Brianna could get that second Olympic spot for ice dance." Chloe Desjardins and Phillipe Vincent had come out of retirement and would be first without doubt.

Practically bouncing, Sam fought a grin. "They really might make it! They're so glad they didn't give up, and they're loving training again. Etienne's taking time for piano, and I swear it's helping his skating to relax more. And now Anita's injured!" His smile vanished. "Not that we wanted her to get hurt. Geez, I sound like a monster."

"You're not a monster. Injuries can create opportunities, even if we don't wish them on anyone." It was simply the truth. "It's a long season ahead of us. Etienne and Brianna still have to earn their spot."

He nodded vigorously. "Absolutely. Bree's concussion symptoms are finally gone, and they're working so hard on their levels. Most nights, Etienne practically falls into bed."

For a strange moment, a pang of envy filled me at the thought of coming home to a partner after a long day of training. How ridiculous. I had Esmeralda, and she was more than enough.

"*Sooooo.*"

I frowned at Sam. "Hmm?"

He rolled his eyes. "How was the first week with Theo?"

I swallowed a bite of cauliflower and rice. "Fine."

Truthfully, it had been stressful and irritating. He was all anyone could talk about, the other skaters flocking around him like moths to a flame. Or flies to dung. He'd been late to practice three times already, and "jet lag" had become a running joke. I'd ignored it all as best I could and stayed focused on my training.

"Oh yeah, I'm sure. Come *on*. Give me the dirt. What's he like?"

"I've known him for a decade. He's the same."

"Yeah, but you don't, like, *know* him, know him."

"I'm more than familiar enough."

Sam huffed. "Are you seriously going to pretend you're totally unaffected by seeing Theo Sullivan every day? Not distracted at all?"

"It's good practice for competition."

"Well, sure, but you have to be a little pissed."

"No, I don't."

"Fine, fine. What's he think about Kuznetsov?"

"I have no idea."

Sam threw up his hands. "How have you not talked to him about Kuznetsov? He could beat you both!"

Stomach tightening, I feigned nonchalance. "Kuznetsov is irrelevant to our training."

"Even if he lands the quad Axel? Don't tell me you haven't heard the rumors. He landed one on Instagram!"

Julien, Ivan, and Ga-young had been breathlessly gossiping about it and I'd tried to ignore them. "Instagram isn't competition."

"If you say so. How's the Lutz?"

A topic I wanted to discuss even less than Theodore Sullivan. "Fine."

"Are you sure it's worth the risk? You've always been so consistent."

This was true, and it was a valid question. Still, I bristled. "You don't think I can do it? I've landed it in competition before."

Sam sighed. "Don't pull that shit. Of course you can do it. You know I believe in you."

I took another bite and nodded.

"Is Theo dating anyone?"

"He's been here a week."

"I mean back in California. They never mentioned a boyfriend in the press, but we all know that doesn't mean shit in skating even if he's openly gay."

"Mm." While Theodore had come out officially a few seasons before, the US federation rarely mentioned it, if ever. I hoped my federation in Canada would be more supportive, but it hadn't been discussed since I'd never felt the need to come out in the media.

I'd informed my family and coaches I was gay, but it mostly felt irrelevant since I didn't date. And the one time I'd tried—

I caught myself and refocused on Sam. "How's school?"

"Okay. Hard to believe this is my last year of undergrad. Fingers crossed I get in to do my MSW."

He was passionate about social work. "You'll be accepted. They'd be lucky to have you."

He beamed. "That's what Etienne says. Did I tell you he and Bree got three key points from the judges on their pattern dance at Nebelhorn?"

I listened as Sam went on about Etienne. He'd had girlfriends before, but his relationship with Etienne was on a new level. There was a glow in his eyes and a reverent tone in his voice.

It seemed he was actually in love, which I couldn't imagine. Or I could, since I'd once briefly thought I was in love. But I'd only been caught in an immature delusion. Love wasn't for me.

"You visiting Ojiichan this weekend?" Sam asked.

"Yes. I'm taking him to the JCCC for a Kendo exhibition."

Sam shuddered. "So many lost Saturdays there. At least Kendo is fun."

"Shodo was fun too."

"Only you could think fancy calligraphy lessons were fun. Forget about the language classes. And you got out of everything thanks to skating once you won the national novice title."

Our parents had met at the Japanese Canadian Cultural Centre in Toronto as children when they'd taken lessons there on weekends. They'd carried on the tradition with me and Sam, and though I'd lost all but the basics of the language, I'd enjoyed the challenge.

I said, "Once we moved to Vancouver they let you do what you wanted."

"Yeah, 'cause they were too busy with all your skating stuff. Then you went and abandoned us by moving back to Toronto."

The guilt was familiar now, less of a stab than an ache. "You know I had to move to the highest tier coaches, even if it meant coming back here." It was true—Jillian, my coach in Vancouver, had been perfect for me through my teens, but I'd needed to step up to the next level.

It was also true that I'd had to escape that rink and the daily reminders of what a stupid, pathetic fool I'd been about *him*. I'd never confessed that part to my family. They'd moved to Vancouver for my sake, but it was their home now, and they'd always been hands-off about my skating.

Our dad's parents had stayed in Toronto, and I visited Ojiichan every weekend I could. Our grandmother on that side had died a few years ago, and now he lived alone in a small apartment in an assisted living complex.

"I'm just busting your balls," Sam said. "Besides, you'll be back at Halloween for Skate Canada. Everyone'll be there with bells on."

I gripped my fork. I had to win. Theodore would be there too, which was aggravating especially since the ISU usually tried to keep the top skaters from competing directly on the Grand Prix circuit until the final in December.

But he'd insisted on doing Skate America and Skate Canada back-to-back. Then he'd have uninterrupted training time before the final. Other skaters had used this strategy too, but I preferred to spread out my competitions.

Later, while I was holding my evening planks with Esmeralda watching from her favorite cardboard box, I found myself wondering if Theodore had actually left a boyfriend behind to train here.

Not that it mattered. Not that I cared. I lowered to my elbows and pushed up and down between the hover and plank positions, lifting one foot, then the other.

I wondered what Theodore was doing right now. Probably eating fast food or something equally irresponsible and lazing on the couch. I did an extra fifty reps, imagining the top of the podium and Theodore below me.

THEODORE WAS SUPPOSED to be transitioning with a falling leaf after his step sequence into his combination spin. Instead, he'd come to a dead stop, his music still playing. This was a run-through, which meant performing the whole program from start to finish. Not standing around during the spins before starting again.

My session was over, and I watched from the low bleachers along one side of the ice, taking my time lacing my running shoes. My feet were sore from breaking in new boots, and though I'd never admit it, I was relieved to have my skates off. I'd still finished two complete run-throughs. They hadn't been perfect, but acceptable enough.

As I'd learned the past two weeks, Theodore didn't like spinning and often left out those elements. He was an average spinner, and was it any wonder why?

His laziness grated on my nerves even though I should have been glad he wasn't preparing the way he should have been. It surprised me Mr. Webber had let him get away with it, but maybe he hadn't.

Manon and Bill encouraged him to do complete programs, but hadn't forced the issue yet. I supposed it made sense since they were still getting used to each other. Theodore was probably still claiming jet lag, as if we weren't used to traveling all around the world for competitions.

His long program music was building as he restarted, stroking across the rink into his next jump. The quad Sal was textbook, but he'd been resting for a good thirty seconds beforehand.

Still, I knew he could pop off jumps in competition the same way, so his laziness in practice was irrelevant. The unfairness burrowed under my skin like slivers.

He was skating to a Rolling Stones medley—mostly the song "Sympathy for the Devil." Audiences would love his cocky grin and explosive jumps, and they wouldn't care that his transitions were simple and the footwork more upper body motions than putting in the effort to carve intricate edges. If he nailed the jumps, the judges wouldn't care either.

When he hit his ending pose, fist in the air and head back after a hip swivel, a few traitorous people in the arena clapped. I grabbed my equipment to shove into my locker before heading out into the drizzle for a run.

I splashed through puddles and ordered myself to stop thinking about Theodore's hips.

It wasn't too long before I ran the trail down into the gully. I'd timed my breathing perfectly to my pace, my lungs working at the optimal level for conditioning.

At some point, footsteps thudded dully behind me, but I didn't pay much attention, focusing on staying in the perfect training zone.

"Hey!"

My heart lurched as Theodore ran past. I was in danger of tripping over my own feet as he spun around, jogging backward and smiling at me. He had the energy of an unruly dog, and I thought of my parents' rambunctious sheepadoodle.

Albeit an unruly dog wearing just shorts and a white T-shirt despite the wet chill. The cotton clung translucently to his firm chest.

"This is a great path!" He faced front again, now running ahead of me. "I hate running, but Manon and Bill are making me."

All that extra energy from not doing his spins was clearly coming in handy. As I chased him, I wanted to demand who'd told him about *my* running trail. But now my heart was pounding and my breath came raggedly, my optimal coordination vanished.

And he was *winning*.

Not that it was an official race, but we were running, and he'd passed me. So yes, it was definitely a race. Core tight, I sucked in air and powered forward, overtaking him. He said something else, but I wasn't listening. He was behind me again, and that was all that mattered.

"What do you do for fun around here?" he asked as he pulled

up next to me, his strides matching mine.

I increased my speed, lactic acid flaring in my quads as the trail turned upward. Why did he insist on talking so much? Particularly to me. His persistent friendliness wouldn't affect my hate for him.

Whether it was fair or not, I'd hated him successfully for years. I wasn't going to be fooled into thinking Theodore Sullivan had any genuine interest in me. That saying about "fool me once" was most definitely accurate.

At my heels, he was still talking. "Ivan said—"

Concentrating on the blood rushing in my ears, I ignored him, blocking out everything but winning. We took turns overtaking, and I was calculating the distance remaining as the trail looped back toward the starting point so I could expend the correct amount of energy to win when he disappeared from my peripheral vision.

If he'd made a noise when he tripped, I hadn't heard it over the roar of my pulse. Still running, I turned to find him sprawled on his stomach in the wet dirt. I was on higher ground, and my shoes slipped in the mud, adrenaline spiking as I threw out my arms to stay balanced.

Stopped now, I watched and waited. Not moving, he'd surely knocked the wind out of his lungs. I didn't see how he could have hit his head, but after a few seconds, adrenaline spiked again. I took a step closer.

He wasn't really hurt.

Was he?

I took another step down the slope. The drizzle was a light rain now, and the ground had to be freezing. Granted, we were used to the cold, but...

Was he actually injured?

His shoulders shook, and for a terrible instant I thought he was crying. Sympathy flared, and my rubber soles dug into the mud as I inched closer.

With a groan, he rolled over, looking at me upside-down, his perfect teeth flashing into that irksome smile as he continued laughing. "Even the Russian judge would give me positive GOE on that landing."

Strange relief gave way to stabbing irritation. He was fine, yet of course he was making a big production as usual. Not to mention bragging about his inflated grades of execution.

He rubbed his chest, still laughing. The muddy white T-shirt had rucked up over his stomach, and my eyes were drawn to the damp strip of pale skin.

"Oh, come on. Are you actually a robot? Don't tell me this isn't funny! That was an epic splat."

As I imagined running my fingertips over his exposed belly, he held up his hand in a wordless request for assistance. With a sigh, I walked several steps down until I was by his feet and took his hand—and he yanked me down into the mud.

On top of him.

Because of course he did. As he laughed, I braced myself on his chest with my free hand, my shoes slipping as I tried to find purchase. Our legs were tangled, my fingers dug into his pectorals, and it *wasn't funny.*

Especially when Ga-young and Julien appeared over the rise on their way up the hill. She was a medalist in South Korea, but at fourteen she was still too young to compete internationally as a senior. Her eyes were wide as she gaped. Beside her, Julien laughed, sweat glistening on his brown skin.

He called out something in French that I thought was the equivalent of "get a room," and I shoved to my feet, face burning. Theodore was still laughing, and Ga-young pressed her lips together, clearly trying not to giggle.

Seething, I powered up the rest of the hill with burning lungs, mud splashed all over my black pants. He was ridiculous! Such a childish trick to pull me into the mud. Right on top of him. Why did he insist on being so, so—

To my horror, I realized I was half hard. Gritting my teeth, I bit back a growl. No matter how much he smiled at me, no matter how tight and see-through his T-shirts were against his enticing body, I would not be taken in.

Like the flash of a camera going off, I remembered the first and last time I'd trusted an easy smile and pretty face. Cresting the hill, I sped back toward the slick road and red taillights passing by, beating Theodore Sullivan soundly even if he wasn't racing me anymore.

Chapter Four

Theo

IT WAS BOUND to happen sooner or later, and apparently today was the day.

The elevator door slid open at the eighth floor, and Henry stepped on. Well, he half stepped on, stopping dead and staring at me like I was a ghost, and this was some horror movie. The guy hated me, but come on. I wasn't *that* bad.

"Hey!" I gave him a little wave. "I guess we're neighbors."

He blinked, so at least he hadn't been magically frozen into stone with the shock of it all. Manon's assistant had mentioned Henry lived in this condo too, and that Ivan had until he moved in with a girl he met.

The door bounced back open. Henry hadn't moved, and the door tried again valiantly to close and do its elevator duty. After two more denials, an angry beep sounded. I tugged Henry inside by the dangling strings of his hoodie.

"So you're on eight, huh?" I said, stating the obvious. "I'm on eleven. The building seems nice enough. You like it here?"

Swiveling his eyes to the bank of numbered buttons, he nodded, then pressed P1 with a frown. The door opened at the lobby, and I said, "See you in a bit!" before he could question why I wasn't going down to parking.

I waved to the concierge as I hurried past, pulling out my phone to check on my ride. Fuck. Fuck! It'd been canceled and the app was searching for another driver. It wasn't always easy to get someone out here midday for some reason. In the distance, cars zoomed by on the 401, the major highway cutting across Toronto.

Since the Ice Chalet was in the middle of nowhere, some drivers didn't want to go up there. It was weird that they'd built an arena so far away in the seventies, but apparently there had initially been a big outdoor adventure park beside it that was long gone now.

I'd tried the bus, but I had to take three to get close to the rink, and it took way too long. At least I'd convinced Manon and Bill for a one p.m. start on Tuesdays and Thursdays. Only problem was that this was Monday.

I'd missed not only the obligatory team session at the crack of dawn, but by the time I'd woken, there was no point in going until after lunch. I'd texted Manon my apologies and explained that my alarm hadn't gone off. Which was true! Because I'd blanked on setting it. My phone usually reminded me at night, but it had betrayed me.

"Come on, come on…" I almost shook my phone like that would help somehow.

Henry had surely been at the rink obscenely early and had likely come home for lunch before heading back. An engine rumbled close by, a red Civic passing the front doors on its way down the driveway. It was Henry, and because I'm an idiot and didn't keep my head down, our eyes met through his window.

He kept going. Which was both a relief and annoying because what a dick for not offering me a ride. Not that he owed me anything, but most people would have at least asked since we were going to the same place. My mother would surely praise his killer instinct.

An icy wind blew crunchy orange leaves around my Converse. My fingers were going numb. It was expensive paying for a Lyft to and from the rink, but it was the best option since I couldn't rent a car.

Red flashed in my peripheral vision. I gaped as the Civic returned after a precise U-turn. It pulled up to the curb, and the passenger window rolled down.

When I leaned low to see him, Henry asked one question. "Why?"

Excuses popped onto my tongue, but after a moment I went with the truth. "I can't drive."

His brows met with a little furrow that was honestly adorable. "Why?"

"My mom didn't want me taking time out from skating to learn. I should have done it when I moved to California, but there was another skater who had a car. Emily Lee? She has a sweet Jeep Wrangler, and she gave me rides." My face burned, and I knew I was beet red. I'd been lazy not to learn when I'd had the chance, and now here I was. Not that I cared what Henry thought.

Still, I squirmed. "My ride will be here any minute, so."

"Who drives you?"

I held up my phone. "Whoever's working Lyft."

A frown pinched his face. "That's expensive."

"Yeah, well. My fault for not learning how to drive."

He didn't say anything for a few moments. Then he faced forward and popped the lock on the passenger door, which released with a little *thunk*.

"Are you sure? You don't have to."

He just gave me a long-suffering glare, so I hopped in before he could change his mind. "Thanks, man. I really appreciate it."

Being unfailingly friendly would surely chisel a dent in his brick wall eventually. I'd get him to like me. Or at least coax a real smile out of him if it killed me.

After clicking on my seat belt, I ran a hand over the immaculate dashboard. "Nice car! I'm surprised you got red. I'd think you were more into gray or black or maybe white? It's a nice cherry red too. Is there a backup camera? Do those come standard these days? Ohh, do you have seat warmers?" I flipped a switch under the heating controls.

Henry sighed as he took a right turn and headed north. "The car was used for test drives. The price was excellent, and it costs too much to repaint."

"Ah, that explains it. Oh, my ass is getting toasty! This must be awesome on those cold winter mornings."

"Mm."

Henry's phone was connected to the radio, and I blinked at the words on the screen. "Dua Lipa? You're not listening, to, like, NPR? What else is on here?" I scrolled through the playlist while Henry gave me stink eye. "Is there K-pop? Lady Gaga? I love this song!" I tapped it.

I sang along, and from the corner of my eye I could see Henry's death grip on the wheel relax. After a minute, he tapped a finger.

"You listen to this to pump you up for practice, right?" I didn't wait for an answer, but he nodded. "Em and I would do the same thing." I looked out at the housing developments, the rows and rows of narrow lots crammed in together. "I miss her. What do you guys do for fun around here? Are you dating anyone?"

As soon as I asked the question, I realized it was hard to imagine Henry in a relationship. Given how tightly wound he was, he'd be a nightmare.

He didn't say anything, so I looked at him and waited more. Then I asked, "Is there a special girl? Or person?" He still didn't answer, and my curiosity only grew stronger. I went with my gut and added, "Or maybe you're into guys? That's what I heard."

That got a sharp glance as he went rigid. "What did you hear?"

he demanded.

Whoa. Why was he freaking out? "*Weeeell…*" I tapped my chin thoughtfully, trying to come up with the best joke, but suddenly it didn't seem funny.

Adam's apple bobbing, Henry watched me with his hands clenched on the steering wheel, his eyes flicking between me and the road. I wasn't sure if he was angry or…scared? I couldn't understand his reaction, but I knew I didn't like how it made me feel.

I smiled reassuringly. "Hey, it's okay. I'm just joking. I didn't hear anything." Everyone in skating knew he was gay. What was the big deal? What rumor was he afraid of?

Lips parting, he took a shuddery breath. I reached out, but he jerked so hard I was afraid he'd veer into oncoming traffic.

"Why are you so freaked?"

Naturally, he said nothing, his eyes locked on the road now. At least we were staying in our lane.

"Is it…" I tried to think of the right thing to say since obviously this was a touchy subject. Maybe everything was a touchy subject with Henry. Was he afraid of being outed publicly? "You know I'm gay, right? It's okay if you are too. Or if you aren't. Like, whatever you are is okay."

He seemed to consider this. Finally, he asked, "You haven't heard anyone gossiping about me?"

"No. People don't really talk about you." Well, not about his sexuality, at least. He was so uptight that most people joked about how he was a robot or alien. "But I thought you were cool with being queer? If you are? My finely tuned gaydar says yes, but I might be wrong. It's happened once or twice." I shrugged carelessly, but the curiosity was killing me.

Henry's tense silence was a little freaky. When I was about to make another joke, he said, "I am. It's not a secret, but I don't…" His gaze flicked to me as he stopped for a light, then dropped. I wasn't sure how that little movement could be so *sad*. "I don't have time for anything but training."

I was weirdly pleased that he'd told me. "Yeah, I hear you. I'm not seeing anyone either." I wanted to pat his arm or something, but he might freak out again. "I really didn't hear any rumors about you. I swear."

The song was still playing, and it filled the silence as he stopped for a red light. I jiggled my foot, more questions burning on my tongue. Now that I thought about it, hadn't he gotten a boner looking at me in the shower when we were still juniors? I vaguely recalled him avoiding me like the plague afterward even though it happened to the best of us.

I couldn't hold it in. "So, you just hook up? Definitely hard to find time for an actual relationship with training. Which app's the best around here? I need to get laid."

He stared straight ahead, knuckles pale on the steering wheel again, cheeks flushed pink.

"Oh, come on! We all have needs. Or are you ace? Not that ace people don't have needs. But maybe you're not into sex with other people, which is totally cool, obviously."

"Please stop talking."

"It's not like I asked you about your fave rimming technique. Seriously, it's okay if you're not into sex. My sister Veronica identifies as gray ace."

"I'm not asexual. Stop." He turned up the music.

Honestly, it was adorable. So easily scandalized! Okay, so he wasn't ace. But for someone always so cool and in control, his reaction fascinated me. Was he super repressed in bed? Did he even make noise?

Was he a virgin?

As we headed into the arena, I imagined him being blown. Did he moan, or was that not allowed? He walked ahead of me, and I watched his firm ass in his tight black pants. If I licked him open, could I get him to let go and be loud?

My balls tingled, and I shook away the stupid thoughts. I really did need to get laid if I was imagining fucking Henry of all people. He was no fun, and I liked fucking fun people. And it was none of my business what he did or didn't do and who he did or didn't do things with.

I seriously appreciated the ride though and said, "Thanks again!"

His Canadian politeness had apparently been short-circuited, and he ignored me. He continued ignoring me during our sessions, doing run-through after run-through after jump drills. I tried to focus on my quads and stop thinking about licking Henry's ass until he screamed. That would get a smile out of him.

I took my time changing out of my skates at the end of the day and chatted with Ga-young and her dad, in no rush to return to my empty condo. My Lyft was still fifteen minutes away when I left the rink.

In the lot, headlights flared to life, and a car approached in the early November darkness. It was only when it pulled up to the curb that I realized it was the red Civic. That it was Henry.

That he'd waited for me.

Grinning, I hopped in. "You didn't have to wait! Thanks. I wouldn't have taken so long if I'd known. You really don't have to give me rides all the time. I don't expect that."

"It's wasteful not to drive together."

"That's true. This is better for the environment." I couldn't stop grinning. "I'm not getting up at the crack of dawn every day like you do, but this is awesome. I'll give you gas money, obviously. Hey, where's your second Grand Prix? You're doing NHK in Osaka, right? Do you know who's on the panel? The technical specialist for the Junior Grand Prix Final is Edgar Stein, and Ga-young is shitting bricks since he's such a hard-ass on edge calls. Her Lutz is definitely more of a flutz."

Henry gave his usual short answers. In the elevator at the condo, I almost invited him to my place for dinner, which would have meant ordering pizza and eating on a cardboard box since I had no furniture. I was clearly lonely since Henry wasn't even good company.

Except maybe he kind of was? He didn't talk much, and he hated me, but he was always listening in a way I was drawn to. Still, he was my biggest rival, and it probably wasn't a good idea to spend too much time together.

He probably had zero desire to hang out. So I said goodnight when he got off the elevator. I tried to FaceTime Em in LA, but she was busy. I tried a few other LA friends, but they were busy too.

I texted with people regularly and saw them on Insta and wherever, but it was a busy, stressful Olympic season, and pretty much everyone I knew at this point was in the skating world. In LA, we'd trained together and partied on the weekends when we didn't have competitions coming up.

But now that I was away from them, I realized it was all kind of on the surface. We'd had a ton of fun, and they understood skating angst. But when I tried to think of times we talked about other things—real life or family stuff—I came up blank.

I wondered if Henry had friends. He must have, though he'd always seemed a loner at competitions. Maybe we could hang since we were neighbors. Right. Neighbors and *bitter rivals for Olympic gold*, I reminded myself.

Well, not that *I* was super bitter, but it wasn't a good idea to spend too much time with the person most likely to beat me. I could imagine my mom grinding her teeth that I was even getting rides from him.

Which of course made me want to hang out with Henry even more.

After a frozen dinner—an organic brand with actual vegetables, so at least healthyish—I called Mr. Webber.

He'd never been much for small talk, and answered with, "I heard from your mother."

I groaned. "Seriously? Sh—" I caught myself. "Shoot. I'm sorry she bothered you. She has no right."

"I've dealt with skating parents for decades. I let her say her piece and told her I appreciated her perspective before I hung up."

"Oh, snap!" I laughed, imagining the steam coming out of Mom's ears. That's what she got for butting in. "Still, I'm sorry she bugged you."

"Chemo is worse than your mother, I assure you."

I hated how tired he sounded, small and almost frail. While he'd never even raised his voice once to me, he'd always had heft and strength when he spoke. He wasn't a big man, but he had a commanding presence.

"Yeah, but still. You'll be glad to know my quad Sal is feeling great."

"Are you doing your run-throughs?"

"Mostly. Did you know Henry will do them over and over if he even makes one mistake?"

"He's dedicated."

"Yeah, but so am I. I'm just not going to give myself an injury going too hard. It doesn't mean I don't want to win."

"Wanting to win and dedication aren't quite the same thing," Mr. Webber said dryly.

That stung, even if it was true. "But Henry's so cold. There's no passion there."

"It's true that he's very internal. He interprets the music beautifully, but he doesn't connect to the audience the way you do. I wouldn't say there's no passion. He's controlled, but he loves skating. He puts effort and care into every movement."

I got up from my bed, which was a mattress on the floor of my small condo. It was a studio with only the bathroom truly separate, the kitchen half open to the living space. Pacing, I insisted, "I love skating too."

"If you say so."

"I do! I'm good at it. I've always been good at it."

"You have, Theo."

Now he was humoring me. I wanted to argue more, but he said he was going to nap, so we said goodbye. I still paced, weirdly unsettled.

Even though I probably wouldn't have made skating my career if my mom hadn't pushed me, I couldn't imagine what else I'd do. I'd graduated high school, but what would I even study if I went to college?

I was good at skating. There was money to be made on Asian tours and through endorsements. I'd always thought I'd be a good coach one day. Working with kids would be awesome, though I wasn't the organized type. Henry would be great at that, but he'd be no fun. Though he'd probably be excellent at teaching technique.

Why was I thinking about Henry so much? Shaking my head, I flopped back on my mattress and logged in to Twitch to see what my favorite streamer was playing today. I wished I had a couch. Henry probably had a couch. He probably had a matching living room set like my parents. He—

There I went again, thinking about Henry.

"THEY'RE SPENDING MORE time with Sakaguchi than you."

It took every ounce of control not to hang up without saying a word. Why had I answered? Well, because she had called ten times in a row, and it was easier to just talk to her and get it over with so I could go back to my Instagram scrolling.

"Hello to you too, Mom."

"Why were you working with the assistant today?"

"Because Manon and Bill were busy with their other students. There's a schedule, and I have no problem doing sessions with Marc."

"Well, I have a problem with it!"

My control frayed. "Good thing I'm an adult, and it's not up to you anymore!" Breathing deeply, I glanced around the bleachers. It was just after six p.m., when there was a dinnertime lull before the evening city-run recreational lessons for kids started.

"All those years, I sacrificed to help you, and this is the thanks I get."

Thumping my head back against the orange brick wall, I closed my eyes, gripping the phone's screen to my ear. "I never had a choice. *You* were bound and determined to make me a champion."

"And I did!" Her voice wavered, going tight and high. "I just want what's best for you."

"I know." We'd had this conversation hundreds of times. I knew exactly what she'd say next, and she did, right on cue.

"It's only because I love you." She sniffled.

"I love you too, Mom." What else could I say? I did love her. And she did love me, even if her ambition and obsessive nature drove me bananas. She wasn't going to change, so I had to deal with it.

"I just want you to have the best. You're so talented, my darling. If those coaches—"

"*My* coaches are doing a great job. I'm sure your rink spy reported that I'm even doing full run-throughs. Sometimes." Her spy was likely another skating parent—there were few secrets at a training rink and even more gossip.

"You should be doing as many as Sakaguchi. I can hear his music!"

"Moonlight Sonata" was indeed echoing through the almost-empty rink. "My sessions are over for today. I started early and everything." Now I was waiting to catch a ride back with Henry, though I sure as hell wasn't telling my mother. It was only a matter of time before her spy filled her in on that development. "How's Dad?"

I could practically hear the shrug. "Fine. Working late."

"And the girls?"

Here was Mom's chance to bitch about my sisters, and she seized it in her jaws like a crocodile. I hmmed and ahhed, tuning her out while I watched Henry launch into his flying sit spin.

He didn't have my natural flexibility, but he still got down really low, his free leg extended ramrod straight and his upper body in a difficult twisted position. His spins didn't drift, and he kept the speed even with the harder variation.

I watched him transition into his straight-line footwork and thought about what I'd said to Mr. Webber about Henry being cold and his disagreement with my assessment.

As Henry lunged and glided on gorgeous edges, almost closing his eyes as he moved to music he'd heard a zillion times now, he looked so peaceful in himself. You'd think he was completely alone, and that was generally how he always skated.

And it really was beautiful, like a painting in a museum. But watching him, I wanted him to look up, to reach out and let me in. Not me personally, but the audience in general.

Or maybe me personally too.

The commentators loved to call me a "showman" and a "performer." I got so much energy from the crowd when I skated, but audiences seemed to make Henry tighter. I could imagine he'd love to actually be completely alone so he could just skate and skate and try to be perfect for himself.

Meanwhile, as long as I was getting good scores from the judges who dug my personality and jumps, I was happy. I'd honestly never cared about trying to be perfect.

"You're not even listening to your poor mother."

Sighing, I tore my gaze from Henry. "Of course I am. Hey, did I tell you I'm getting a new short program costume? Can I get your opinion on the color? I'll text you the options, hold on."

I'd already decided with Manon and the designer, but nothing made my mother happier than telling me what to do. I sent her the pictures and watched Henry begin his free skate again even though I hadn't seen him make a single mistake.

Chapter Five

Henry

*I*T'S JUST LOVE.

Manon's voice rang in my ears, but my heart still thumped as I gave the Skate Canada audience a small smile, lifting my arms out as I glided across the ice to take my starting position.

I'd always felt crushing pressure skating in front of a home crowd, and Manon had worked to reinforce that the audience only wanted to support me.

Canadian fans were nothing if not loyal, and they cheered and stomped and whistled in greeting. Sam, Mom, Dad, Obaachan, and other family and friends were here too. Not so much *my* friends, since I'd always been far too focused on training for socializing.

I'd stumbled on my quad toe in the short, though I was still in second place. Behind *him*, of course. I didn't want to disappoint, and if I didn't skate perfectly… Ugh.

Performing was honestly my least favorite part of skating. I could happily train every day without needing an audience. But the audience was part of winning, and I definitely wanted to win.

I lowered my head for my starting position, one leg back with my toe pick in the ice, my hands resting lightly over my heart atop my long-sleeved shirt, which was a lightly shimmering silver on top, fading down into a rich navy blue under my chest that matched my pants. My newly trimmed hair made a perfect swoop over one side of my forehead.

Be perfect. Don't fall. Don't fail. Don't let everybody down.

Stomach fluttering as the first piano note echoed through the arena, I pushed off, stroking to gather speed for my first quad, the dreaded Lutz. I tensed, rushing the takeoff. My timing was critically off, and I opened up too late, over-rotating it and barely staying on my feet.

I could just imagine the negative GOE displayed in red on the top left of the screen for TV viewers beside the base mark. I'd already thrown away too many points, and it was only the first element. I had to focus and shake it off as much as I wanted to start again.

Focus or he'll beat you!

After an okay quad toe-triple toe, I nailed my first triple Axel before transitioning into the choreographic sequence, where I had time to catch my breath and express the music. But I could barely even hear Beethoven over the buzzing in my ears. I couldn't stop thinking about the Lutz.

What would he do?

Theodore would switch up his program on the fly and try the Lutz again, this time in combination. The month he'd been training in Toronto, Manon and Bill had been trying and failing to get him to stop changing his choreography and leaving out transitions. I'd done my best to ignore him.

I knew every moment of choreography as though it had been imprinted in my DNA. As I performed my combination spin, I scanned through the program for the right place to try the quad Lutz combination instead of a planned triple-triple.

Heart racing, I went through the motions, thinking ahead. My quad Lutz combination wasn't consistent enough yet, but wasn't this my chance to get it out in competition? If I did it, my score

would shoot up, and the audience would roar. I could do it. I had
to try.

My legs burned, but I flew across the ice and reached back
with my toe pick, vaulting up into the Lutz.

Pain flared in my hip as I crashed onto the ice, sliding with
momentum before popping back up onto my feet. Worse than
falling again on it was that without another jump on the end, even
a single toe, I'd repeated the same solo quad jump twice, which
wasn't allowed.

The audience clapped, trying to boost me. I'd made a mess of
my program, but I managed the rest without any more major
mistakes. I finished in a haze, the audience applauding despite
how terribly I'd performed.

All I could do was try to smile as I took my bows, shame burning my face. I'd failed miserably not only in front of the fans, but
my family. I would have loved nothing more than to crawl into a
hole and bury myself in darkness, but the cameras were on me, the
microphones strong enough to pick up every word in the Kiss and
Cry.

Steeling my spine, I gave Manon a stiff hug as she reassured
me that it was okay and I'd done my best. The Kiss and Cry area
for this competition had been adorned with a maple leaf-covered
bench and backdrop, the Canadian federation's logo prominently
displayed in a red and white theme.

It was my job now to sit on the bench with Manon and pretend all was well while the cameras zoomed in on us. As the judges
finalized their scores, the technical specialist reviewing any
questionable elements, slow-motion replays of key moments from
my performance unspooled on TV for the home audience, the
arena scoreboard, and on a monitor by my feet.

I had never actually allowed myself to shed tears in the Kiss
and Cry, and even in celebration, kisses were rare. Manon still
reassured me as we watched the replays, and I nodded, keeping my

face impassive as I watched my failures.

Theodore hadn't skated yet, and I'd kept on my noise-canceling headphones backstage. I'd heard the score of the previous skater, but he'd clearly made too many mistakes for me to worry about him ranking above me.

Skate Canada was part of the Grand Prix circuit of six competitions in the autumn, culminating in the Grand Prix Final in December for the top six skaters or teams in each discipline. We earned points for our placements at our two assigned events.

My mouth was painfully dry, and I gulped from the water bottle Manon had handed me. My chance of making the Grand Prix Final in Torino would depend on how I placed here and at my second assignment: NHK Trophy in Japan.

NHK would be a tough field—minus Theodore, who'd already won Skate America last week. If I were off the podium here at Skate Canada, even if I won NHK, which I was favored to do, would I earn enough points to make the final? It would depend on how other top skaters performed at their events.

Cold sweat clung to my skin. The judges were taking their time. The replays were over now, and all eyes focused on me like ants swarming my body. The longer the judges took, the more elements were in question, and the lower my score could be.

What had I been thinking? Why was I so stupid? I never switched around my choreography. It wasn't prudent, and I knew it. I'd lost focus and possibly destroyed my chances at the Grand Prix Final, which I was certainly expected to make.

If I didn't, it was the chance the skaters on my heels needed to gain momentum and favor with judges and spectators.

I was going to vomit.

Sometimes I wondered why of all sports, I'd chosen one that was judged. The panel of experts analyzed my every move, as did the viewers and the commentators. If I were a hurdler, either I'd win the race or I wouldn't. But from the moment I'd first tried on skates and fallen flat on my back, I'd craved the challenge of mastering the ice.

As the announcer finally read my free skate score—180.72—I squinted at the monitor by my feet and then up at the scoreboard, waiting for the standings. I saw my name appear at the top a moment before the announcer said, "And he is currently in first place."

There were two more skaters to go, including Theodore. I'd be bronze at worst, but I should stay ahead of the skater from China unless he truly excelled. It seemed I wasn't the only one who'd faltered, and despite the relief, I still felt sick to my stomach.

Manon patted my knee and told me I'd done well, which we both knew was a bald-faced lie, but the world was watching and listening. Backstage, she sighed heavily and muttered, "You got lucky," followed by something in French I didn't particularly want to translate.

But she did give me another hug before I had to run the gauntlet of waiting reporters and cameras. Making my way down the line, I gave stock answers about how unworried I was about the Olympics, and oh yes, it was great having Theo Sullivan pushing me in training, couldn't be better.

In the end, he didn't have a great free skate either, though he beat me by 9.63 points. I could admit that I'd let the performance go and probably hadn't deserved the program component scores I received, but Theodore's PCS were still unfairly high.

All I could do was make it through the medal ceremony and required press conference. I'd been told often that I had "resting bitch face," but I'd given up trying to smile all the time years before. My skating could speak for itself, though it hadn't said anything complimentary today.

Theo waited atop the podium with a huge grin when I skated out to thunderous applause. I bowed to the audience, who really were too kind and loyal to me even though I was a disgrace.

As much as I'd have loved to ignore Theo, I stopped in front of him and held out my hand. He shook it, then bent down with arms open because he was terrible.

I had no choice but to hug him back or appear churlish. Appearances were vital in skating. I had to be seen as a gracious loser even when I seethed with frustration and anger—most of it directed at myself. I stiffly embraced Theodore.

"Tough break with the Lutz," he said, his breath tickling my cheek as we parted.

If I'd spoken, I'd either have snapped in fury or—even worse—burst into tears. So I nodded and skated around the back of the podium to climb up to the silver position I'd managed to hang on to by my fingernails. Wang Zhan had won bronze, and he was thrilled by it, grinning madly and hugging us, practically bouncing onto the podium.

Suddenly, it struck me that I couldn't remember the last time I'd felt such *joy* at a medal, even a gold. When I'd captured my last world title, the overriding sensation had been relief. Satisfaction, yes, but *joy*? I watched Wang Zhan with a pang of envy, wondering if Theodore was joyful. He was always grinning in that infuriating way with his perfect, beautiful smile, so he must have been.

"YOU CAN DO better."

"Mom!" My mother huffed at Obaachan and drew me into a hug, and I allowed a moment to breathe in her favorite tropical perfume that smelled subtly of coconut and made me think of summer. "We know you did your best and we're always proud of you."

I stepped back and nodded, though I preferred Obaachan's honesty. We understood each other. I hadn't done my best—not remotely—and what did I have to be proud of?

Perhaps that I hadn't completely imploded and could still make the final, but this silver medal was going in the garbage. Either that or I'd wear it to practices to remind me of what not to do.

Dad hugged me too in the quiet corner of the arena concourse. The women's free skate had started, though there were still some people milling around and buying revolting-looking pizza. Arena food was uniformly disgusting and overpriced, and I wouldn't touch it if I was starving.

None of us were particularly tall, but Obaachan was so short I had to stoop to embrace her. She pinched my waist with a familiar, sharp little twist, and whispered, "You're in your own way." She stood back. "Annabelle won't like it."

I winced and agreed. Annabelle, my choreographer, was visiting Toronto from Montreal next week to go over programs with multiple skaters in the area and make tweaks. She would not be pleased at my butchering of her work today. Since I hired her and could easily not work with her again, she would go about it delicately. But I deserved the criticism.

"How's Ojiichan?" my father asked. "Is he wearing his hearing aids?"

I sighed. "No. He says he doesn't need them." Which we all knew wasn't true. But I didn't mind it too much. When I visited him at the retirement village, we often sat in peaceful silence for hours doing crosswords.

"He's always been stubborn as hell," Dad said. "Did I ever tell you about the time when I was five or six and—"

Sam groaned as he arrived with Etienne. "*Yes.* You've told us a million times." He hugged me. "Don't freak out. It's better to bomb here than later in the season."

Mom huffed. "He didn't *bomb.*"

Obaachan made a noise that was decidedly dubious. As Sam

spoke to her, Etienne quietly said to me, "Tough skate. You'll bounce back at NHK."

I nodded. Bouncing back was the only option. "How was the rhythm dance?"

His handsome face brightened. "Awesome. We moved up a slot and we're in the final flight tomorrow."

"Excellent." I truly was happy for him and Brianna.

Sam kissed Etienne's cheek. "So proud of you."

I truly was happy for Sam and Etienne as well, though watching the easy way they kissed and linked hands made me… What? Wistful? It was ridiculous. Even more bizarre was that it made me wonder where Theo was. Probably off celebrating without a care in the world.

My phone buzzed with a text update from the cat-sitting service feeding Esmeralda. As expected, she was still hiding every time the woman went over to check on her. I hated leaving her alone, but I had to compete.

"All right, we'll leave you and your friends to catch up," Mom said, waving to someone down the concourse. "See you tomorrow after the gala. We're cooking all your favorites for dinner." She pulled me into a hug.

I glanced behind to see who Mom had waved at. There were a few Canadian skaters I'd trained with here in Vancouver before I'd moved back to Toronto. Hannah Kwan gave me a cheery smile, her dark ponytail swaying. Her pairs partner stood beside her.

My eyes met Anton Orlov's, and I tasted bile. My ears buzzed, and though Etienne and Sam were saying something to me, I had to escape. Hannah called to me, and I ducked into the closest bathroom, breathing hard. Sweat prickled my brow. Mercifully, Etienne and Sam didn't follow.

It was inevitable that I'd encounter Anton at events. He and Hannah were vying for the silver at Nationals behind the top pairs team, who were world medalists.

We'd surely be on the Olympic team together, and I'd have to smile for pictures and be in the same room with him. On the same flights, the same buses.

It had been years now—three-point-seven to be exact—and I should have been able to move past it. But just seeing Anton hurtled me back, humiliation and hurt tying my stomach into knots. I hated—loathed, despised, detested, abhorred—my weakness.

Strangely, I thought of Theodore and what he'd do in my shoes. He'd probably have shrugged off the whole experience and moved on to the next hookup or relationship or party. With that smile firmly in place.

I waited thirteen minutes in a stall, and when I slipped out, Anton and the others were gone. I'd see them at the event banquet that night, but I'd be sure to keep as much distance as I could.

HOURS LATER, I'D escaped the banquet after making my obligatory appearance. It was a damp, drizzly night, which was the norm for Vancouver.

After putting on sweats and lacing up my shoes, I slipped out of the hotel and ran to the seawall and along the path there, replaying my free skate and itemizing the mistakes I'd made.

It was late by the time I crossed a park, the trail muddy. My feet skidded coming down a slope, and an image of Theodore sprawled in the mud—laughing as usual—filled my mind. Those gleaming teeth and almost-dimples in his cheeks. How red his lips looked when they were rain-wet...

Increasing my strides, I forced my thoughts from the memory of his body beneath me and the warm brush of his breath on my face.

In the hotel lobby, I sped to the elevators with my head down and hood raised. The banquet had surely ended by now, but plenty of people would have spilled out into the bar. I kept my eyes on my mud-flecked shoes until I stepped off on my floor, relieved at the hush that greeted me.

A hush demolished by Theodore calling out, "There you are!" and flashing one of his smiles.

He loitered by my room, so I had no choice but to approach. Leaning one shoulder against the wall, blue dress shirt hugging his lean torso and suit jacket slung over his shoulder, he asked, "Can you do me a favor?"

No. "What?"

"I lost my card." He seemed to read my mind. "And my phone's dead. Can you call reception for me? My room's just down the hall."

It was preferable to spending any more time with him than necessary, so I nodded. Then he followed me into my room because he was insufferable. Also clearly intoxicated judging by his bright eyes and slight stumble.

"I have to piss. Can I?"

"Presumably."

He laughed, tossing his jacket onto the wooden desk chair and missing by a mile. "See? I knew you were funny under all that seriousness."

"I'm not."

This only made him giggle and hiccup. "Sorry. I had too much wine. Or cocktails. Or maybe both. You should have stayed. There are lots of Russians here, and they know how to let loose."

Ignoring him, I dusted off his jacket and hung it over the chair before calling the front desk. They agreed to send someone up with a key but of course had to see ID before handing it over.

I'd forgotten to ask him his room number. The receptionist wouldn't tell me, so they'd come up to my room. Which meant I was still stuck with Theodore.

He emerged from the bathroom talking as if we were in the middle of a conversation before *flopping onto my bed*. "So I dared them to shoot tequila instead of vodka."

I had to be dreaming. He was not really here in my room with his dress shirt now unbuttoned down to his chest and hanging out of his trousers, his tie unaccounted for. Sprawled on the bed I'd been using. Still wearing his leather dress shoes. Dark chest hair peeking out of the wide collar of his aforementioned shirt.

On. My. Bed.

He gave me a dazed smile. "Don't you think?" When I didn't answer, he added, "That the Russian ice dancers aren't as good as that new hot Italian team, but they'll probably win anyway. And they can hold their tequila surprisingly well."

"Your shoes are on my bed."

"Oh. Sorry!" He looked at his own feet as if surprised to see them. "I figured you'd take the bed by the window. It's funny how most of the rooms at this hotel have two beds even if you ask for only one. I used to get a roommate to split the cost, but I made great money touring Japan last spring. But you know, these coverlets are probably covered in jizz, so don't worry about shoes."

Correction: this had to be a nightmare.

He bolted up to sitting. "Not my jizz. I didn't, like, jerk off on your bed." He laughed. "Wait, you were in here, so you know that. You would have seen me jerking off. Not that you would have just watched."

Our eyes met, and his laugh faltered. My face was hot.

His Adam's apple bobbed, and he laughed again. "What I mean is, I saw this thing on TV where they brought one of those UV lights or whatever—like they use to find blood splatter that's been cleaned up—and they examined hotel rooms. The bedspreads don't get washed very often, and it was cum city."

Which was disgusting, but hearing him say "*cum*" sent entirely inappropriate desire bolting through me. That word should have been distasteful, yet...

Glancing around the room, I had to look anywhere else but at his parted thighs.

"Gross, right? The remote is apparently super germy, which makes sense."

He rattled off more repulsive facts, and though I'd known hotel rooms weren't as clean as I'd like them to be, they'd been a staple of my life for years. I hadn't wanted to think about it. I'd taken off my running shoes by the door, and now I was glad to be wearing socks on the carpet.

"I need to shower," I blurted.

Theodore's gaze dragged up my body. "Oh, right. You were running. Why didn't you stay to celebrate?"

I spat the word like poison. "*Celebrate?*"

"Yeah. I mean, I know you came second, but..." He winced. "Sorry. I shouldn't have brought that up."

"Neither of us has anything to celebrate. We're lucky the rest of the field was weak."

He shrugged. "It wasn't my best, that's for sure. But I still won. And I won Skate America last week, so I'm through to the final for sure. That's definitely worth celebrating."

"But you were sloppy. Your transitions were barely there. If you'd show up to practice on time and do your run-throughs and stop being lazy, you'd—" I broke off. Why was I trying to help him?

With an eye roll, he said, "Yes, *Mom*. I still beat you."

I clenched my jaw at the reminder. "Don't you care that you didn't perform as well as you could?"

"Why do *you* care? It's not very killer of you."

I had no idea how to respond to that. He was laughing to himself in that way drunk people did sometimes.

Apparently my confusion was evident because he said, "Oh, I mean you're supposed to have the killer instinct. My mom is always praising how ruthless you are." He wrinkled up his face. "But I dunno. You could have left me in the hall, but you're helping me. Here I am." He motioned to himself and the bed. "I don't think you're as cold as people say."

It hurt, but only a twinge. I'd much rather everyone thought I was ruthless and steely than betraying the truth about my weakness. I said nothing.

Theodore eagerly filled the silence. "Anyway, it's done now. No point in beating myself up about today. Who cares about one Grand Prix event? It was good enough. It's the Olympics that matter."

Good enough? Who cares? I clenched my fists, a tide of fury rising. How could he not *care?* He could be truly great—perhaps the greatest of all time—if he put in the effort instead of the minimum. With his natural talent, he'd be unbeatable. He almost was already. It was such a *waste.*

"Do you care about anything? Don't you want to make Mr. Webber proud?"

Face paling, his smile vanished. He opened and closed his mouth. "I…"

Then Theodore shot off the bed and into the bathroom. I listened to him vomiting, guilt washing away my resentment. I considered bringing him a bottle of water from the mini bar, wondering whether it was better to try and help or give him privacy and not intrude. Even though it was my room.

In the end, I was still debating when he emerged red-faced with his hands in his pockets. "Sorry. Tequila was a bad idea. I forgot that it makes me puke."

There was a soft knock on the door, and Theodore showed his ID to the employee and took the new key card. He smiled at me, but it was more of a grimace. "Thanks, man. Sorry for barging in. See you at gala practice. I'll try not to be too hungover." He waved and was gone.

His suit jacket remained where I'd hung it properly over the chair. I folded it over my arm and opened the door, but the hallway was already empty. His room must have been close by.

Suddenly, I wished I knew the number so I could return his jacket and give him the water. Did he have toothpaste and a toothbrush? Surely he did. I had Listerine, and it would help to gargle with it to get the acid aftertaste out of his mouth.

I considered knocking on every door on the floor until I found him, but eventually retreated into my room. I pulled off the coverlet, folding and leaving it on the spare bed.

I discovered Theodore's tie crumpled on the tile floor in the bathroom and ironed it before carefully rolling it into the pocket of his jacket.

Chapter Six

Theo

EVEN THOUGH I was in a new city, launching the hookup app was like opening the fridge and seeing the same chicken breasts and broccoli inside.

Granted, it was barely eight o'clock in the morning and the rink was in the middle of nowhere so no one was raring and ready to go nearby, but I could still scroll the local options who weren't online.

Meh.

I'd caught a ride with Henry even though my first session wasn't until nine. I figured I could still relax while I was waiting and drink my extra-extra-large black coffee.

I'd convinced Henry to hit the Tim Hortons drive-through since it was on the way. I wasn't picky about coffee as long as it was full of caffeine, but Henry had turned up his nose, sticking to his thermos of whatever he brewed himself. I thought it was green tea or something.

Watching Henry drill his quad Sal, I licked the last crumb of sugar from the maple dip donut I hadn't been able to resist, trying not to feel too guilty. I'd had an egg and ham breakfast sandwich too, though Henry had clearly disapproved.

He probably made his own power bars of oats and tofu or

whatever. But I'd be on the ice four hours total today with two hours of cardio off-ice, plus strength work. A little sugar boost wouldn't hurt, even if my mother would really, really disagree.

I scrolled the app. It was all cauliflower and protein shakes when I wanted...what? Chocolate cake? Filet mignon? Mmm, bacon. Hell, I'd settle for a butternut squash. Or maybe a rutabaga. Radishes. Anything but more carrot sticks. I wanted the hookup equivalent of that maple dip donut.

I watched Henry power around the rink and land Sal after Sal consistently. He missed a few, but not many, and the running edge on his landings really was gorgeous. He didn't rush through elements like I did sometimes. And his black pants clung to his long, lean legs and his ass...

Jesus, I really was horny if I was thinking about Henry Sakaguchi's ass.

I opened the virtual fridge again, knowing the same shit would be inside. I tried another app, scrolling aimlessly past headless abs. Did Henry have a profile?

He'd seemed adamant that he didn't, but hmm. I tried to remember glimpsing him in the locker room and what his chest looked like, but I'd really never paid attention.

Probably not much hair. Lean muscles, flat stomach. Pinkish nipples. Would he have a little hair under his bellybutton? Was he cut or uncut? What did he like? Was he as innocent as he seemed?

I gulped down the rest of my now cold coffee and fidgeted on the bench. Popping a boner at the rink wasn't in my training plan, but it sure did wake me up.

Enough pondering Henry's imaginary hookup app profile. He was way too uptight to have one. I couldn't imagine him relaxing enough to actually have sex or have fun doing it. He'd be the most boring lay ever.

A few hours later, I sat in the small linoleum-floored, orange-walled lunchroom in the dungeon by Manon and Bill's office.

There was a microwave and fridge and a few round tables.

I moaned as I bit into my oxtail curry roti from across the street. I sat with Julien and tried to reassure him as he angsted about his triple Axel. Ga-young and her mom were at another table eating big salads in Tupperware containers.

"I just can't get the timing on my takeoff," Julien said glumly.

"You will. Didn't you grow four inches or something this year? Throws everything off. We all go through it."

"Even you?" He looked at me hopefully.

"Absolutely! You'll get it back."

Honestly, I'd transitioned from junior to senior without my jumps being too affected. I could naturally spin so fast that my triples and quads had grown with me. My issue had been patience and focus. But *so* many skaters struggled, especially girls since their bodies changed even more.

"Thanks. It's hard not to get down. I want to win so badly."

I grinned. "Winning's awesome. But it's not everything."

He rolled his eyes. "Says the guy who can't lose these days."

"Fair point." I took another bite of my roti. "Mmm."

Henry waited by the microwave, looking lost in his own thoughts as usual. When the machine dinged, he removed a glass container using a folded paper towel and headed to the one empty table. I said, "Hey, do you want to sit with us?" and pulled out the remaining chair. It just seemed wrong for Henry to eat alone.

He stopped, seeming to debate before joining us. His knee bumped mine under the table, and he jerked back, stirring his lunch, the fork clinking on the rectangular glass container. It looked like salmon with a ton of mixed veggies and a bit of wild rice. I couldn't see any sauce. Did he even put salt on that?

I took another bite of my roti and mumbled, "Have you ever tried this? So good."

Henry raised an eyebrow. "Are you having a cheat day?"

"I guess!" I shrugged. "I've got a month until the final. But

I'm out of food at home. I really need to stock up. Ugh, I hate cooking and bringing my lunch."

Julien was eating chicken and veggies. He said, "My mom fills up the freezer with these lunches for me."

"Yeah, my mom used to make every one of my meals." I shrugged, shaking off the tension that gripped me. I took another bite and imagined how pissed it would make her. "I'm pretty good most of the time, and I'll be better closer to a competition. One cheat day won't kill me."

Henry made this little sound of…disagreement? Disgust?

I asked, "What?"

"So undisciplined," he muttered under his breath.

I rolled my eyes. "Yeah, but I still beat you at Skate Canada, didn't I?" This got a glare from him, and Julien watched us warily. I added, "I pull it off when it counts," and took a giant bite of oxtail. It was a little spicy, but I refused to cough.

He shook his head, eating his bland fish and vegetables and ignoring me. Look, he wasn't *wrong*, but I knew what it was like to count every calorie obsessively, and fuck that. Before I could control it and put on a smile, anger flashed hot.

"Maybe I'm undisciplined, but at least I'm not boring AF. You know, if anyone actually wanted to fuck you, they'd have to take the giant stick out of your ass first."

It was a dumb thing to say, and *why was I thinking about Henry having sex*??? In the sudden, suffocating silence of the lunchroom, Henry flushed with this weird little wince. It was more than just embarrassment or anger—the split second of hurt was unmistakable.

Ga-young's mom said sternly, "What kind of talk is that?" Beside her, Ga-young gaped at me, fork frozen halfway to her mouth.

Julien muttered something in French, shaking his head, and Henry put down his fork, snapped the lid on his container, pushed back his chair, and stood.

"I'm sorry!" I blurted. "I don't know why I said that." I leapt to my feet. "I didn't mean it. I'm sure lots of people want to—" Wait, nope, that wasn't the direction to take this. "I'm sorry. Food is a touchy subject."

Henry still left without a word. Not that I could blame him. I slumped back into my chair and picked at the rest of my lunch, the joy gone.

"That really wasn't like you," Ga-young said when her mom left to go to the bathroom.

"I know."

"I mean, Henry hates your guts, and he was definitely judgy about your lunch, but I didn't think you had a problem with him," Julien said as he peeled a banana.

It shouldn't have bothered me at all, but it did. It nagged at me all damn day.

Did he really *hate* me?

Yeah, we were competitors and the two top skaters in the world for four years now since the last Olympics. But he was giving me rides now. Surely he wasn't *that* Canadianly polite.

I had a late off-ice strengthening session with the trainer in the windowless dungeon gym, so I texted Henry that I'd get a Lyft. I could have just told him, but I figured he didn't want to talk to me after what a dick I'd been. It was only fair to let him off the hook.

I worked with the trainer on strengthening my non-dominant leg and the whole left side of my body as well so I wasn't off-balance. I did a hundred jumps a day landing on my right leg, so the left couldn't be left out.

"You coming to the extra session tomorrow morning?" the trainer, Maggie, asked as she sat on a weight bench and watched my one-legged squats. I was barefoot, my toes spread wide.

I opened my mouth to say hell no, Saturday was for sleeping

in, but hesitated. "What's the focus again?"

"Natalia Platova is teaching a masterclass in edges."

"Oh, right." She was a legend, and it was amazing she was still traveling around giving seminars in her eighties. "Yeah, for sure."

Mr. Webber would love the idea since he'd always been a Natalia fanboy. My theory was that they'd had a torrid, forbidden affair a million years ago when they were both competing while she was trapped in communist Russia.

Yes, he'd like me taking her class, even if it was a group thing. The last few times I'd called, he'd sounded really tired and hadn't been able to talk long.

I kept thinking about what Henry said after Skate Canada. I really did want to make Mr. Webber proud. I was determined to crush it at the Grand Prix Final in December.

My quad burned as I lowered into another squat and then pushed up to a calf raise, core tight for balance with my hands held out in front of me. "It would be stupid to miss it."

"It would," Maggie agreed with a shrewd look. "So I'd skip the partying tonight." She made a circular motion with her hand, and I performed a series of quick twitch jumps on one foot—backward, then forward.

"I haven't even had a glass of wine since Skate Canada!" I swiped at the sweat on my forehead, indignant. "Just because I like to relax and have a good time once in a while doesn't mean I do it all the time."

She held up her hands. "I believe you."

But I could tell she didn't. Not really. I mean, yes, had I gotten wasted in the past? Sure. Especially when I was a teenager and living in the prison of my parents' house under the watchful eye of Warden Mom.

When I'd had the chance to go to a competition without her because she couldn't take the time away from my sisters to go to Asia or Europe, I'd let loose.

But I'd moved to LA to train with Mr. Webber when I was twenty-one. Yeah, I'd had some fun there, but I'd calmed down a lot compared to when I was a teenager.

In skating, reputations were hard to shake, and I was the party boy to some people no matter what. I'd been training in Toronto more than a month now, and I'd gone nowhere and hooked up with no one.

"I'll be there!" I told Maggie.

"Do you want a lift? I'm sleeping at my girlfriend's tonight, and she's in the condo next to yours. I assume you won't want to ride with Henry."

Oh.

Obviously word had spread about what a jackass I'd been, because of course it had. There were zero secrets at a training rink. "Sure. You're going? I didn't think you skated."

"I barely do, but I'm trying to learn. It helps me help you if I can understand the sport better. Now let's do some burpees."

Groaning, I did as I was told even though burpees were created by the devil.

Obviously Henry was going tomorrow since an edge class by Natalia Platova was probably his wet dream. Not that I was still thinking about what turned him on. I wasn't. I wasn't thinking at all about Henry and how much he did or didn't hate me.

EVERYONE CAME FOR the class even though it was meant for kids. This was Natalia Platova, so you showed up no matter how good you were.

The arena pulsed with skaters, parents, and coaches, the row of bleachers full. In his usual all black, Henry watched Natalia intently, carving out beautiful edges and following her instructions perfectly.

"Hey!" A sharp finger jabbed my hip, and I tore my gaze from Henry. A little girl grumbled, "Watch where you're going." Then she looked up and apparently realized who I was, her freckled face paling. "Oh my God. Theo Sullivan."

I grinned. "Good morning. What's your name? Sorry I was in your way."

She forgave me. During the break, she produced a Sharpie, and I signed her skating club jacket. Her parents were thrilled, and I chatted with them and a bunch of the other parents who gathered. The elite skaters didn't usually share the ice with the club kids, but it was fun to answer their questions.

It was on the second break that morning when I blinked at my phone, the letters in the text from my sister Veronica suddenly unreadable. I rubbed my eyes and looked at it again, blinking forcefully. But my vision wouldn't clear, and the screen seemed too bright, the words obscured like there was some kind of filter—

The horrible sinking sensation hammered me. I closed my eyes, and there it was on the left in my field of vision—the aura warning of an impending migraine. It only happened every month or two, so I shouldn't have complained, but it was the worst.

I hated it. I hated how helpless it made me feel when the aura appeared, and there was nothing I could do to rewind.

Fuck. I had to go. The break was ending, and I didn't see Manon or Bill so I could explain. I went to grab my stuff as the aura grew and obscured my vision. I thought of it as a prism or crystal.

It was multifaceted, a 3D entity that began on the left and grew bigger and bigger before fading away. Sometimes I imagined it too big for my eyes to handle, encompassing my brain and constricting as the pain set in.

Digging in my sports bag, I prayed I'd remembered to throw in the new bottle of ibuprofen gel caps. It would come as a shock to no one that I hadn't. The bottle was probably sitting in a plastic bag on the kitchen counter with whatever other shit I bought the other day at Shoppers.

The huge florescent lights overhead seemed brighter than ever, and I held my hand over my eyes. I finally spotted Manon amid a group of parents and waved her over as I quickly took off my skates, trying to breath through the low-level panic. I reminded myself I'd had migraines before, and I'd be okay no matter how helpless I felt.

"What's up?" she asked.

"Sorry, I need to go home."

An eyebrow arched. "Jet lag?"

The few people in earshot laughed, and I couldn't blame them. I tried to laugh too. "No, not this time."

"Hungover?" Ivan suggested.

Manon's lips thinned. "All right, if you're hungover you'd better make your exit."

It was probably dumb for me to feel quite so offended, but for once, this wasn't my fault. "I'm not hungover!" I cringed at how whiny I sounded. Why should they believe me? "Honestly. I'm getting a migraine."

Manon nodded as Bill appeared. "Okay. Go on home, Theo. We'll check in on you tonight." To Bill, she added, "He has a migraine."

Bill simply said, "Okay. Feel better."

I couldn't tell if he believed me or not, and I hated that I *cared*. Now I had to either wait for the torturous bus or hope a Lyft driver was willing to come out to the arena. I grabbed my bag and made my escape, wishing I'd brought my sunglasses even though it was cloudy.

Outside the arena doors, I squinted at my phone. The pain hadn't hit yet, but the aura made it so hard to see. It would disappear soon, and then *bam*.

"You're leaving?"

Was this migraine causing auditory hallucinations? I turned to find Henry, skate guards on his blades. I said, "I don't feel well." He frowned, and I wasn't sure he believed me. I wasn't sure what that expression was on his face. Disappointment?

Nausea gripped me so hard I clamped my jaw shut, but it was no use. I lunged to the curb, bending and puking into the dead leaves scattered on the cracked pavement.

This happened sometimes when a migraine hit, and at least I'd only eaten a power bar, so there wasn't much in there. I coughed and spat, dropping to my knees.

In the corner of my eye, Henry's skates appeared. I rasped, "I'm not hungover!" It was stupid since he didn't even like me, but it mattered that Henry knew this wasn't because I'd been irresponsible. "I'm getting a migraine, I swear." I coughed, more bile coming up.

His hand squeezed my shoulder gently. "I'll drive you. Hold on."

The relief was warm sweetness, but I shivered there on the curb, spitting and drinking little sips from my water bottle, which at least I'd remembered.

Henry returned, and I managed to get up and walk to his car. The aura was gone now, so the pain would start any minute, growing until my head felt trapped in cement.

In the car, I leaned against the window as he drove. "I really do have a migraine. There was an aura and everything."

He kept his gaze on the road, slowing for a red light. I didn't think he'd say anything, which probably meant he thought I was full of shit, which really *bugged* me.

Then he asked, "What's that like?"

"The aura? I see it like a prism, kind of. It's usually a little crescent moon, and then it gets bigger and bigger until it's gone. Then the pain hits." Eyes closed, I wished desperately for sunglasses.

"Do you have medication?"

"Just over-the-counter stuff. If I catch it early enough and lie down in a dark room, it's usually manageable after a few hours. But I forgot to put the Advil in my bag."

"Mm."

In the underground parking lot, I shuffled along with my head down as Henry walked beside me. I complained about how damn bright it was everywhere. The elevator was torture, the movement making my empty stomach gurgle with a wave of fresh nausea.

It wasn't until we were at my door that I realized.

First off that Henry was still with me, and secondly that my keys were in my jacket—which I'd tossed on a bench by the ice that morning. I groaned. "Oh, fuck me. I don't have my keys. We need to get the concierge."

Henry looked at his phone. "They'll be on their lunch break."

"Fuuuck." I was ready to curl up in a ball on the ugly beige hall carpet.

Henry's long fingers grasped my elbow, and he led me back to the elevator. I followed, figuring he'd fix this somehow. The electrical storm in my brain made it hard to focus or think. I just needed darkness and Advil.

Henry didn't take me down to wait for the concierge, though. He guided me into his condo, telling me to take off my shoes when we got inside. I did, glad my stomach was already empty when I bent to unlace my sneakers.

"Thanks. I'm sure he'll be back soon," I mumbled. "Lunch isn't that long."

Saying nothing, Henry led me into the main area of the condo. It was a studio like mine, but he had a real bed with a frame and everything across the far wall under the big window.

A leather love seat sat across from a TV on a chest of drawers, and a little round table and chairs were squeezed in by the kitchen. It was all so grown-up.

He turned from the drawers, holding out a plaid bundle. I stared in confusion.

"There's vomit on your pants," he said.

"Oh! Fuck. Sorry. Did I get any on your car seat?"

He was still holding out the bundle. Pajamas? I took the soft material, and he disappeared into the bathroom. I guess he wanted me to change into these? It was so hard to *think*.

I stripped off my practice pants—yep, splashes of puke on one leg—but Henry was already back holding a bottle of Advil and staring at me with wide eyes.

Maybe I wasn't supposed to get changed? But I couldn't just stand there in my boxer briefs, so I kept going while he turned sharply toward the kitchen.

The green plaid PJs were super soft flannel with a matching shirt and bottoms because of course Henry wore full sets of pajamas and not a T-shirt and boxers or whatever.

He returned with a glass of water, and I fumbled with the buttons on the PJ top, which was tight over my chest. For a second, I thought he'd offer to help, and excitement flared through the stony pain. Then he motioned me to the bathroom and gave me the water and Advil.

He'd also left out a new toothbrush on the counter still in its packaging. Probably a freebie from the dentist. A half-used tube of toothpaste sat beside it, the end efficiently rolled. Was he secretly my nana in disguise? If Henry had a purse, he'd carry mints.

When I went back out, I stumbled. Henry knelt on his bed, pulling the gray curtains shut and reaching out with his ass on display.

Definitely not my nana. Nope.

Standing beside the double bed, he wordlessly pulled back the duvet, which was a silvery blue that reminded me a bit of his free skate costume. I gratefully slid between the sheets, my whole body aching and exhausted, feeling like the cement had encased all of me.

"This isn't how I imagined the first time in your bed."

Oh, Jesus, wait. Had I said that out loud? What was I even talking about? I pried my eyes open, but it was too dark to see if Henry was blushing. I was afraid if I tried to explain the joke that I'd make it worse, so I quit while I was ahead and shut my mouth.

I'd just take a little nap, and then we could get my keys from the concierge, and Henry could have his Saturday back...

I wasn't sure how long it had been before I blearily blinked. The condo was still dark, a faint red glow coming from the kitchen. Henry sat on the far end of the love seat with his legs curled under, socked feet peeking out.

He'd changed into sweats and a hoodie, and under the soft yellow light of a reading lamp positioned away from me, he wrote with pencil on a clipboard.

Surely the concierge was back from lunch and could open my condo, but the thought of returning to my mattress on the floor and not much else did not appeal even a little.

I snuggled under Henry's duvet and breathed in his rich scent from the pillow. Eyes closed again, my head still painfully heavy, I listened to the occasional scratch of the pencil and wondered what he was doing.

I slept more. Henry's pillow-top mattress was amazingly soft yet still supportive. I was dozing lightly when I felt a cat jump up. I'd noticed a fleeing feline butt earlier, and now it was apparently curious about who was in Henry's bed.

It was weird that thinking those words—*in Henry's bed*— excited me. I'd been in my fair share of beds, but now the thought of someone else between these quality sheets—not just here, but with Henry in bed too instead of sitting nearby—had jealousy spiking through me.

I imagined him holding me. Kissing me. Touching me all over, both of us naked—even though his PJs were really comfortable, and I loved wearing them.

I imagined coaxing moans of pleasure from him and finally making him smile. Clearly the electrical storm in my brain was causing a misfire.

The cat brushed my bare skin where I'd stuck out my foot, the PJ leg bunched up. After a while, I always got too hot to sleep all tucked and bundled.

I didn't want to open my eyes or move and frighten it, so I stayed motionless in that twilight state. At some point, a rough little tongue licked my shin experimentally, and I smiled.

"How do you feel?"

I opened my eyes at Henry's question, the black, orange, and white Calico cat leaping down to safety. Henry made a little clucking noise that apparently beckoned it. The cat jumped onto the love seat and walked across the back before settling by his head.

Realizing I hadn't answered and was staring at Henry like a creeper, I said, "Better. Thank you. Who's that?"

"Esmeralda."

"Big *Hunchback* fan?"

He seemed surprised. "Yes."

"What? I know literature. Okay, fine, I know cartoon musicals. We had the DVD when I was a kid."

His eyebrows shot up even higher. "It's under-appreciated."

"It is!" So Henry liked cartoon musicals too? It was weirdly comforting, though for all I knew he also read ancient books. "She's sweet. A little skittish?"

"Mm." He shifted to face me, stroking her idly with his left hand. I could hear the low vibration of her purr.

"What are you working on?" I nodded to the clipboard on his lap, relieved that my head felt more normal.

"Crossword."

"Oh, that explains the pencil. I've never really done one.

78

When I was a kid I liked word searches. They're probably super easy for you. Is that the *New York Times* crossword? I saw a video on YouTube about how it gets harder every day of the week. Also, crosswords have themes? I had no clue. Heh, *clue*. I'm surprised you don't do it in pen and force yourself to start over if you make a mistake."

For a second, I thought he was going to get pissed. But a tiny smile tugged at the corner of his mouth. *Yes!*

He said, "Touché."

It wasn't a real, beaming smile, but it was major progress. My stomach growled, but I ignored it. Being here in Henry's darkened condo in his pajamas felt so comforting. Like we were in a little cocoon. It was surreal and strange but kind of amazing.

"You must be hungry," he said.

I stretched and yawned. "Yeah. What time is it?"

"Four twelve."

"Shit, really? I've taken up your whole afternoon. I'm sorry."

"It's not your fault."

"I swear I didn't have any chocolate. Or red wine. Sometimes citrus can be a trigger, but I didn't have any this whole week."

Henry's brow furrowed. "It's not your fault you have a migraine."

"I shouldn't have had that roti, but I don't think there was anything in there that would do it. Sometimes the migraines just seem to happen even if I do everything right. Honestly."

"I believe you."

"Oh. Right." I cringed. "Sorry. I get defensive about food. Have I mentioned that?" I plowed on before I lost my nerve. "I was an asshole yesterday."

He pulled Esmeralda into his lap, eyes on her as he stroked. "I shouldn't have criticized your food choices."

"Look, we both know a donut for breakfast wasn't the smartest start to my day. I'm supposed to be an actual adult, but sometimes I think I'm still rebelling against my mom when I eat junk."

"She always seemed…challenging."

I barked out a laugh. "That's a nice way to put it. If she was here now she'd be ripping me a new one for having a migraine. She'd insist it was my fault and search my room for evidence of cheating on my diet and grill her spies at the rink for intel."

Henry watched me with his brow extra furrowed. I shrugged. "She was always *really* invested in my skating. When I grew and got zits in middle school and put on a bit of weight, she started locking the fridge and pantry."

He blinked. "How?"

"Like, actual chains and mini padlocks on the doors attached to brackets she installed. After a few months, my dad stepped in. He usually lets her do whatever she wants because it's easier that way, but my sisters were embarrassed to bring their friends home. Not to mention pissed that they couldn't grab a snack when they wanted. I guess my friends were other skaters who weren't as shocked by it. But she was right that nutrition is important. I'm sure she'd approve of your eating plan."

He shook his head firmly. "I don't approve of her approach."

"Yeah, well. At least Manon and Bill don't do public weigh-ins. Mr. Webber didn't either," I added quickly. "But my Mom insisted on it with my old coach in Chicago, and I guess he agreed. Pavel's originally from Russia, so he grew up in that Soviet system. If they gained an ounce there was no borscht that night. Do Russians actually eat borscht? Hmm. Did you read that interview with the Russian girl who quit last year? They don't even drink water some days because they're afraid they'll gain. It's so fucked up. But I'm fine. I try not to obsess about it, but I really do need to get my shit together to buy more groceries and bring my lunches to the rink. I need to plan ahead better."

After a few moments of silence while he studied me—*in his*

bed—Henry said, "I'll make dinner now."

I guess I could have argued and said I'd put him out too much already, but… A home-cooked dinner sounded amazing. So I drank more water and sat up in his bed, still feeling muzzy and tired out after all that talking even though talking was one of my favorite things.

Esmeralda meowed at Henry as he moved around the kitchen. I couldn't see exactly what he was making because the pass-through was higher than the counter, but I watched him concentrating as he chopped, the rhythmic sound of the knife soothing. He bit his lip at one point, and all I could think about was kissing him.

"Is she hungry?" I asked as the cat meowed even louder. Onion and garlic sizzled in a pan, along with spices. Cumin, maybe? Whatever it was, it smelled amazing.

"Always," Henry said. He scooped her up, nuzzling her head.

I was officially jealous of a cat.

Wait, what? No. This was only my post-migraine brain being a dick. Definitely not jealous and didn't want Henry to nuzzle me. But I had to admit I wanted his approval. Which made no sense! Why should I want that?

I was the two-time, current world champion, and most importantly I'd beat him at the last four—no, five!—of our matchups. I was on top. I shouldn't need anyone's approval but the judges'.

My face went hot as he approached, still holding Esmeralda. He crouched and released her next to the cat scratching tree at the foot of the bed, then returned to the kitchen.

"Watch," he said, opening a cupboard. He took out a package of red lentils and crinkled the plastic.

"Okay." I waited for the punch line. Was this a lentil joke?

Then he slowly picked up a thin plastic pouch. I couldn't see what was on the label. Looking toward the cat, he crinkled the plastic a tiny, tiny bit. Barely audible.

Esmeralda practically *flew* back into the kitchen, mewling at his feet. Henry shook out two little beige-brown shapes into his palm and said, "Her favorite treats. She never mistakes any other package for this one. Never." He bent and disappeared out of sight behind the counter.

"Wow. Impressive!"

Soon, chicken sizzled, and I belatedly asked if I could do anything to help. But Henry said no, so I settled back against his pillows and watched him cook for me. Again belatedly, I said I should get dressed, and he told me my clothes were still in the dryer.

He'd done laundry for me, and I liked it.

We ate at his little table with cork-backed place mats of Van Gogh's "Starry Night" under the white plates. He'd made fajita filling with chicken and peppers, the whole wheat tortillas tucked into a fabric warmer that looked like a big round oven mitt.

I quickly rolled a fajita. "Mmm," I groaned as I took a bite. "Oh my God, so good."

He'd set out all the fillings, taking up the rest of the table. As he spooned salsa on top of his fajita, he looked pleased at my enthusiasm, his eyes lighting up. There was no cheese, but he'd included thick, organic sour cream, and I slathered it on my next creation.

We watched a home renovation show and ate delicious food. A sleek, black SodaStream sat on the counter in his kitchen, and even though he didn't have any of the sugary flavors to add, the plain soda water went perfectly. I mean, an ice-cold Corona would have been great too, but that definitely wasn't part of a pre-Olympic eating plan.

The thought of the Olympics made my stomach swoop. Here I was with my biggest rival for gold, sharing a meal and wearing his PJs while his cat rubbed against our ankles. I could imagine my mother's fury at my softness and how shocked our competitors and everyone else would be if they could see us now.

A thrill rippled through me. It felt wonderfully forbidden even though all we were doing was eating dinner and watching a *Property Brothers* rerun.

It wasn't like we were fucking—which wasn't something I should think about, so I tried to shut it down immediately. But my mind still whirled, shaking off the lingering migraine slowness.

Under the table, if I moved my left leg an inch or two, my knee would touch his. If I leaned over and kissed him, what would he do?

My heart skipped as I looked at him. A chunk of salsa had caught on the corner of his mouth. He glanced at me, going still as he swallowed, a question in his deep brown eyes.

I reached out and swiped the tomato from his lips, touching him for a fleeting moment. "Salsa," I said.

Henry was like a statue as I turned back to the TV renovation and took another bite of dinner. I ate and pretended everything was completely normal. He started eating again too, and when I wiped my mouth with a sharply folded cloth napkin, I darted out my tongue to lick the salsa from my thumb.

Chapter Seven

Henry

WHY WAS THEODORE Sullivan so persistently nice?
  Well, I supposed he wasn't *always*, but neither was I.
He was generous more often than not, regularly going out of his
way to encourage others.

As I ate a banana and circled my ankles, sitting on a chair
backstage at the Grand Prix Final with my socked feet straight out
in front of me in the air, I watched him comfort his young
American teammate as she cried in frustration.

He sat on the floor in the corner with June across the nonde-
script open space, and though I couldn't hear, from the way she
was gesturing as she spoke I was sure she was complaining about
her under-rotations. She wore a tracksuit, but her hair was still
twisted into an intricate knot and her glittery makeup smudged
her cheeks.

I sympathized, but what could really be said about it? She
needed to go higher. If she persisted in completing more than a
quarter rotation of a jump on the ice as she landed, the jumps
would be downgraded. It had to be corrected, and better to do it
now while she was still relatively young.

But Theodore could apparently find quite a bit to say about it.
He gesticulated and smiled encouragingly and talked and talked.

June sniffled and nodded and eventually gave him tentative smiles. He wrapped an arm around her slim shoulders, giving her a squeeze.

A shiver rippled through me as I imagined what it would feel like.

When I finished fifty ankle circles in both directions, I stood to do some shaking, starting with my hands, then my arms, then bouncing into my knees as well, waking up my body. I was used to jet lag, but some days it was harder than others. I'd won NHK in Japan with a clean short and one major mistake in the long—a fall on my quad toe combination. The quad Lutz had been my best yet, though.

Of course it bothered me not to go clean in both, but there was the Grand Prix Final here in Torino, Nationals, and of course the Olympics, plus Worlds a few weeks after that. There was danger in peaking too early in the season.

As I sat again, listening to the muffled music playing in the rink for the pairs' short program—some terribly dreary old song about chasing cars—Theodore plopped down on the floor at my feet and huffed with his phone in hand.

"I swear to God, if my mom annoys Mr. Webber one more time… He's not even coaching me right now! And I'm an adult!"

It truly was inappropriate. I was fortunate that while my parents had always supported my very expensive skating career, they would have been just as happy for me to quit.

They had jobs and interests and had always deferred to my coaches. But there were many parents in the sport who were far, far too invested in their children's skating.

"Does she contact Manon and Bill too?"

"She tried, but they blocked her. Mr. Webber still uses an old landline, so he's just hanging up on her now. He's got too much to deal with right now without her piling on." He shook his head, lips pressing into a thin line. "As if it's his fault I was second in the short? You were clean, and I popped my Axel. Of course you're in first place."

I was, though it was difficult to be too happy about it in the face of Theo's anxious discontent. Missing his triple Axel was very unusual for him, but he'd lost focus.

He added, "As if chemo isn't bad enough without my mother asking him if he'll be able to make it to the Olympics to make sure I do better."

I murmured softly in agreement and said, "That's unacceptable."

"Yeah." Theodore's throat worked. A hint of stubble remained on his skin. "And when we talked yesterday, he didn't sound—" His voice suddenly broke, and he blinked rapidly.

Oh no. I didn't want anything to happen to Mr. Webber, though he was elderly, and statistically it was unlikely he'd live very much longer. And I didn't want Theodore to be upset. In fact, my heart thumped, my stomach roiling.

He shook his head, sucking in deep breaths and clearly trying not to cry. He sat cross-legged, and his knees jiggled. I reached down, taking hold of his shoulder. His eyes met mine, and he gave me a tremulous, grateful smile.

I thought about slipping off the chair and pulling him close, running my fingers through his fine hair that looked soft…

I regained my senses as he cleared his throat and said, "Anyway, he doesn't sound great today. But I'm going to do my best and make him proud."

The reminder of the cruel words I'd said to him after Skate Canada flooded my face with heat, and I let go of his shoulder, nodding as I folded my hands in my lap.

"And hopefully my mom will back off already. I mean, she's gotten more than she ever could have wished for when she forced me to keep skating."

"Forced?" I knew his mother was very invested, but that was a strong word.

He shrugged. "I tried to quit a million times in high school. At least when I moved to LA on my own—Jesus, did she put up a fight about that—it wasn't so bad. But when I was a kid, it's not like I had a choice."

I couldn't begin to understand not wanting to skate. "You do now."

"I'm too good to quit now. It would be stupid. I *do* like it. I put in all this work my whole life. After the Olympics, I can retire and do shows. All the fun stuff without judges and required elements and PCS and all that shit."

I gaped. But we were at the very top of the sport. Here at the Grand Prix Final, only the top six finishers in each discipline from the autumn circuit were competing. And of course we were world champions. This was where all our training paid off—though I preferred the routines of the rink to the stress and travel of competition.

He added, "I think her only regret was not naming me after one of the greats so she could talk about it in TV fluff pieces and make Brian Boitano or whoever say he was so honored."

I'd always been enraged by how flippant Theodore could be. How easily everything seemed to come to him and how he could shrug off mistakes and pressure. But I'd somehow never imagined that he didn't actually want all of this deep down.

I asked, "What does your father say?"

Theodore snorted and tapped his phone. "Not much. He's busy with his lawyering. That's the official term for it."

I chuckled. Theodore's head snapped up, looking at me excitedly. I glanced behind me, puzzled. Down a gray corridor, the edges of the press area were visible. "What?"

"Nothing!" He went back to his phone, but he looked unfathomably pleased with himself.

My phone buzzed in my pocket, and my brother's face filled

the screen. I calculated the time difference to Vancouver. It was a strange time for him to be trying a video call. Uneasiness tugged in my gut as I swiped to answer. "What's wrong?"

"Bro! Good morning to you too. Or afternoon? I have no idea. Why do you always think something's wrong? Loosen your screws already."

Relief flowed, and I exhaled. "That's not a saying."

"Sure it is! I just said it."

Theodore laughed. Then he grabbed my wrist, his fingers wrapping around bare skin where my warm-up jacket rode up a few inches. He twisted my hand and said to the screen. "Hey, Sam! Seriously, have his screws always been this tight?"

"Dude, you have no idea. I hope Henry hasn't been too frosty. He doesn't like change."

I tried to yank my hand back, but Theodore's warm grip on my wrist was too strong. He said, "No, he's been great! I'm impossible to resist." With a laugh, he let go.

I shifted in the chair, ignoring my brother's smirk when I looked at the screen again. "Yes?"

"Just wanted to say don't break a leg." It was an old family joke my parents and grandma had also made when we spoke earlier. Sam added, "Crush the competition. No offense, Theo!"

"None taken!" Theodore called back.

"I want to do my best," I said.

In unison, Sam and Theodore groaned, my brother grumbling, "We're not the media. Be real." He looked away from the camera and said, "Be there in a sec."

Judging by his dreamy expression, he was speaking to Etienne. I said goodbye and chewed over his words. *Be real.*

I *was* real. Yes, it was a stock statement from skaters and other athletes, but aside from obviously wanting to win, I truly did want to do my best. I couldn't control the judges—I tamped down a swell of irritation at Theodore for his inflated artistic scores—but doing my best was wholly in my power. And if I did my best, obviously the odds of winning were greatly increased.

The pairs skaters were finishing, and my Canadian teammates passed by. At least Anton and Hannah weren't at this event, though I'd see them soon enough at Nationals in January. I pushed that thought away, nodding to Rebecca and Brent, who were sweaty and grinning and seemed surprised to see me for some reason. I wasn't sure why since the men's short program was next after a dinner break and all the competitors had surely arrived.

"Way to go!" Theodore said, jumping up to hug them quickly. They'd clearly skated well, and I congratulated them too as Theodore bumped his fist with their coach as Rebecca and Brent continued on to do press. "Henry, you know Dev Avira, right?"

I stood and shook his hand, my stomach fluttering ridiculously. "Yes. How's Bailey?"

"Great! Having her first baby any day now and finishing her degree." Dev grinned, his very straight teeth flashing bright against his brown skin. With his thick, glossy curls brushing the tips of his ears, he was very handsome, and when I was younger, I'd had a bit of a crush on him. And his husband. "Misha and I are going to be the godparents."

"Awesome!" Theodore bumped his fist again. "He's here, right?"

"Yep. Commentating for Russian TV."

"I hope he said nice things about his husband's team." Theodore laughed. "Gotta love the incestuous world of skating."

"Indeed. He rarely pulls his punches, but Becky and Brent nailed it today."

"Clearly made the right move going to LA to train with you." Theodore's smile dimmed. "I miss it there."

"I bet. I was so sorry to hear about Mr. Webber. Hope he's doing okay?"

Theodore nodded too rapidly. "Yeah, yeah. He's tough. He'll

be fine!"

Dev nodded too. "I really hope so." He cleared his throat. "Speaking of the incestuous world of skating, I didn't expect to see you two so buddy-buddy. You're the talk of the event. People are frankly shocked there hasn't been bloodshed."

That took me aback. The talk of the event? I glanced around, and sure enough a few people looked away suddenly. My skin prickled.

People were watching us? What were they saying? My pulse kicked up, though I wasn't sure what exactly I was afraid of. I typically tried to ignore it, but gossip was in skating's DNA.

Naturally, my mind leapt back to Anton, and the terror that it would all come out. No. Surely it would have already. It had been almost four years. Still, it was possible. Of course it was.

An iron band tightened around my chest, shame crashing through me like an explosion of lava. I'd been so gullible and weak and—

"Henry?" Theodore's fingers touched my wrist. I whipped my hand away, crossing my arms as Theodore and Dev shared a frown.

Dev laughed uncertainly. "Hey, it's okay. Didn't mean to freak you out. The Gillooly thing was just a joke."

I blinked. Apparently he'd said something else, but I hadn't heard it in my panic. I swallowed hard. "I know."

Theodore elbowed me. "Don't worry. Everyone knows you're way too honorable to have me whacked in the knee. I mean, you're *Canadian*. I'm way more likely to take out a hit on you."

"You wouldn't do that. You're annoyingly nice."

They burst out laughing, and Theodore's eyes lit up, his smile dimpling his cheeks. More heat washed through me. I hadn't meant to say that aloud. This was why I didn't like talking. But it didn't seem like they were laughing at me, at least.

In fact, Theodore's cheeks had gone pink. He said, "See? I

really am impossible to resist." He beamed at me and seemed about to say something else when he motioned with his chin. "Here's Misha."

Like Dev, Mikhail Reznikov was long and lean, though he was even taller than his husband. The male pairs skaters were typically the biggest of any skaters, and I'd often been attracted to them. As Misha greeted Dev with a warm, casual kiss on the lips, my belly somersaulted.

Dev and Misha had battled for gold, yet they'd ended up falling in love. When they'd gone public with their relationship, I'd devoured every interview and scrap of media coverage.

Though I'd met them before, it still gave me a thrill to see them together right in front of me. I'd kept a tab with their wedding photos open on my phone for longer than I should have.

"Hey, congrats on the book trilogy. Is it going to be translated into English?" Theodore asked. "I love fantasy stuff with dragons and all that."

"I hope so," Misha answered. "*Spasibo.*" He slipped his arm around Dev. "There is time to return to the hotel, yes? I need some quiet."

Dev gave him a little smile. "Yes." To Theodore and me, he said, "Good luck tonight, guys. Glad to see you're not at each other's throats. Honestly pretty surprised."

Theodore laughed. "Well, Henry hates me, but I'm wearing him down with my irresistible wit and charm. Enjoy the quiet!"

I wanted to argue that I didn't hate him. The denial was like a whirlwind inside me, a confusion of emotions and words, but Dev and Misha were already walking away.

A new truth settled through me, squeezing into nooks and crannies.

I didn't hate Theodore Sullivan. Not anymore.

His breath tickled the shell of my ear, and I shivered as he whispered, "They are relationship goals. You know 'quiet' was code for sex."

I followed his gaze to where Dev and Misha had stopped to talk to a journalist, their arms around each other's waists. They were so comfortable and affectionate with each other even though they'd started as bitter rivals.

Theodore moaned softly. "Oh my god, can you imagine them fucking? So. Hot. I heard they had secret hookups in the Athletes' Village at the Olympics."

Yes, I could certainly imagine Dev and Misha together in the most intimate ways. But with Theo's warm exhalations on my skin, his body leaning close, I could imagine far, far too much. I could imagine Theodore saying other things in my ear.

Filthy things.

Desire coiled in my belly, blood rushing south and threatening to expose me. We were standing backstage at the Grand Prix Final, and there was Kuznetzov and his coach, and were they looking at us?

Everyone was looking at us. What was I doing? How had I allowed this distraction?

I jerked away and fished my noise-canceling headphones from my bag. "Time to prepare."

He was my rival. My enemy. I had to focus. I had to go back to ignoring him. It didn't matter if Theodore wasn't the villain I'd always relished imagining him to be. He'd gotten under my skin for years as a competitor, and I couldn't allow him to get to me now with his kindness and dimples and whispers.

Theodore sighed. "Yep, I guess so. Okay, see you later. May the best man win, right?"

Not responding, I turned on the soundtrack to the *Hunchback of Notre Dame*, which I listened to before every competitive performance. I had to start my pre-skate routine. I shouldn't have gotten distracted.

Theodore was saying something else, but I couldn't hear him.

I sat back down, closing my eyes and beginning my visualization of my program.

It was one thing not to hate Theodore Sullivan. But I still wanted to win.

Chapter Eight

Theo

THE CROWD CHEERED, clapping along with the Rolling Stones as I gave it my all through the footwork. My quads burned with lactic acid, my lungs strained, but I gave the audience all the face I could, smiling and winking and feeding off their energy.

I'd pulled it off. It was good enough at least for silver. I'd tensed going into the Sal today, but I'd muscled it out and managed to let go and just feel the music and the crowd.

I swiveled my hips into my final pose, and they were on their feet. It was always a great feeling, and I finally let myself think about Mr. Webber while I took my bows with a grin.

Hopefully I'd made him proud.

I helped the flower girls pick up some stuffed toys, waving to the crowd as I made my way to the Kiss and Cry. From the corner of my eye, Henry shot out onto the ice through another door in the boards. Manon was there watching as he did a few warm-up laps while I got my scores. Coaches with multiple skaters at events typically split up so no skater or team was alone at any time.

Bill waited for me by the gate, applauding with the US federation rep beaming beside him. I hugged them and soaked up the praise, putting on my skate guards and team jacket before we sat with the cameras ready to catch every reaction.

We watched the replays, which finished with a slo-mo hip swivel. I joked, "Sexy!" and the audience read my lips and laughed, cheering even harder as the judges tabulated.

The stronger the crowd reaction, the higher marks tended to be, and yep—a new world record flashed up on the scoreboard. I pumped my fist, and the crowd thundered.

Wiping sweat from my face, I chugged water before gathering my plushies. There would be a huge bag of them backstage collected from the ice. I always donated the toys to the local children's hospital.

Early in my career, Mom had insisted on keeping every toy and gift, filling the corners of our house until my sisters revolted, and even Dad put his foot down.

I truly appreciated every gift from fans, but there were only so many stuffed animals one person could own. Aside from keeping the odd one, I figured they'd live their best plushy lives being played with by kids.

As we left the Kiss and Cry, I looked back at Henry taking his position at center ice, a hush falling over the arena. I could have sat and watched him for a few minutes, but I didn't want to throw him off or anything.

Obviously he'd heard my marks and the crowd reaction, so the pressure was now on him to hold his lead. It was only a few points, so this was going to be a close result.

And obviously I wanted to win—*duh*, winning was the most fun—but I weirdly found myself...kind of rooting for him? Not that I'd ever wished *harm* to a competitor, but... As much as I disliked Mom's killer instinct bullshit, I didn't become world champion by rooting for the other guys.

Backstage, "Moonlight Sonata" more distant now, I handed off the toys and went to take my seat with Kuznetzov and Nakamura, who were currently in second and third. But instead of the expected high fives, they watched me approach with tight, weird expressions.

Huh. Were they pissed I'd taken first place? I mean, yeah, obviously they were on one level, but it wasn't unexpected, and we'd all learned as kids to paint smiles on our faces and hide our real feelings in skating. At least until you were alone.

Bill was saying, "What are you talking about?" to someone.

It all happened in slow motion.

Everyone was watching me—skaters, coaches, federation officials, event coordinators, camera operators. I was used to having eyes on me, especially after a skate like that. New world record score! Yay!

But something was wrong.

I turned to Bill as he gripped my arm. Tears shone in his eyes, and my stomach dropped like a rock, icy dread washing through me.

Bill said, "Theo. There's bad news." His voice got hoarse, and he cleared his throat. But I didn't need him to say it.

Mr. Webber was gone. I knew it. Not in a woo-woo *I can feel his cosmic absence from the universe* way, but because it was the only thing that made the unbearable weight in the air make sense. Unless it was my family or something—fuck, was it?

I went rigid, croaking, "What?" I was ready to shake it out of Bill, my mom and dad and sisters' faces wheeling through my mind.

He'd gotten his shit together and said, "I'm afraid Mr. Webber passed away a few hours ago. His children and grandchildren were at his side. It was peaceful."

For a terrible moment, I was relieved. My family was okay. But Mr. Webber was gone, and even though he hadn't been my family, he *had* been actually, even if I paid him to coach me, and we'd had contracts and a business relationship. I'd loved him, and I think he'd loved me.

And he was gone. It wasn't fair even if he was old, and I'd known deep down the cancer was bad and that he probably wouldn't make it, but *it wasn't fair.*

"I just talked to him yesterday," I said stupidly.

"I know." Bill squeezed my arm. "He stopped treatment last week, and it was quick. He didn't want you to know. He didn't want to distract you."

Did I make him proud?

I wanted to scream it and shake the answer out of Bill, but I could only nod, the hot needles of eyes on me prickling my skin. I stood there nodding as Bill hugged me.

Bill and other people were talking at me, platitudes all over the place, and I didn't want any of them. I wanted them to shut up, shut up, *shut up.*

For once, I didn't want to talk. I nodded and nodded, and an official told me I could talk to the press tomorrow, and they were delaying the medal ceremony too, that we'd have it before the gala. I was grateful, but couldn't they just be quiet?

Apparently I won, beating Henry by less than a point. I didn't care, though I'm sure Henry did—it was brutal to lose by fractions. I was probably the last person he wanted to see.

After practically ripping off my costume and shoving my bag at Bill, I made my escape, insisting on walking the short distance through Torino to the hotel where we were all staying.

Cool, steady rain soon soaked me. The mountains were shrouded in thick clouds as night set in. It felt later than it was, the rain apparently keeping people away from the restaurants and bars.

I didn't bother with the hood of my jacket, weirdly enjoying the wet. The streetlights gleamed in puddles between dark, locked-up cafes. A Mini zoomed by on the narrow road, tires sending up splashes before the muffled silence settled in again.

I stopped for a while in front of a clock shop with an intricate

Christmas-themed display in the window. The swaying chimes, spinning wheels, and cuckoo clocks mesmerized me, keeping the grief at bay. I felt strangely empty and light-headed.

It was hard to imagine that I'd never see Mr. Webber again. He'd never give me the cocked brow that spoke volumes. He'd never offer a hard-won smile after I worked my butt off and did everything he asked without complaining for once. He'd never again pat my knee in congratulations or condolence in the Kiss and Cry.

Why hadn't I called him again this morning? I was struck violently with the need to know exactly when he'd died and what I'd been doing, and if I'd had time to call and hear his gravelly, sardonic voice one last time.

I didn't think anything of the footsteps behind me until I turned down an even narrower side street a block from the bright windows of the hotel. My Chucks squelched as I headed down the steeper road, not ready to leave the shadows. When the footsteps followed, I turned just in case I was being a dumbass and was about to get mugged or something.

Henry stopped about fifteen feet back. On the higher ground of the sloping alley, he looked tall. I could just make out his typical serious expression, though for once he wasn't frowning. His eyes looked soft with concern even at a distance, and my heart felt like it expanded even as my breath caught.

I realized it wasn't true that I wanted to be alone.

My gratitude in seeing him standing there—soaking wet in the miserable December rain, not intruding but watching over me—was overwhelming.

I wanted *Henry*. No one else. His steady presence reassured me in a way I didn't think anyone else could. That was actually a scary thought, and I almost bolted into the mess of narrow old streets.

Heart thumping, I closed the distance between us. I was still downhill, and it reminded me of the times when he stood atop the podium and I was a step below at silver, though it had been a couple of seasons since he'd beaten me.

He'd always seemed so unknowable—a robot, an alien, *ha ha*. He still watched me silently, rain dripping down his nose.

On my tiptoes, I slowly pressed a kiss to Henry's rain-damp cheek.

After lowering my heels, I rested my temple featherlight against the side of his jaw, arms hanging at my sides.

I trembled—did Henry too? Holding my breath, I longed for more. More warmth than his ragged exhalations tickling my left ear. More contact. More skin. More, more, more.

What was I doing? Why was he letting me? This wasn't—we weren't supposed to be...

What?

For a horrible moment, I thought he'd shove me away or even just step back, and it *hurt*. I wanted to beg him to just let me...what? I wasn't even sure.

Let me in.

Since when did I want that? What did that even mean? This was all getting too big, too out of control. It didn't feel like a game at all anymore, and I guessed it hadn't for a while.

We stood frozen with my lips a whisper from his skin. We should both run. I should never have gone to train in Toronto, even if Mr. Webber—

The sob burst free. I had to run, but hot tears choked me, my throat closing. And Henry let me in, enveloping me in his arms, my face buried in his throat as I cried.

Which didn't really do it justice. I was *weeping*, and I was so relieved my mom wasn't there ordering me to pull myself together. I reached around his waist and clutched him, hands squeaking on the slick rubbery material of his jacket.

Honestly, Henry had every right to tell me to get a grip already, but he only held me close. It should have been humiliating, but I was safe.

A Vespa approached up the hill with a thin, tinny hum of its engine as it passed. We stood locked together in the rain's steady fall.

Eventually, I mumbled, "I'm sorry. I don't know what's wrong with me."

All he said was, "I liked Mr. Webber."

I sniffed loudly, tasting the salt of my own snotty tears. "He liked you too. He always admired your discipline and work ethic. He'd say stuff like, 'Henry Sakaguchi isn't complaining about an extra run-through.' And he was right, of course. He was always right. I should have listened more. I should have—"

Henry rubbed up and down my spine slowly as I cried out the fresh burst of tears. I didn't know how long we stood there before he guided me along the narrow streets with a gentle hand on my back as I word vomited all over him, telling stories about Mr. Webber and how I'd been such a pain in the ass sometimes.

I didn't even know what I was saying, but Henry listening to my bullshit like it mattered was somehow what I needed. He ushered me through the side entrance to the hotel using his key card and then through another door. Stopping, I blinked at the gray stairwell.

"We shouldn't run into anyone this way," Henry said.

Duh, of course. The hotel was full of skating people—from skaters to judges to coaches to federation officials to fans. The lobby and bar downstairs would be crammed.

Nodding gratefully, I plodded up the stairs, Henry still attentive at my side as if he was afraid I was going to fall or something.

Outside my door, I fumbled for the key card, which I'd fortunately zipped into my jacket pocket. A thought floated by. "How did you know this is my room?"

He shrugged, looking at the striped carpet. "I'm in four-oh-five."

"Oh. Right. I guess that makes sense we're on the same floor."
I shoved the card into the reader, and the light flashed red. I tried
again. Red. I wiggled the metal handle as if that would help.

Fingers brushing my wrist, Henry eased the card out of my
grip and flipped it around before sliding it into the reader. Green.

Laughing somewhat hysterically, I pushed inside. "Thanks." I
unzipped my jacket, fingers shaking and cold, and dropped it.
Henry watched from the threshold, keeping the heavy door open.
"Thanks," I repeated. "I'd probably have gotten stupidly lost.
Thanks."

He nodded. He took a breath, and I thought maybe he was
going to say something? Then he nodded again and eased back,
and the door was going to thud shut and I'd never hear what he
was going to say.

"What?" I demanded desperately. I tried to smile. "What did
you—" I waved my hand toward him.

Henry only watched me with that cute little furrow between
his brows. Wait, was it cute? I mean, it was. There was no
debating it—the furrow was adorable. Had I always thought that?
Maybe. I wasn't sure. Did it matter?

"Will you watch a movie with me?" I blurted before he could
disappear. "Please?"

For a horrible moment, I thought he might say no, but he
nodded. "We should shower first."

My mind exploded with images of steam and Henry's slick,
naked skin, desire rocketing through me and leaving a trail like a
comet. I could barely breathe, knees unsteady, my dick going
hard. Before I could respond, the door swung shut, and he was
gone.

I had to laugh because Henry had obviously meant we should
shower alone, which made all the sense since it would be very
weird to shower together considering we'd never even kissed.

But fuck, I was dying to.

I tore off my wet clothes and practically dove into the shower, my cock so hard it almost hurt. Under a stream of wonderfully hot water, I flattened one palm against the white tile wall, leaning forward as I stroked myself roughly.

My head filled with visions of Henry's mouth and tongue and hands and the firm lines of his lean body against me, but this time we weren't in the rain with our clothes on. We kissed and rubbed together in my mind as I toyed with my foreskin, legs spread for balance.

I imagined him behind me. Inside me. Grunting in my ear with hot breath, filling me, coming inside me. I traced the sensitive ridge along my shaft, wondering what Henry would sound like when he let go. Wondering what he'd sound like moaning and groaning as our wet skin slapped together.

My balls tightened, pressure building through my body as I strained and stroked harder, my cock throbbing in my familiar grasp. What would Henry's hand feel like on me? His mouth? What would he taste like?

Seizing tight, I shot my load over the tiles, shuddering, my groans muffled in the steamy enclosure. I milked myself and fondled my balls, little sparks licking up my spine. With my elbow bent and forearm against the tiles, I cushioned my forehead on my arm, panting.

Well. Either it had been way too long since I'd hooked up or I really, truly wanted to get busy with Henry. A lot.

I laughed, and maybe I was losing it, but *damn*, I really wanted to fuck Henry. Not just fuck. I wished he was holding me like he had on the street, strong and stable while these bursts of grief and hysteria came and went.

But what did Henry want? Was he only being nice to me? It had to be that. Or he was being a good friend because he'd proven himself a kind person underneath his uptight, careful exterior. He'd seemed so humorless over the years, but really he was shy and careful.

Could I make him moan and come and laugh and lose control?

I stayed in the shower too long imagining it, my dick twitching. I was barely into the white, terrycloth hotel robe when there was a soft knock at the door. My ears burned as I tightened the sash around my waist. Here was Henry being generous by hanging out with me, and I was jerking off about him. He'd be horrified.

I yanked open the door before he had second thoughts. Henry's hair was wet, and he'd changed into sweatpants and a gray Skate Canada T-shirt. I was honestly disappointed he wasn't in his adorable plaid pajamas.

His feet were socked, and it made him seem so vulnerable somehow, even though I was the one in a robe. His gaze flicked down my body, then settled around my chin like usual.

"Hey!" I said too brightly as I stepped back. "Thanks for coming."

He entered, and I motioned to the king-sized bed, suddenly glad my room didn't have a sitting area and that the one chair in the corner was piled with my stinky practice clothes. He looked at the neat bed, which housekeeping had made up.

"Ah! Let me…" With a flourish, I peeled down the coverlet and pushed it on the floor, shoving it half under the bed. I managed to avoid talking about cum, but I knew we were both thinking it, which made me flush hot again.

As Henry perched on the edge of the mattress, I wrapped the end of the terrycloth sash around my hand, my stomach fluttering. "Can I get you a drink?" I asked, like this was a date. No, I was only being polite. "We should order food. You must be hungry."

Henry watched me warily as I grabbed the room service binder and shoved it at him. I opened the mini fridge and started rattling off the contents out loud. I zipped with nervous energy, and what the fuck was the matter with me? Mr. Webber was gone, and here

I was crushing on Henry.

Shame spiraled through me, and my voice broke on, "Stella Artois." Shit. I blinked away fresh tears.

"It's all right." His low voice was soothing. He didn't say anything else, just waited for me to get my shit together.

I shut the fridge and gingerly sat beside him on the end of the bed, leaving a good two feet between us. Henry opened the menu and held it between us, slowly turning the pages. This was an English version, but the words danced in front of me like they were foreign and unintelligible. My bare foot jiggled.

"Are you starving?" I asked. "You should treat yourself. Have pasta."

"Mmm." He turned the page.

"We're in Italy, after all. What's that saying? When in Rome. You should eat all the carbs."

He turned another page. "As long as you eat them too."

I laughed. "So we both pack on a few pounds? That's fair."

"So you eat," he said simply.

My chest flushed with warmth. "I guess I should. I'm hungry, but not. You know? I should be too sad to eat." I should have been too sad to jerk off. More guilt flooded me. "My mom would be yelling at me if she was here. She says I'm too emotional. God, I'm so glad she didn't come."

My laugh was a little too loud now. "That sounds horrible. But she's just a lot. I can't stop her from coming to Nationals or the Olympics, but at least my sister had an important piano recital this week. Frankly, my mom would have ditched it in a heartbeat to be here, but I made sure I brought it up at a family party in front of a bunch of people so she was stuck doing the recital. She never paid as much attention to my sisters' stuff growing up. Veronica is studying music now at Julliard. Do you play the piano? I could see that. Not because you're Asian! Since you have such musicality on the ice. You look like you feel every note. I'm performing to the audience and shaking my ass to the beat. And with Kuznetzov, I don't think he even hears what's playing."

"The music doesn't bother him at all."

It took my spinning brain a second to get Henry's dry joke, and a genuine giggle slipped out. Who knew he actually had a sense of humor?

He added, "Yes, I took piano lessons growing up. And it doesn't sound horrible."

Again, it took me a moment to understand what he was saying—that it didn't sound horrible for me to not want my mother here. Gratitude welled up in me for his understanding and the mildly catty comment about Kuznetzov. Of all people, he got it. He got me. My life was so fucking weird.

Henry squeezed my shoulder, and my breath caught. His thumb rested a fraction from the edge of the robe and my bare collarbone. God, I wanted him to touch me. It didn't have to be sex or anything. I just wanted to feel his skin on mine.

He motioned toward the headboard, which I took to mean I should sit back. So I crawled over to the pillows while he called down and ordered a bunch of things. Then he went through the movie selection and picked one. I was absurdly grateful not to have to make any choices.

Henry sat on the end of the bed again, and I reached forward with my right hand to tug his arm, a thrill shooting through me as my fingers curled around his bare elbow. He briefly looked at me over his shoulder before scooting back and sitting cross-legged, maintaining the couple of feet distance between us given how huge the bed was.

We stacked the extra pillows to lean against, and I idly tugged at a loose thread on the robe. Because I'm the worst, I said, "I wonder if there are jizz remnants on everything in hotel rooms. I remember something about fluids sprayed on walls."

Henry jerked to look at the padded headboard behind us. He

fiddled with the pillows. Then he looked down at the remote with sudden alarm. "I hope you disinfected this."

"The remote?" I stared at it blankly.

With a sigh, Henry got up and left. I sat there puzzling over it until he returned a minute later with a package of antibacterial wipes. He picked up the remote with two fingers as though it might bite before wiping it thoroughly, between the buttons, and around all surfaces. He proceeded to disinfect every handle and touch surface in my room.

It should not have been sexy.

It should have been annoying or something. It should have been weird. But it made me want to pull him close for a kiss, even if he wiped my lips with Clorox first. Except that might be poisonous.

He disappeared into the bathroom. After a minute, the tap ran, and he was surely washing his hands. When he returned, he went to the newly sanitized mini fridge and pulled out a bottle of white. After a brief inspection of the glasses by the empty ice bucket, he poured the wine.

We settled again and drank Chardonnay or maybe Pinot Grigio and watched the latest Marvel movie. He dealt with the room service guy and brought in the massive tray, spreading out our dinner on the mattress.

"Aren't you afraid of crumbs in bed?" I asked.

"It's the best option in this room. We're not eating on the floor." He shuddered.

"Good point."

Besides, having the bedspread gone meant I was *in* bed with Henry as opposed to just on top of it. There was a distinction, and the intimacy of sitting cross-legged together on the sheets eating our gnocchi and caprese salad and so many delicious, carby, fatty things comforted me.

Henry ate slowly, clearly savoring every bite. It was probably the understatement of the century to say it was unlikely he allowed himself to indulge very often. That he was doing it with me—*for* me—was powerful in a way I couldn't really explain.

Thoughts of Mr. Webber flitted in and out. Never really gone, but not crushing. The distraction of food and wine and superheroes and Henry was everything I needed, and I was intensely grateful.

As I ran my spoon through a pot of seriously the best chocolate mousse ever, I quietly said, "Thank you."

Henry swallowed a bite of tiramisu, and our eyes met. The moment stretched out, the people on TV shouting about something, the *rat-a-tat* of gunfire echoing. A cocoa-dusted crumb from the top layer clung to his bottom lip, and I almost reached over to brush it free.

He gave me a little nod before turning back to the movie and his dessert again.

I blurted, "I hope he was proud of me." I couldn't look at Henry, afraid I'd see a horrible truth written on his face since he was so bad at lying. "Do you think so?"

I *had* to look.

Lowering his spoon, Henry regarded me with his usual silent intensity, his eyes serious under those thick lashes. "Yes."

With that one, beautiful word, I knew he was telling the truth. And I knew I wanted Henry to be proud of me too.

When I looked over to ask him if he wanted more wine, Henry wasn't watching the movie. His gaze whipped up to meet mine, and he turned his face back to the TV, his always impressive posture straightening even more.

There was *so much* I wanted to say, but I rolled my lips inward and forced myself to stay silent. I glanced down, and *oh*. My robe had gaped open, and half my chest was exposed, including a nipple.

And Henry had very much been staring at my bare chest.

And that had very much been desire written all over his gorgeous face.

It was seriously amazing that I used to think of him as a robot or alien with a consistently flat expression. Once you knew what to look for, Henry's face practically shouted his feelings.

The flicks of his gaze, the minute tightening of his mouth or lifts of lips. The wrinkle of his nose, the widening of his eyes. The faint blush on his cheeks. All of these appearing for brief flashes before he seemed placid again.

That had been desire blazing from beneath his thick lashes. If I kissed him? Maybe he wouldn't be so horrified after all. Maybe he wanted me too. But I didn't want to ruin everything by leaning over to test my hunch.

Stomach full, I slouched against the pillows, getting lower and lower. I'm not sure when I fell asleep, strangely lulled by the fight scene sound effects, but it was the middle of the night when I woke.

The sheets and soft blanket were tucked around me, and I blinked at the murmuring TV, set to BBC and showing some cooking show, the woman stirring a pot at a huge gas range barely audible.

Most comforting of all was that Henry hadn't left me alone.

I blinked at his curled outline in the blue light from the TV, his lips slack. He was under the covers too, and I was officially in bed with Henry Sakaguchi. And funnily enough, the earlier lust didn't return. All I wanted to do was cuddle close and feel the whispers of his breath on my skin.

Afraid I'd wake him, I didn't move a muscle, watching the curve of his cheek and dark fan of eyelashes in the flickering light, his eyes moving in a dream I hoped was about me.

Chapter Nine

Theo

ONE WHEEL ON my suitcase was out of whack, and I yanked it back just in time to avoid a collision with the woman beside me. Customs forms in hand, we filed slowly through the exit from baggage claim, giving our pieces of paper to officials and praying we wouldn't be pulled aside for inspection.

For me, it wasn't because I was carrying anything I'd get into trouble for—though I'd said I wasn't bringing in any food to Canada, and there was a Butterfinger and a half-eaten bag of Doritos in my little carry-on backpack. I just hadn't been hungry on the flight to eat them.

I'd flown from Torino to LA for Mr. Webber's funeral, and now I was back in Toronto for the last week of training before the rink shut down for Christmas.

It was closed completely that one day, and the next was a weird holiday called Boxing Day. The rink was open for public skating since Manon and Bill and the whole team took it off before we went back to training the twenty-seventh.

In a non-Olympic year, they'd probably take the whole Christmas-New Year's week off, but every day counted with our Nationals in mid-January, a couple of weeks earlier than usual. Every day counted for me especially since I'd taken time off for the funeral.

I shuffled forward in the line, peeking at my phone even though there were signs saying not to. Plenty of other people were ignoring that rule too. The screen filled with texts from my mom, because what else was new? She'd been dead set against me going to the funeral, but obviously I'd ignored her.

It was a few days of training, and I'd be fine. It was good to get some California sun and catch up with Em and my friends from the rink in LA. I'd even managed to get through the funeral without crying. Apparently I'd wept so much on Henry's shoulder in Torino that I was all out of tears.

I held my breath as I scanned my texts, but nope. Nothing from Henry. It was seven p.m. Toronto time, and he'd be home with Esmeralda after a long day of training. Why would he be texting me? I'd wanted to text him a million times since I'd left Italy, but I'd only typed them out and never sent them.

I'd bothered Henry enough. Hell, coming to train at his rink in the Olympic season was a *lot*. Leaning on him emotionally while I came apart at the seams in Torino had been even more.

Still, I'd sent him a message from LAX saying I was on my way back and asking if I could get a ride tomorrow. I reread his reply now.

Yes.

Obviously it was dumb for me to keep looking at that one word like I could decipher some hidden meaning. I'd asked a question, and he'd responded. The end. Sure, I'd blubbered all over him, and he'd been sweet and kind and we'd slept together—but not like that.

It didn't mean anything had changed. I was his rival for gold, and I'd just beaten him again in Italy. He'd been far, far kinder than most people would be.

What was I even expecting?

The customs guy took my form and marked it with a line before telling me I was free to go. I hurried through the automatic frosted glass doors that sprang open to reveal clumps of people waiting for passengers.

One family had a bunch of helium balloons and flowers. There were drivers holding passenger names on cardboard signs, but I was just going to call a Lyft and—

At the bottom of the little ramp to the waiting area, I jerked to a stop. A man behind me banged my heels with his suitcase and muttered a curse. I was blocking the way, and I ordered myself to move and stop staring at Henry.

And I was staring at Henry because Henry was here.

He waited alone near the back of the waiting area in his black practice pants, sneakers, and blue puffy winter jacket, and he was beautiful.

My stomach flip-flopped as I bit back a shout of pure, unexpected joy. I was probably grinning like an idiot as I practically ran toward him, dragging my suitcase instead of pushing it on the wonky wheel.

"What are you doing here?" I asked because I'm a dumbass. I quickly added, "I mean, I guess you're picking me up? Thank you! Awesome. I had no idea. You really didn't have to. Traffic must have been terrible coming out here!" How had he known my flight number? Sure, I'd texted about the ride tomorrow, but…

"I had some errands to run, so I was in the area."

Wow, he really was a bad liar. His gaze flicked around, and he shifted from foot to foot, and it was honestly hilarious and adorable how obvious it was.

Not to mention the airport was all the way west of the city, and we trained all the way east. What errands would he have out here? During Toronto's hellacious rush hour that rivaled LA's?

I let him off the hook and said, "Cool. Thanks."

I insisted on paying the ridiculous airport parking fee, and we merged into heavy traffic on the highway, a sea of red lights ahead in the night. At least it was moving decently even if we were only going three quarters of the speed limit.

Henry hadn't turned on the radio, and I could only take the silence so long. I jiggled my foot restlessly. "Aren't you going to ask me how the funeral was?"

That cute little furrow appeared between his brows. "Do you want to talk about it?"

"Well… Not really. It was a funeral. They pretty much suck. I've only been to my grandparents' before. Separately. They didn't die at the same time or anything, like in an accident or whatever."

"Mm."

"I'm glad I went, though. It was good to see my LA people. There was a huge turnout. Everyone loves Mr. Webber. *Loved.* Still getting used to it, I guess. Maybe I do want to talk about it."

"Okay."

"I miss him. Like, *duh*, what an obvious thing to say. But even though I knew he probably wouldn't make it, he was just so…*much*. He had such presence. You know what I mean?'

"Like you." Henry seemed to regret saying that as soon as it came out, his lips tightening and fingers flexing on the steering wheel. He opened and closed his mouth, but didn't add anything.

I laughed, trying to hide my pleasure and rambling on. "I'll take that as the ultimate compliment. Anyway, it's weird that he's gone. It shouldn't have been a shock. It wasn't, I guess. But it was. I'm probably not making any sense."

"It makes perfect sense."

"Okay. Thanks." Now I really didn't want to talk about it anymore, so I said, "You must be starving," I said. "Do you want to hit up a drive-through? My treat. Oh, or I have some snacks." I reached behind for my backpack that I'd dumped on the backseat.

Henry looked at the junk food I pulled out like I'd just offered him a plate of steaming turds.

"I know, I know! I shouldn't. But I'm jet-lagged."

Eyes on the road, Henry said, "Eating that will only make you feel worse."

"I know, being a pig won't help me win." I laughed. "You should be feeding me Doritos all day."

Henry apparently didn't see the humor. An awkward silence filled the car at the reminder that we were competitors. Why did I say that? It was the last thing we should talk about.

"You're not a pig," he said, nostrils flaring. "No one should ever call you that."

"My mother disagrees." I tried to laugh it off. "Don't worry, I'm fine. She used to get to me a lot more. I've had tons of therapy. Anyway, maybe we should have a pact."

"A pact?"

"That we don't talk about skating. Well, that's probably impossible. How about we don't talk about competing against each other. We can just park the elephant in the room over in the corner, or stuff it under the bed."

Saying the word *bed* out loud sparked a rush of highly inappropriate thoughts that I definitely shouldn't talk about either.

After a few moments, Henry nodded.

"Cool. We're both going to work hard and do our best, and it'll be up to the judges at the Games. And until we leave for Calgary in February, we can hang and stuff."

Henry nodded again, then said, "I have curry in the slow cooker."

"Mmm. That would be amazing." The idea of a hot, home-cooked dinner at Henry's place with actual furniture and Esmeralda filled me with a kind of peace I hadn't felt since I woke up in Torino with him still snuggled in bed beside me. Watching me.

As I'd blinked blearily at him, he'd whipped his head away, pink flushing his cheeks. It had taken all my willpower not to roll on top of Henry and kiss him until nothing else mattered.

"What kind of slow cooker do you have? Is it the Instant Pot? I heard that thing makes yogurt too. I should cook more. Actually,

I was thinking maybe we could, like, divide and conquer when it comes to food? I'm not a great cook, but I can do a few things all right. I should be better about packing lunches and stuff. My mom used to say—"

Ugh, why was I bringing her up? I was still holding the small rolled-up Doritos bag, and shame shuddered through me. I crushed the remaining chips into crumbs, crinkling the bag.

"We'll get groceries Saturday morning and prepare for next week."

"Yeah, okay. Cool. Thanks."

I exhaled, shoving the massacred Doritos back in my bag. I'd throw them out later, along with the Butterfinger. It really would make me feel shitty in the morning. Not that I was never going to enjoy sugar again, but Henry was right. I didn't like feeling ugh.

"Tomorrow's Friday? My days are all messed up. And I guess Christmas is next week? You're not going to Vancouver? Obviously not. I'm not going to Chicago either. Too much training to do. It'll be weird to have two days off during the week. We could do more cooking, maybe? Unless you have local plans for Christmas. Not that you have to spend Christmas with me!"

"I'm visiting my grandfather at his assisted-living facility in the morning."

"I didn't know you had any family here. Cool. That'll be nice. Do you see him a lot?"

"Most weekends."

"Cool." I was saying that too much. "Thanks again for picking me up." We were past Scarborough now and into Pickering, so it wouldn't be much longer. "It's good to be back. And thanks for—" I waved my hand, trying to think of the best way to say it. "Hanging with me in Torino."

He nodded and looked over his shoulder before changing lanes. He was so *responsible*. Since when had I found that unbearably sexy?

After we'd woken together in Torino, we'd had to get our shit together for gala practice. Henry had barely said a word like usual. But I'd missed him as soon as he'd left my room.

And now being back in his practical Honda—I bet he knew the safety ratings off the top of his head—I felt settled again.

"I'll cook for you tomorrow," I said. "And for me. Oh, but we need to get groceries first, so I'll order healthy takeout for you tomorrow. And for me. Then I can cook on Saturday. What should I make?"

"I'll send you a recipe."

"Okay! Nothing too fancy."

"Stir fry isn't fancy."

"Yeah, I'm sure I can do that. Mostly. Probably!"

Getting back on the ice tomorrow would be hard—it was amazing how less than a week off could feel like eons when you laced up again—but I couldn't wait for the weekend. I'd cook Henry the best stir fry ever. Or die trying.

"WATCH THE ALMONDS. They'll burn."

"Yep." I glanced at the raw slivered almonds in the little frying pan before turning back to the fridge.

Saturday night dinner was almost done. We were in Henry's condo since he had all the cooking stuff—not to mention chairs and real furniture—and he'd hovered until I'd shooed him out of his own kitchen. I had this covered.

He sat at the little round table beside the kitchen doing one of his crosswords, one foot tucked under him. He said again, "Careful with the almonds."

With an exasperated eye roll, I glanced at the stove before turning back to the green onions that needed chopping. They had to be added at the end so they didn't wilt, which was apparently what happened if you put them in earlier according to Henry.

I said, "Almonds are still raw."

I started chopping the onions, and what seemed like a split second later, the unmistakable smell of burning tickled my nostrils. I whirled and yanked the pan off the burner. "Damn! They burned!"

Sitting at the table, Henry gave me a look that said, *no shit*. Esmeralda came out from where she'd curled by Henry's feet and crossed to the windowsill over the bed, as far from the stench of my shitty cooking as she could get.

I stirred the burnt almonds glumly with a wooden spoon. "But they were raw a second ago!"

"This is why you have to monitor them."

"I was trying to multitask."

"If you'd allow me to help—"

"No, no. I'm doing this for you." I lamely added, "And me. Gotta pull my weight here. It's fine—I've got it."

I really, really wanted to get this right. I didn't care if I didn't like it as long as he did. I took a minute to reread the recipe. Okay. I had this. I'd redo the almonds. No big. I dumped the burned ones in the green bin.

"Okay, give me another clue," I said.

"Contrast between two things. Ten letters."

"Hmm." I stirred the ground turkey and veggies, which were pretty much done. "Opposites?"

"That's only nine."

"Right. Do you have any letters?"

He told me, and a lightbulb went off. "Antithesis!" I frowned. "Wait, how do you say that?"

"It's 'an-ti-thuh-sus.'"

Laughing, I went back to chopping the green onions. "I didn't think it sounded right. I never said I was smart."

After a few moments, I felt the itch of Henry's intense gaze like a laser beam and looked over, taken aback by his intensity. "What?"

"You *are* smart. Mispronouncing a word only means you probably learned it by reading it instead of hearing it aloud."

"I was pretty much homeschooled so I could focus on skating, so I did the minimum to graduate. It's okay, at least I have my looks." I struck a model pose with my hip out and head tilted coyly, batting my eyelashes. He didn't even crack a smile, and I straightened. "What is it? I'm not upset about saying that word wrong. Honestly. Actually, I'm stoked I figured it out! But you're sweet for trying to make me feel better."

Still gripping his pencil, Henry flushed and dropped his gaze. I guessed it was the first time I'd called him something like *sweet*. But he was, damn it, and I wished I could cross the little kitchen and kiss his pink cheeks. Then straddle his lap and—

Nope! Back up that train of thought. Beep, beep, beep!

But why had this upset him so much? My flash of lust faded, and I set down the knife. Biting back the urge to pepper him with questions, I watched him and waited.

And waited.

I shifted my weight back and forth. Crossed and uncrossed my arms. Picked up the knife. Put down the knife. It was probably nothing? Was it nothing?

Why did I feel like it was something, though? That there was some hurt there, and I wanted to dig it out of him and make it better. Why had he reacted so strongly? Why?

Teeelll meeeeee.

As my bones felt like they were about to burst through my skin with the pressure of being patient, Henry finally met my eyes and sighed.

He said, "It's nothing."

The volcano of questions rose up. "Hmm?" I asked, impressed at my cool facade. Then I wondered if I'd been pronouncing *facade* correctly or not, but that was beside the point.

Henry turned the pencil, running his fingers up and down and around the tip, and I valiantly kept my mind out of the gutter. Mostly.

Finally, he said, "It's ridiculous to remember this so well. I was in grade four. It was nothing."

"Okay."

He shrugged. "I was reading something aloud in class. I don't remember what it was. The word 'monastery' was in the passage. I didn't go to a Catholic school, so I don't know why that would come up. I was in a special advanced class, and we were reading a short story, I think. I pronounced it 'mon-*ass*-tery' with the incorrect emphasis. Everyone laughed really hard. Even Mrs. Markham smiled."

I chuckled. "Ah. Okay." I waited for him to say he'd been beaten up on the playground later or something.

He stared into space like he was remembering the class laughing at him. "A boy named Tyler teased me about it all that week and called me stupid. I was afraid to say anything at all in case I pronounced something else incorrectly." He shrugged again. "So I spoke less after that. I was already quiet anyway."

Whoa. I almost said, "*That's it?*" but thank God I didn't. Henry had clearly been scarred by this incident a lot of people, including me, would laugh off.

How he'd gone into a judged sport was beyond me, but I guessed he loved being on the ice so much that he'd worked through it. Pleasing the judges had to fuel his perfectionism.

I wished I could reach back through time to tell baby Henry that it was okay, and he didn't have to be perfect. Also I'd kick that Tyler's ass.

What I did say was, "I'm sorry."

He wouldn't look at me. "I don't know why I remember that like it was yesterday."

I did cross over to him now, but I resisted straddling his lap, plopping down in the other chair instead. "Because your big brain has a scary good memory and likes to torture you."

His mouth quirked, and I felt a victorious rush like I'd landed the illusive quad Axel right there in the condo. What would it be like to kiss him? If I leaned across the table and licked across his bottom lip, would he let me in?

"Houlihan's moniker."

I tore my eyes from Henry's mouth. "Huh?"

"Eight down. 'Houlihan's moniker.' Seven letters." Pencil in hand, he tapped the paper of the crossword book.

"Oh, right." It was my turn to blush, my cheeks burning as I jumped up and returned to the cutting board. "I have no idea. I mean, 'moniker' means name. But what's a Houlihan?" I grabbed the remaining shoots of green onion and massacred them.

"Most likely a person. This is an older puzzle book, so it might be from the nineties. Or the eighties, even."

Spilling more slivered almonds into the pan, I frowned. "Why are you doing such old ones? Isn't it way easier to do new crosswords?" I laughed as soon as I said it. "Of course that's exactly why you do the old ones."

"Mm."

With a rush of fondness, I toasted the nuts, forcing myself to watch them the whole time aside from little glances at Henry I couldn't resist.

Chapter Ten

Henry

TEETH CLENCHED, TRYING to hide my grimace, I hit my short program final pose. In the hush after the music ended, the sounds of the rink came back to me. The murmur of conversation—Bill correcting Ivan on his spin position, the assistant coaches working with younger students, a few parents on the bleachers watching.

"That's enough for today," Manon said. "You need to rest—no arguments."

My pulse was elevated, and with each rapid breath I took, my ribs ached. I wanted to argue for one more run-through—especially since I'd put a hand down on my triple Axel. My skin prickled with the surreptitious stares around the rink.

Everyone had heard I'd strained the intercostal muscles between my ribs on my left back. Everyone was watching and listening even though they were pretending not to, an unnatural hush descending. Mitigating injury was part of the sport, but this close to the Olympics, it was fodder for gossip even more than usual.

"It's already much better," I told Manon. This was true—I'd rested for a whole day, and it was only a strain. I'd gotten twisted up on an awkward landing. I knew my body, and it wasn't serious.

It was annoying.

"Good!" She gave me a smile with steel in her eyes. "And now you're going to rest. You have an appointment with Dr. Shankar soon anyway. Bye!"

There was no sense in arguing, even though I detested finishing without a completely clean run-through. At the edge of the ice, I bent to slip on my skate guards, careful to keep my face neutral even though my back twinged.

"Hey! That was a great Lutz. How are your ribs feeling?"

Muscles protesting, I straightened to face Theodore. "Perfect." My *ribs* weren't injured.

He raised an eyebrow dubiously. "Yeah? You know, I was thinking of a better way to do the hot-cold therapy." He bent to take off his guards, tossing them onto the closest bench, one teetering on the edge before falling to the concrete with a dull clatter. "My plan is—"

"Theo!" Manon called, tapping her wrist even though she wore no watch.

If anyone hadn't been looking at me before, assessing the state of my injury, they were certainly watching Theodore and me now. He gave Manon a wide smile and yelled, "One second!"

After the first week when we'd skated on the same sessions before Manon and Bill had had time to adjust the schedule, Theodore and I didn't train at the same time. Though I was still driving him most days since he'd been getting up early more often. The rides were naturally the subject of arena gossip, but no one knew about our dinners and cooking. At least not to my knowledge.

But the more we interacted at the rink, the more gossip would spread. I hated the hot prickle of stares and whispers, and I snapped, "It wasn't a great Lutz. It was acceptable." And considering he had the best quad Lutz in the world, I didn't need Theodore's encouragement.

He'd been about to say something, but frowned. "No, it was good. You've been holding back, but that one was perfect. I know what it's like when you have an injury. Anyway, I just… Hey, Ivan."

Ivan stepped off the ice and put on his guards, giving Theodore a nod.

"Theo, let's go!" Manon approached, frowning. "Everything all right?"

"Yeah, totally!" Theodore said.

She nodded decisively. "Warm-up laps. Crack that walnut between your shoulder blades. Core on and get into your knees. Firm and stiff are two different things."

He did as he was told for once, though his posture still needed work. I crouched to pick up his errant skate guard, placing it on the bench beside the other.

"What was he saying?" Ivan asked, dropping to the bench and pulling a banana from his bag.

I shrugged. "He was just talking."

Ivan grunted and bit off half the banana. "Don't let him get in your head."

"I'm not." I sipped from my water bottle, tearing my gaze from Theodore.

Ivan mumbled through another bite, "He's a nice guy, sure, but don't forget he's the enemy."

I wanted to argue. A few months ago, I would have agreed wholeheartedly. A few months ago, I'd hated Theodore. I watched him now begin jump drills, reeling off one of his exceptional quad Salchows.

I reached for the resentment that had once flowed like water. Theodore was laughing and saying something to Bill, and then he gathered speed for another perfect Salchow. It came so easily to him—the natural snap and quick spinning motion.

The memory of his hot tears on my neck as I held him on a

rainy street invaded. The way he talked and talked to Esmeralda as if she understood him. Curled on my couch dozing. Following a recipe with earnest effort. The tightness in his jaw when he spoke of his mother's abuse though he'd likely never use that word.

"Everyone thinks you're going crazy." Ivan laughed. "Be careful."

On the drive to Dr. Shankar's office in Markham, I tried not to imagine Theodore on the top of the podium in Calgary while I was a step below. But I could hear "The Star-Spangled Banner" in my mind instead of "O Canada" and see him with his hand over his heart, singing along.

A surge of petty jealousy took over, and I let it flourish. I encouraged it with more memories of losing, trying to fan the flames. I would beat Theodore at the Olympics. Once we left for Calgary, he would be my enemy. I could close the door on this strange…what? Friendship? I was still in control. Everything was fine.

At the appointment, Dr. Shankar asked, "How are you doing with your visualizations?"

"Well," I lied.

Even if I did my very best, would it be enough to beat Theodore? The judges would put him in front if he landed all his quads. He had one more in his planned free skate than me, and it would be all the difference he needed no matter how shallow the edges on his footwork. His hip swiveling would be more than enough for his PCS even if Manon couldn't improve his posture.

"Henry?"

I blinked at Dr. Shankar. She watched me with her head tilted slightly, brown eyes almost squinting. I answered, "Yes?"

Sitting across from me in her neutral-toned office, she uncrossed her legs, her slacks making a *shushing* sound. I shifted, the pristine leather of her couch squeaking.

"You seem distracted today. Restless. You mentioned you have a new injury?"

I waved a hand dismissively. "I strained the intercostal muscles around my ribs." I motioned to my left lower back, not letting myself wince. "It's improving daily. Very minor."

"Glad to hear it. How are things going with Theo?"

My spine stiffened. "Fine." I couldn't hold her gaze and looked at the sage throw rug on her wooden floor.

She chuckled. "I don't think that's true. Neither do you. Remember, if you focus too much on your competitors and not your own performance—over which only you have complete control—that's when distraction can lead to mistakes."

Control. Dr. Shankar was correct. I'd remained in control in so many aspects of my life for years. After my shameful stupidity in Vancouver, I'd rededicated myself to skating. Yet now I was letting Theodore distract me.

The worst part was that it wasn't on the ice. It was at home.

My eyes flicked to the round metal clock on Dr. Shankar's office wall. Dinner was scheduled in two hours. Since he'd returned from the funeral, he'd eaten dinner at my condo every night. I typically cycled through the same handful of recipes, and Theodore eagerly sliced vegetables, both of us in the kitchen now.

When toasting nuts, he watched carefully, wooden spoon in hand.

"Henry, have you considered visiting a personal therapist?"

I snapped my attention back to Dr. Shankar. "I need a sports psychologist."

"Yes, absolutely. But you might recall a couple of years ago when I suggested you might also want therapy that doesn't center on skating and your career. I have many clients that do both."

"Skating is all that matters. Being the best. Winning."

"Mmm. Yet you've told me you prefer training to competing. Do you want to win for the accomplishment or the validation?"

Leather squeaked as I shifted. "Perhaps both."

"You haven't brought up Theo since before the Grand Prix Final."

"We just discussed him."

She smiled. "I'm not sure I'd call your one-word answer a discussion. And I raised the subject. Which, having gotten to know you, indicates to me that there's a reason you don't want to talk about him. How did it feel when he beat you by such a slim margin at the Grand Prix Final?"

"Fine." I couldn't tell her that I had only cared for a few minutes before learning of Mr. Webber's death. That I'd scoured the dark, sleepy streets until I found him, content to watch from a distance to make sure he was safe.

I couldn't tell her because I hadn't fully acknowledged to myself how Theodore sobbing in my arms in the gray drizzle had somehow broken me. Or had at least cracked the surface, and now I was…leaking. I thought about him constantly. Not about how to beat him or how annoying he was and how much I hated him.

No. I thought about him stirring almonds and scratching behind Esmeralda's ears. Looking up new recipes he thought I'd like and beaming at me with that beautiful smile that crinkled his eyes.

I couldn't tell her I was still as stupid and pathetic as I'd been in Vancouver when I'd let myself believe I was understood. Wanted, even. She'd give me self-talk exercises and tell me I was harder on myself than even the Russian judges, and I'd be expected to find it humorous.

"I realize it's easier said than done, but can you put on your mental blinders over the holidays and concentrate on the choices and actions that are in your control? Can you stop obsessing over Theo Sullivan?"

"Absolutely."

Another lie.

"TAKE OFF YOUR shirt."

It was absolutely ridiculous that my heart thumped at those words. Theodore knew I had a muscle strain, and after our dinner of leftover curry and freshly steamed broccoli, he'd gone up to his condo and returned with a blue bead ice pack that had a soft fabric covering on one side.

"I have ice packs," I said.

With a low *riiip*, he pulled apart the black fabric straps. "But this one stays on really well. Here." He beckoned me closer.

I stood at the sink rinsing Esmeralda's dish. I'd given her too much food again, but only a bit. "I'm fine."

Rolling his eyes, Theodore crossed to me, his socked feet silent. Before I could object, my hands still full with the dish and sponge, he lifted the hem of my T-shirt. I made a sound that could have been called a squeak.

"It's okay," he murmured. "You can keep it on." He slipped his hands around my ribs, his breath warm on the back of my neck. The cold pack touched my back, and I gasped softly. He shifted it, asking, "Is that the right place?" His right hand was splayed on my stomach, and I shivered.

"A little to the left," I whispered. "There."

Standing close to me, he tightened the straps around my stomach, sealing the Velcro. "Okay?"

I couldn't breathe, let alone speak. But I managed, "Cold."

His laugh tickled my ear. "That's the whole idea. You're doing cold-hot, right? I have a brilliant idea for the hot part."

My belly somersaulted. Did I want to know?

BEFORE LONG, I followed Theodore out of the changing room

and across the tile pool deck to the condo's hot tub. We had the entire area to ourselves, which perhaps wasn't surprising for later on a weeknight. There were cold puddles of water on the tile from earlier users.

"I was like, you can't be serious. You want me to skate to *Phantom* and wear a bodysuit with the white mask design over half of me diagonally? What is this, the *eighties?*" Theodore scoffed as he tossed his towel over a hook on the wall and continued on to the shower in the corner. His towel had barely caught, and it slipped to the floor.

Picking up his towel, I hung it properly before doing the same with mine. Nerves skittered across my bare skin. I'd actually never used the condo's pool facilities, and my dark surf-style bathing shorts were a few years old and felt tight over my glutes.

But Theodore had me beat in the tightness department. He turned on the shower, waving his hand through the stream of water before stepping under it.

"Why not just do *Cats* and make me wear a full face of whiskers makeup? Sure, I was still a junior, but it was beyond tacky. It's like, there are other musicals in the world."

Water ran down his body as he turned under the shower, the short bathing suit that looked like skimpy red boxer briefs clinging to his backside so tightly they could have been painted on. I'd been pointedly ignoring the bulge in the front of his shorts, and I ripped my gaze away as he faced me, still talking. I took my turn under the shower as he pressed the big red button that switched on the hot tub.

"Well?" He climbed down into the tub and watched me expectantly. "Have you seen it?" He hadn't sat yet, the water swirling around his lean thighs.

Whatever it was, I probably hadn't, so I shook my head.

"Oh my God, it's seriously horrible but hilarious. We should watch it one night. Esmeralda will love it."

I said, "Okay," wondering why the idea of watching a movie or TV show or whatever it was he was talking about didn't seem like a bad idea. It should have. It was a *terrible* idea. It was one thing to share coaches. I shouldn't have been spending my evenings with Theodore.

I should have been asleep already or practicing bedtime yoga instead of sitting in the hot tub with him. I'd convinced myself this was an acceptable activity since it was a component of physiotherapy, which was vital to training.

I hadn't considered that we'd be half naked. Three-quarters naked, more accurately.

He lowered himself into the water with a long, low moan.

"This is amazing." He moaned again, closing his eyes. "Get in here."

I did, because I was about to humiliate myself, and at least my groin wouldn't be visible under the white water. I bit back my own groan. The heat really did feel wonderful. I stretched out my legs, brushing his calf and whipping back my feet.

He was talking, talking, talking, and laughing about something, and every flash of a smile made my arousal throb. His smattering of chest hair was wet and dark around his nipples, and my throat was dry…

For years after he'd smirked at my pubescent erection in the communal concrete shower room in Croatia, I'd resented him. Where was that lingering enmity now when I needed it? How had it vanished so quickly?

The more time I foolishly spent with Theodore, the less I hated him, and now I found the one emotion that had been so reliable for years had abandoned me. That irrational hate had fueled me.

Could I even beat him without it?

"Turn around." He made a spinning motion with his finger. "It'll help."

I'd lost the thread of conversation, but I didn't want to admit it. I tentatively shifted to sit sideways on the hot tub's tile bench. Before I knew what was happening, Theodore surged across the water and tucked himself close behind me, his right leg bent and shin pressing against my backside.

My lungs stuttered as his left hand spread over my ribs. Slowly, using thumb and fingers, he massaged the sore area of my back. He was saying, "I strained these muscles a few years ago, and it's so awkward to reach yourself. Not that I'm an expert, but does that feel okay?"

"Uh-huh."

All the deep breathing and meditation in the world couldn't stop my simmering arousal from boiling over into a full-fledged erection. I kept my gaze high on the reflection of the empty pool in the wall of dark windows.

Then I lowered my eyes to the image of Theodore close behind me and my own parted lips. We were small in the glass across the room, but seeing us excited me.

I could feel his breath on my neck like I had standing at the sink. I could imagine his lips touching my skin, his body covering mine, bending me over the side of the hot tub…

"Why are you helping me?" The question scraped out of my dry throat.

His fingers flexed on my side, his tone teasing. "I want to beat you fair and square. It's no fun if you're injured."

I jerked away from him with a splash, sliding to the other side of the hot tub.

He blinked at me before forcing a smile that didn't reach his eyes. "Sorry! No competition talk, right? We agreed. There's no winning and losing here." He made a zipping motion across his mouth, his lips glistening red in the steam.

I could only stare at him, my breath too fast and my head spinning with confusion. We shouldn't be doing this. I should get up and leave and stop talking to Theo until after Calgary.

Not Theo. *Theodore.*

A voice boomed, "Time to lock up the pool area!"

The concierge's announcement made me jump half out of the hot tub. Unfortunately, it didn't put a damper on my erection in the slightest, and as Theodore exchanged pleasantries with the man before he left and presumably returned to the front desk, I willed my body to cooperate.

What was wrong with me? I shouldn't be attracted to Theo—**Theodore**—and I clearly couldn't let him get so close to me ever again. I had to put a stop to this, yet no matter how hard I attempted to focus and control my body, I couldn't.

Climbing out and grabbing his towel from the hook on the wall, Theodore ran it over his hair. And pressed the red button, sealing my fate. The camouflaging swirl of frothing water flattened, steam still rising.

Frowning, he gave me an awkward smile and hesitantly asked, "You coming?"

Humiliation had me in its jaws, and I wished there was a way to slip under the water's surface and swim back to my condo in darkness.

He crossed the deck, feet slapping on the wet tile to loom on the other side of the hot tub. "Are you feeling okay? You're really red." I nodded, but his frown deepened. "Are you dizzy? That can happen if you spend too long in the water and overheat."

I shook my head. "Go on without me."

He sighed. "Seriously? Look, I'm sorry I said that. I know we have to keep competition separate from this. Don't be mad, okay?"

"Just go," I rasped.

"You sound weird. I'm not going to leave you here. What's—" He crouched low, scanning me, and his eyes popped comically wide. "Oh! Are you—" He bit his lip, trying not to laugh. His smile grew quizzical. Then hopeful.

His face was so expressive that I could see the progression of his thoughts to the inevitable eyebrow-raising conclusion that my erection was a reaction to him. Perhaps drowning myself was the best option, because surely I was going to die of embarrassment.

Yet his surprised laughter wasn't cruel. Thinking back now to that horrifying moment in the shower room in Croatia when I'd been similarly aroused by him… Perhaps his laughter then hadn't been cruel either. Only teasing. We'd both been young, after all. He likely didn't even remember that fleeting moment that had haunted me far too long.

But here I was making a fool of myself again.

"Oh!" He ducked his head, smiling shyly in a way that made my heart skip a beat. "Hold on." He returned with my towel, thrusting it out.

All I could do was leap up to grab it and wrap it tightly around my waist to hide my shame. I practically ran to the changing room, flip-flops slapping as I bypassed the shower, chlorine be damned. I grabbed my T-shirt and keys and escaped.

"Henry!"

I jabbed the elevator button repeatedly with my thumb, dripping all over the floor. It was very inconsiderate to the cleaning staff, but I had to get away.

The *ding* finally sounded, but of course Theodore barreled onto the elevator after me, shirtless too with his towel around his hips and a cloth tote bag in his hand.

"Don't you think we should talk about this?"

I stared at him in mute horror as the elevator rose. This had to be some kind of cruel nightmare. It was bad enough how pathetic I was, and now Theodore was trying to be *nice* about it, which was so much worse.

When we reached my floor, I lunged past him. And he followed, because naturally he did. Still talking, because naturally he was.

"It's okay." We reached my door, and he grinned cockily. "I'm tough to resist. You're only human."

I glared at him as I jammed the key in my door and shoved it open. I tried my best to close it in his face, but he was halfway in and I might really hurt him, the wood thick and heavy. He was trespassing, and I shouldn't have cared about hurting him. Frustration surged.

I need to hate him again. Throw him out. Now!

I kicked off my flip-flops, fisting my hands and close to hyper-ventilating. "Go ahead. Mock me." *Please.* I could process that. That was familiar. That I could resent and cling to.

"I'm not here to make fun of you."

Pity was worse than mockery, but there was something in his low tone that made me shiver. Goosebumps rippled over my bare chest, still damp in the cool air. My nipples were hard, and my groin throbbed.

"We agree we have to keep this separate from competing." Theo stepped closer in the little foyer. The red light from the rice cooker illuminated the space just enough. Esmeralda appeared to investigate before disappearing again.

"I haven't told anyone about our dinners. Have you?"

I shook my head.

"And I know no one at the rink has a clue or my mother would have found out, flown to Toronto, and banged down your door during *House Hunters* to drag me out of here."

I almost smiled at that.

Theo did smile, a devilish grin in the red glow. I could only stare as he closed in. Slowly, he loosened my towel and tugged it free.

"It's always the quiet ones. Or what's that other saying? Still waters run deep? I bet you run *really* deep." Biting his lip, he ran a fingertip down the center of my chest. My breath seized, my cock swelling fully again simply from that. "No one has to know about what we do together. And we'll stop before we go to Calgary. It'll be all business during the Olympics."

I panted shallowly through my mouth, torn between squirming away and throwing myself into his arms.

He drew his index finger down over my sensitive belly, making me flinch, the muscles jumping. Then over my shaft through the wet, clingy material. All I could do was tremble, biting my tongue so I didn't make any embarrassing noises.

"You really are a dark horse. That's another saying, right? I bet that's been an answer in one of your crosswords." Without warning, he grasped me with his whole hand, rubbing and sending shockingly pure bolts of pleasure through my whole body.

Somehow, he was still talking about crosswords. "You know, I tried the Monday one the other day. It's the easiest, right?"

My knees were weak as he stroked me, and without the wall behind me, I would have collapsed. He was laughing now, but not with derision, and as he leaned in, I almost let him kiss me.

I turned my face at the last moment, fear surging through the pleasure. It would be too much. I'd come as soon as his lips met mine, and it was too humiliating. Too exposing. If I let him kiss me, all the walls would crumble. There'd be no protection left.

Hand on my shaft, he stilled. I blinked at the red-lit coat closet, my face turned, his gaze hot on my cheek. He murmured, "It's okay." With his free hand, he caressed my arm, sending more goosebumps rippling. "Have you done this before?'

The memories from Vancouver invaded along with indignation. I went rigid. "Of course! I'm not a virgin."

"Okay." Theodore still caressed slowly, his tone soothing. "It would be all right if you were."

"I'm not!" I glared at Theo, gritting my teeth. "I'm not."

I remembered the narrow bed in the dorm room in Vancouver, and *him* and how shameless I'd been. How pitifully stupid.

I asked, "Why are you doing this? You don't really want me."

He seemed taken aback, blinking owlishly in the red glow. "Uh, I beg to differ." Taking my hand, he pressed my palm over his erection through the rough towel. "Henry, I want you."

I couldn't hold in a moan, and his beautiful face lit up. His gaze flicked between my mouth and my eyes, and he very deliberately took my chin and turned my head so he could suck on the side of my neck.

His damp mouth locked onto my ticklish skin, and I bit back a gasp. That he was respecting my refusal to kiss had warmth pulsing in my chest.

Even as he stroked and nuzzled me, a steady stream of groans and moans and mumbles poured out of his mouth. I stayed quiet, my lips pressed together, nostrils flaring. He pulled my damp bathing suit down to my thighs and dropped to his knees, and I nearly had to slap my hand over my mouth.

Spreading his hands wide, he circled my inner thighs rhythmically with his thumbs while he peered up at me. "Can I suck you?"

Did he really want to? Was this a trick? I stood frozen, my hands at my sides.

Theo sat back on his heels, dropping his hands. "Do you want to stop?"

I shook my head so hard it was a miracle I didn't dislodge my brain. Or what was left of it. A coy little smile tugging on his lips, Theodore watched me through his eyelashes as he leaned forward and licked my balls. I had to whimper. He opened his mouth and sucked one, the heat incredible.

He smiled around me before moving to the other ball, lips and tongue gentle. My whole body shuddered at the featherlight sensation. I felt like I would float away if not for his mouth grounding me, if not for his hands strong on my hips. I had to touch him, and he purred like Esmeralda as I threaded my fingers through his soft hair.

This had to be a dream. I'd wake up alone in my bed any minute now. Theodore Sullivan could not actually be on his knees for *me*, teasing and touching. Then he sucked my shaft down to the root without warning. After three hard pulls of his mouth, I came, gasping as I spilled down his throat.

I shattered into too many pieces. The release was shockingly intense compared to using my own hand when I was too pent up. I shook and quivered, my back arching. This time, I wasn't alone.

Theo was with me, all heat and muscle and moaned encouragement. He swallowed it all, and when I realized with horror that I was gripping his hair so tightly it must have hurt, I jerked my hand to my side.

He released me, my shaft and his mouth shining wet in the crimson light. He shoved down his ridiculously small bathing suit and placed my hand back on his head. I tentatively tightened my fingers, pulling his hair just a bit.

Groaning, he leaned into my touch as he jerked himself roughly, eyes closed and mouth open. He spurted over his hand, splashing my knee and muttering a string of obscenities.

He slumped against my legs, keeping me on my feet for at least a few more minutes. I couldn't resist caressing his hair as we panted harshly. It felt like being in a cocoon, just the two of us in the ghostly light from the kitchen. If only we could stay this way…

Esmeralda's outraged meow made us both jump. Somehow laughing, Theodore pushed to his feet. "Sounds like the princess is jealous. Or hungry. Like always, right? I can relate, sweetheart. Mmm, what I wouldn't give for a Big Mac and large fries. Plus a shake. Shamrock is the best, obviously, but otherwise I go for vanilla. I like chocolate—I mean, who doesn't—but not in a milkshake for some reason."

I blinked at him as he shimmied back into his bathing suit, my heart fluttering from the way he'd said *sweetheart*. Which he'd directed at my cat, I reminded myself.

Wake up!

I tugged up my cold, damp bathing suit and tried to shake off the hazy aftershocks.

"Can I give her a treat?"

I nodded, and Theo disappeared into the kitchen, opening the right cupboard with a familiarity that swelled my heart dangerously. Esmeralda zoomed after him, and he murmured to her, the package crinkling.

When he returned, he watched me carefully. "Do you want to lie down?"

What was he saying? Did he want to go to bed together? Did he think I was about to pass out? Had we really just done that? What did this mean? What was going to happen next?

I thought of sleeping beside him in Torino, or when he'd napped in my bed during his migraine. How innocent he looked as he slowly woke, licking his lips and blinking blearily.

"I have early practice." It was true. I didn't know what I wanted or what to say, so I said that.

For a moment… Did he look disappointed? *Hurt* even?

But in the next breath, he was grinning carelessly the way he did so often. "Think of me fast asleep when you're dragging ass out to the Chalet in the dark. And I'll see you for the Christmas Eve group session thing. Right?"

His smile faltered, and my heart skipped as I nodded. Biting his lip, he slowly reached out to take my chin. He turned my head and leaned close, pressing his lips to my cheek the way he had in that rainy alley in Torino when I'd followed him to make sure he didn't get hurt in his dazed grief.

I held my breath as he lingered, only a whisper from my skin. When he stepped back, he huskily murmured, "Sweet dreams."

I watched the door thud shut behind him, knowing I had a sleepless night ahead.

Chapter Eleven

Theo

"ARE YOU SURE you don't want us to give you a lift?" Ga-young's mother asked with a polite, totally nosy smile.

"I'm sure!" I replied, jerking my thumb at Henry. "We're already going to the same place. It's cool. We won't kill each other. Not on Christmas Eve, anyway."

"Maybe on Boxing Day," Henry said flatly.

Ga-young, her parents, and I all turned to Henry in surprise. Was that...a *joke*? It made me stupidly happy as I followed him out to the Ice Chalet's snowy parking lot.

I'd been really tempted to haul ass out of bed and come in early with Henry, but I didn't want to... I don't know. Pressure him, I guess?

In the Honda, we were alone for the first time since my favorite blow job of all time. So far. There were some strong contenders in the running, but sucking Henry and undoing his buttoned-up reserve had been amazingly good.

As I fiddled with the heat vents, I stole glances at him. He drove with his hands at ten and two like usual, checking his blind spot before changing lanes and adjusting the windshield wipers to combat the wet snow falling.

Does he regret it? Did he like it? I mean, he came in my mouth, so obviously he liked it on a physical level, but did he like it in his head? Is he secretly mad at me? Would he give me a ride if he was? He'd wanted me just as much as I wanted him. Right? Or would he pop a boner for anyone massaging him in a hot tub? What should I say? Should I ask him to turn on the radio so this terrible silence ends? Or will that make him think I don't want to talk or—

"Do you want to make dinner tonight?"

His question startled me out of my anxiety spiral. "Yeah!" I winced. "But I can't. We're doing our big Christmas thing tonight on Zoom with my parents and sisters and uncles and aunts and cousins and stuff. We're spread all over these days. Everyone makes their own food and we eat it together and talk."

"Mm." He adjusted the wipers. "I'm doing a call with my family in the morning before I see my grandpa."

"Right, cool. Sorry."

His brow furrowed. "Why?"

"About tonight. Because I would really rather have dinner with you."

He glanced at me, and a tiny smile tugged at his lips.

Yes! "And hey, if you want company visiting your grandpa, I could come with you. Only if you want. Would that be weird? I don't want to make it weird."

But if he wanted to see me tomorrow, I could give him my gift. Excitement sparked in my veins. It was probably a stupid idea, but I'd prepared it just in case and figured I could give it to him if the opportunity arose...

After a few moments, he said, "You'd like to come?"

"Sure! It would be cool to meet him. If you want. I understand if you don't. Maybe he hates me like my mother hates you. It's not personal! She hates everyone who could beat me. Sorry, we're not supposed to talk about that. Bad elephant! Get back in the trunk!" I was losing it. Why was I so nervous?

The furrow was back as Henry drove into the condo's underground parking, circling down to the bottom level. There was no one in sight as he pulled into his spot and killed the engine. It ticked down in the silence.

I was sure Henry could hear how hard my heart was pounding. Fidgeting, I took off my seat belt. He did the same, yet didn't move to get out.

I was supposed to be an adult, but I felt like a teenager. Why did I want him so much?

"I'd like you to come with me tomorrow," he said quietly.

"Okay." I nodded. And nodded again. "Do you want to—are we cool? I had a lot of fun last night. I'm up for more if you are. It doesn't have to be—we can just—" I waved my hand.

I almost said that it didn't have to mean anything, but I couldn't. This already meant something. Even if we never hooked up again, this was *something*.

Henry exhaled a shuddery breath and licked his lips, his brown eyes locking on mine. "You really want me?"

The question was barely a whisper, and suddenly he seemed incredibly fragile. Like I could shatter him if I did or said the wrong thing. Protectiveness rose up, and I carefully rested my left hand on his thigh. I stared intensely into his eyes, willing him to believe me.

"I really want you." Then more words tripped out. "It's probably a bad idea with the Olympics so soon, but we're already hanging out. We could agree that we hang until we go to Calgary, and then it's every man for himself." The unsaid question was: What about after the Olympics?

One step at a time.

"You won't tell anyone?" Henry asked.

That question stung, not gonna lie. Was he ashamed of me? But no, that wasn't fair. Of course we couldn't tell anyone. Holy shit, it would be the hottest gossip in skating, and my mom would a hundred percent find out and lose it.

Admittedly, the thought grimly satisfied me, but that could

come after the Olympics. Assuming Henry and I carried on...whatever this was.

One step at a time.

"It's our secret," I promised.

Slowly, I rubbed his thigh, my fingers dipping between his legs. He sucked in a breath, and oh yeah. He was hard. His tight practice pants hid nothing.

"Yeah?" I asked.

Please say yes. Please say yes. Please say yes. Please—

"Yes."

In a nanosecond, I leapt into action. Well, leaned into action since we were in the car. The stretchy fabric was soft under my palm, and I squeezed his dick with enough pressure to make him gasp. God, I *loved* that sound. I chased it, eager for more.

Rubbing him through the material, I flashed him a grin. "Is this okay?" He only blinked at me, pink lips parted, whole body tensed.

Shit. I dropped my hand. "Should I stop?'

For a heartbeat, I swear I could see the war inside him. Then he shook his head an inch and made this tiny, sexy, whimper of surrender.

My grin returned, and this time, I squeezed my hand into his pants, impatiently freeing his cock. He glanced around the garage with adorable franticness.

"It's okay. It's just us." I nuzzled his neck, and he gripped my thigh.

He was uncut, and I eased back his foreskin to tease the glistening head. Jesus, I was ready to swallow him to the root again, but the steering wheel made that impossible. I could bend over to blow him, but I really liked being on my knees for that.

He squeezed his eyes shut, breathing shallowly and practically silently through parted lips as I jerked him. He'd denied being a virgin, but there was something innocent about him that I couldn't put my finger on. A vulnerable spot, like the soft skin behind his ear that I licked.

I reached down to tease his balls, the waistband of his pants digging into my forearm. "Do you want to come?"

A shudder ran through him, his hips jerking. He nodded.

"Do you want *me* to make you come? No one else?"

Shutting his eyes, a blush creeping down his neck, he nodded again. He still clutched my leg with his right hand like I was a life raft and he was drowning.

I loved it. I loved giving him this, because if anyone needed to unclench, it was Henry. I shimmied my free hand under his jacket and the hem of his sweatshirt so I could trace up and down his spine.

Lips at his ear as I worked his cock, I whispered everything that popped into my mind. "It's okay, I'm here. I'll help you. I'll give you what you need. You need this so bad, don't you? Sorry— *badly.* I know how much you like proper grammar."

There! He laughed, just for a moment, the choked sound barely escaping. But it was undeniably a laugh, and it made me happier than it had any right to.

"Oh, yeah. You need this so badly. Do you jerk off a lot? I bet you do. But this is better, isn't it?" His dick throbbed in my hand as I grasped it again. "Mmm. You like this, right? Your cock is gorgeous, you know that?" I bit his earlobe—not too hard, but hard enough.

A sweet, perfect little moan escaped him. I wanted to shout in triumph, and any blood remaining in the top half of my body flooded south. I let go of his junk, and he whimpered.

"Feel how hard you make me?" I guided his hand to the bulge in my pants, groaning when he rubbed me. "Oh, fuck. You turn me on."

He practically squeaked, face adorably red by now. I grinned, stroking him faster and harder. "You have no idea how hot you are. But you feel it, right? I'm about to jizz in my pants for you. But I want you to come first. I want to see you let go. You want to know a secret?"

Panting, Henry opened his eyes, his chest heaving.

"I've thought about you when I jerk off. Fucked myself on my fingers and imagined it's you filling me. I spurt so much cum thinking about you, Henry."

Mission accomplished, because now Henry was the one spurting cum all over my hand, his flushed neck bared as he spasmed, mouth open. I milked his shaft and talked him through it, praising him, not even sure what I was saying.

Then it was my turn to gasp. Henry pushed me back against the seat and freed my straining cock from my practice pants and underwear. Bending over my lap, he swallowed the head of my dick.

"Oh, fuck yes."

With his usual quiet intensity, Henry sucked me like the technical specialist would be reviewing every angle. It was a little clumsy, and I wondered again how much practice he'd had—or hadn't. I liked the idea that he was inexperienced. There was so much we could explore together.

Winding my fingers in the soft flop of his hair, I made sure not to pull. "Feels amazing."

He swirled his tongue tentatively, and I kept talking, encouraging him. I didn't mind when he scraped a bit with his teeth. I liked roughness sometimes, though I was sure Henry hadn't meant it. He was slurping, fingers digging into my knee, sucking harder and harder.

I wanted to tell him it was okay, and he didn't have anything to prove, but it felt too good. All I could do was groan and warn him—a second too late—everything going tight.

He coughed and sputtered, releasing me as my orgasm exploded, my spine arching. "*Henry,*" I moaned.

When he sat up, I didn't let go of his skull, petting the back of his head as I blinked back to reality. I focused on him, my breath catching as I got a good look at his face.

At the milky drops on his chin and red lips.

His mouth glistened, and he blinked at me, looking slightly dazed. I'd officially never wanted to kiss anyone so much in my whole life. Henry Sakaguchi had just blown me, and he looked so nervous, and it was *precious*.

"That was incredible," I murmured.

Eyebrows up, he smiled tentatively. A little twitch at first, then I saw actual teeth. Yeah, yeah, I'd seen him smiling with teeth on the podium and for pictures or whatever, but this wasn't that. This was *real*.

I like you so much.

Honestly, what even was my life? How had I fallen for Henry Sakaguchi of all people? His smile faltered as I leaned in. I paused and whispered, "It's okay. I'm just going to clean you up."

The adorable brow furrow made its appearance, and I slowly, slowly, licked the bitter drops from his chin before swiping the last one at the corner of his mouth with the tip of my tongue.

He shuddered, fingers painful on my knee. I wanted to kiss him so bad—*ly*—but I wouldn't cross his line.

The *slam* of a car door made us both jump. Slapping my hand over my mouth, I peered around, but still couldn't see anyone amid the rows of vehicles. Laughing, I slumped against him, pressing open-mouthed kisses to his throat, feeling the faintest scratch of stubble.

"Guess we'd better go upstairs," I mumbled against his skin.

"Mm." That familiar sound was raspy.

We hauled our skating bags out of the trunk and crossed the concrete lot in silence that I wanted to fill. It was freezing, and I wished we could get in the hot tub.

I said, "Brr," because I was a dumbass.

As we got on the elevator, Henry asked, "What are you eating tonight?"

"I'm ordering Swiss Chalet. I saw a commercial for the special they have with stuffing and cranberry sauce to go with the chicken. And chocolates. My mom won't like it, but whatever. It's Christmas." I fidgeted uneasily. "I should be better, I know."

"You're not bad."

The elevator slowed at Henry's floor, the doors opening with a *ding*. He stepped off, then turned to face me, putting out a hand. The doors bounced back.

"I only asked because I want to make sure you have something nice to eat."

"Oh! Yeah. Thanks. I'm good. See you in the morning?"

Or I could come down after my call and we could watch TV or have sex or do crosswords or have sex or whatever. We could sleep together again, and we don't have to have sex. I just want to wake up with you.

He nodded as the doors slid shut, and I was left with too many unsaid words clogging up my brain.

Chapter Twelve

Theo

"UM, LET ME see." I examined the Scrabble board, my mind spinning uselessly. Henry and his grandpa were *amazing* at the game, and I was putting out sad little words like, "run" and "bike" and "go."

My foot jiggled under the small table. We were in a festively decorated common room at the old folks' home. Christmas carols played on a boom box with surprisingly clear sound, and various families visited residents.

Garlands were strung along the ceiling, and a big tree in the corner was decorated with a lot of handmade paper and glitter ornaments probably made by some kids.

Humming, Mr. Sakaguchi popped a chocolate rosebud in his mouth, sucking loudly. He'd refused to wear his hearing aids, and Henry had only tried to convince him for a minute.

"Okay, I guess I'll go with this." Cringing, I put down my tiles, forming "wake" on the board.

Mr. Sakaguchi shook his head and tapped a gnarled finger on another spot on the board that led to an available letter "e." He pointed to the red square, and I squinted at it.

"Oh!" I moved my tiles. "Triple word score. Cool." I made sure he was looking at me and smiled. "Thank you!" Henry said he could read lips pretty well, and I tried to enunciate and speak more slowly than my usual word vomit.

Smiling back, he nodded. His hair was white and stuck up at adorable angles from his head. He was small and a little stooped, but he'd had a shockingly strong grip when I shook his hand.

We'd gone to his room first, and Henry had given him a bag of presents to unwrap, including the soft green sweater he wore now. Henry wore a similar sweater over a button-up collared shirt and slacks.

That he'd dressed up for Christmas was just so *cute*. My family never did, but at least my dark jeans and Henley looked decent.

I'd picked up the chocolates at a convenience store, and Mr. Sakaguchi seemed to enjoy them. He sucked another as he put down "verdant," the "v" on a triple letter square. Henry marked down his score on a pad of paper with a pencil, his hair falling over his forehead.

He'd need it trimmed before he went to Canadian Nationals. I wanted to reach over and brush it back, but kept my hands to myself. He examined his tiles, then tapped the spot his grandpa had just used with a little shake of his head.

"Ojiichan, I had a great plan."

Mr. Sakaguchi grinned. "Boo hoo," he said loudly.

"Savage!" I added.

Henry gave me a little smirk. "There's no mercy in Scrabble."

"Except you're both helping me."

He lifted a shoulder, eyes on his tiles. "You're still learning how to play."

"Where's your famed killer instinct?" I *tsked*. "My mother would be so disappointed."

He met my gaze. "I work hard to disappoint your mother."

I laughed, but my stomach flipped. He could have been saying he was going to beat me for gold, but I wasn't sure he meant that.

Mr. Sakaguchi slapped the table. "Time's up."

Henry put down "jockeys," which of course made me think of underwear even though he meant the people who race horses. I was pretty sure that was what he meant.

Stop thinking about Henry and underwear!

It was my turn again to come up with a piddly word. Speaking of my mother, my phone was buzzing in my pocket, and I knew it was her. Sure enough, when I checked after my next turn, the screen was full of missed calls and texts. This was why I kept the ringer off most of the time.

"Okay?" Henry asked.

I shoved my phone back into my jeans. "Yeah, sorry. My mom has a lot of opinions about a fluff piece the network is doing for Nationals. They're going hard on the Mr. Webber angle, and I don't like it." I rolled my eyes. "Of course the federation is all about playing up the dead coach angle, and my mom is friends with all of them. You know skating. Everyone knows everyone."

Henry nodded. "And everyone has opinions."

"Yep. Just like assholes." I slapped my hand over my mouth.

Mr. Sakaguchi barked out a laugh that caught the attention of most people in the room. Ears burning, I tried not to laugh, but it was no use. I guess if you could read lips, the bad words probably came easily.

Henry's phone rang, and he tapped the screen. "Merry Christmas." His eyes flicked to me before he scooted his chair closer to his grandpa's, holding out the phone. Mr. Sakaguchi's eyes lit up, and he waved.

Well, this was awkward. I guess Henry's family in Vancouver were awake, so of course they were calling. I jerked my thumb over my shoulder and gave Henry a smile as I stood. He nodded minutely before returning his attention to his phone and the chorus of voices asking questions.

I loitered by the tree, scanning my mom's texts. Like, yes, fine, I'd do an interview on camera with the network's human-interest reporter, who'd try to make me cry.

I hadn't said *no*, but I was busy. My mom was acting like the fate of my entire career hung in the balance. I scrolled down to the first message from the crack of dawn. She hadn't even said merry Christmas.

At least during our family Zoom call the night before, my sisters had changed the subject after I gave a short update on how training was going. I'd asked them ahead of time, and they were more than happy to get the family talking about anything else.

I sent off a quick reply saying I'd email the reporter tomorrow. A knot tightened in my gut, but it would be fine. I could talk about Mr. Webber and answer their questions and pull heart-strings for ratings.

Mr. Webber would have hated it. Grief punched me in the throat, my eyes burning with tears as I fought to get my shit together. I could imagine his long-suffering eye roll and biting comment about the network making a meal of his death. Fuck, I missed him so much.

And it wasn't like I was his only student. Tons of people missed him! His family and friends and people who were way closer to him than I'd been. But as great as Manon and Bill were, I wished so much that I could have finished my career with Mr. Webber at the boards.

The memory of Henry asking about making Mr. Webber proud resurfaced. I did want to make him proud. Even if I didn't really believe in heaven, I was his last champion, and winning Olympic gold in his name would be a huge accomplishment. I loved winning, but if I could do this to honor Mr. Webber…

I shook off thoughts of the Olympics, feeling strangely guilty about it with Henry right over there. We'd both worked our whole lives for this, but only one of us could win.

"No shit," I muttered. "This isn't news."

"Uh, excuse me?"

I spun to find a family standing nearby wanting to take pics in front of the tree. I moved and offered to take a group shot for them. Then another family asked, and I played photographer for a while, making faces and getting kids to smile.

When I looked back across the room, Henry was watching me. My breath caught at the softness in his eyes. He still held out his phone, but his arm had dropped, and Mr. Sakaguchi nudged him.

Jerking, Henry refocused on the screen. They had to be almost done, so I quietly took my seat, scrolling through Insta as a male voice—probably Henry's dad—told the elder Mr. Sakaguchi he really should wear his hearing aids.

"We should finish our game," Henry said.

"Let's see! Who's winning?" someone asked. It sounded like Henry's brother.

Henry turned the phone down over the board, and Sam said, "Wait, who played 'bike?' That's my speed. Ha ha, get it? You and Ojiichan must be having too much eggnog, bro."

Again, Henry's gaze flicked to me. He seemed to be debating, and then he swiveled the phone up to face me. On screen, Henry's parents and brother made identical faces of shock with eyebrows high and mouths open. A tiny old woman who had to be Henry's grandma smirked.

"Hey!" I waved. "I don't really know anyone here in Toronto, so Henry took pity on me." I honestly still wasn't sure if his grandpa knew I was Henry's top rival, but the rest of his family sure did.

"Theo!" Henry's mom said. "Well, uh, merry Christmas. How is your family?"

We small-talked for a minute before Henry's grandma butted in and asked, "How are you and Henry getting along?"

My gaze flicked to him doing his deer-in-headlights routine. "Uh, good!" I said. "We push each other to be better. Henry's taught me a lot."

"Mmm. You know, Henry says he's too busy for a boyfriend, but he sees you every day now. You should—"

"Obaachan!" Henry snatched back his phone. Of course he was too polite to just hang up, so he said, "Merry Christmas" before disconnecting. The tips of his ears were pink, and I wanted to kiss them.

Soon, the residents were called to lunch. Mr. Sakaguchi shook my hand, clasping mine in both of his as I gave him a respectful nod. Henry stooped to hug him, and his grandpa squeezed him tight, saying, "You're a good boy."

I couldn't help but smile. He *was* a good boy, and it was one of the things I loved most about him.

Whoa.

Loved?

Where had that word come from? A few months ago, I'd barely liked Henry. Honestly, I'd barely given him any thought beyond thinking he was boring. Now we were...

What? I had no idea what this was. But it was Christmas, and I had a present for him, and all elephants could proceed directly to the corner. Or I'd have to shoot them.

"SORRY TO BE such a pain. At least there's no traffic on Christmas Day. Well, obviously there's *some* traffic, but it's a lot emptier than usual." Heart racing, I jiggled my leg.

"Mm."

Henry hadn't seemed to mind driving out to the arena after we left his grandpa's retirement home. I told him to go around the rear, blabbering as we went.

"The caretaker said he'd leave it at the back door. Like, who's going to be all the way out here in the boonies on Christmas Day to steal it, right? It's just my team jacket anyway. So stupid of me to forget it when I have to post a holiday pic today wearing it and tag the federation."

"I don't mind."

I was sure he genuinely didn't because he was so *sweet*. He'd always seemed icy cold, but he wasn't at all once you knew him. And I still only knew part of him. There was so much more, and I wanted all of it. *Now.*

But no, I would be patient.

Did I mention I hated being patient?

"I don't see anything." Henry pulled up near the access door and put the car in park.

"Hmm, yeah. Let me check."

Heart pounding, trying not to grin, I hopped out. My boots crunched on the fresh snow, my breath clouding the air. First, I tapped the code into the keypad on the wall. Then, pulling the key from my pocket, I put it in, unbolted the door, and pulled it open with a flourish.

Or I would have, but it stuck. "Oh, for fuck's sake." I tugged on the freezing metal handle. My gloves were in the car, because of course.

The Honda's engine went silent, and Henry got out. "What are you doing?"

Tugging the stupid door, I huffed. Then jiggled the key since the caretaker had mentioned it stuck sometimes, now that I thought about it. There! I yanked and nearly fell on my ass as the door gave way.

"Um, Merry Christmas!" I motioned to the blackness beyond the door.

Henry stared at me, his brow and everything else furrowed.

"I thought you might want to get in an extra session."

He still stared.

Oh shit. Was this the worst gift ever? "I just thought since you love skating so much you'd like to have the place to yourself. You know, because you love training. They practically have to drag you off the ice. But if you don't want to, we can go. This was probably a stupid idea."

My stomach gurgled. I felt sick. It had seemed like a good gift, but maybe I knew him even less than I thought.

"But we're not allowed. The arena's closed."

"I talked the caretaker into it. I'm hard to resist." I grinned, but that worried expression still creased Henry's face.

He pursed his lips in the cutest way. He was twenty-four going on forty, and I wouldn't have changed it for anything.

I said, "He gave me the code and the keys. It's not a big deal. He knows you're the most trustworthy person, like, in history."

"But it's against the rules. We're not supposed to be here when it's closed. And we have to pay for our ice time." Snowflakes drifted into his dark hair, and I wanted to kiss him so much.

"It's Christmas." That admittedly wasn't much of an argument. "I wanted to surprise you."

"I didn't get you anything."

"Sure you have! It doesn't—I don't care about that. Do you want to skate?" I started to close the door. "Or should we go?"

"You did this for me?" A smile dawned over his face. With teeth! Victory was mine!

"Yeah." Grinning, I shrugged nonchalantly.

"I don't have my skates."

"Duh, I snuck your stuff into the trunk. When I came down to borrow your plunger, I swiped the keys." Trust me to make Henry think I'd taken a giant dump and blocked up my toilet, but I couldn't think of anything else I could fake borrow that would be urgent. "I brought my stuff too, but only if you want to skate with me."

He didn't answer, just going around the car and opening the trunk with a beep of his fob. He was actually still smiling when he joined me at the door with our bags. We crept inside, the door shutting behind us with a *clang*.

Squinting down the dark hallway, I whispered, "He said the emergency lights would be enough, and this place is so old they don't have motion detectors in here."

The only light was florescent and all the way at the other end of the corridor. Where we stood, it was black, and I considered getting my phone out of my pocket to use the flashlight. But Henry took my hand, weaving our fingers together, so fuck the flashlight. I could have floated down the hall.

We tiptoed toward the rink hand in hand. I whispered, "So you've never done anything like this?"

He huffed. "Of course not."

It belatedly occurred to me that if we got caught, the police might not care that I had the key, and shit, I wouldn't want to get the caretaker in trouble. Maybe this wasn't a great idea after all. But Henry was holding my hand, so it was clearly the best idea in the history of ideas.

We crept into the rink. The emergency lights high in the corners of the space illuminated the ice like spotlights, casting shadows in-between. The ice had been cleaned by the Zamboni at the end of the previous day, and it had that perfect fresh, cold smell. It was hard to describe.

I reluctantly let go of Henry's hand when we reached the benches along the ice. "I put your practice clothes in there too," I whispered, even though we did seem to be completely alone. I unzipped my bag and yanked off my boots.

We'd had each other's dicks in our mouths, but we hadn't seen each other actually undressed. I hesitated with my hands on my fly, which was dumb since when was I shy? I unzipped and kicked off my jeans. My boxer briefs were gray and tight, and I was going to be hard in a second the way Henry's gaze traveled over my body.

Instead of putting on my pants, I peeled off my Henley, Henry's eyes glued to me as he lowered his trousers and folded them neatly. I picked up my jeans and folded them just to prolong the whole process, my nipples peaking in the cold air even as heat simmered through my veins.

The only sound was the movement of fabric as we pulled on our black practice pants and long-sleeved shirts, watching each other the whole time. We zipped up our team jackets on top—Henry chuckling when I pulled mine out.

His fingers flew over his skate laces, and as soon as I watched him stroke across the ice like he was flying, I knew this was the right gift. We were used to skating in spotlight at galas and shows, so the black pockets weren't a problem. Henry disappeared for moments at a time before sailing out of the darkness.

I took my time lacing up, watching him glide. Soon, I recognized his short program choreo, because *of course* he was doing a run-through. One of his skate guards teetered on the edge of the bench where we'd left our shit. I straightened his guards neatly on the bench the way he liked before dropping mine.

On the ice, I stayed out of his way, feeling the breeze on my face and the smooth ice under my blades. This was when I could love skating—no elements or judges or GOE or my mother telling me what I'd done wrong. The only thing missing was an audience.

But Henry? He could spend all day alone on the ice perfecting every movement, lost in his own world.

After an hour of being (for me) impressively quiet while Henry did his thing, I called out, "Truth or dare!"

Rolling his eyes, Henry ignored me and took another lap around the rink.

Swallowing a mouthful of water from my bottle, I said it again as he neared. "Truth or dare!"

Still ignoring me, he did another lap before launching into a textbook flying camel, the spin centered perfectly and his free leg extended straight as an arrow at waist height where he bent over.

I should have practiced my spins the way Henry did. They weren't worth nearly as many points compared to jumps, though. Whatever. I did them well enough.

There was nothing stopping me now from spinning, but I stubbornly called, "Truth or dare!" as Henry exited the spin, excitement sparking as he sighed heavily. He was getting worse at ignoring me, and it thrilled me in a way I hadn't expected.

"I'll go first." I grinned and waited.

Another sigh. "We're not in grade seven."

I cocked my head. "Did you play a lot of truth or dare in middle school?" He'd always seemed so serious that it was hard to imagine.

He shook his head, frowning. As though truth or dare had always been beneath him, thank you very much.

"Come on." I flashed another grin. "I dare you."

Crossing his arms, he muttered, "Truth or dare."

"Dare!"

"Do a full run-through of your free skate."

My turn to roll my eyes. "Ha, ha. Come on—something fun."

"A back flip."

"Easy!" I skated off, gathering speed around the end of the rink before launching myself backward and landing easily on two feet. "Okay, you try it."

His brows met. "You didn't give me a choice."

"Oh, right—truth or dare."

"Dare. As long as it's to do with skating."

"That's not a rule, by the way. But okay: I dare you to do a back flip and land it on one foot. There. Are you happy?"

He was already stroking down the ice, concentrating before executing an almost perfect back flip even if he had to put his other foot down on the landing. We took turns, each of us trying our back flips until we were breathing hard.

Sweat dampened my forehead, and I wiped my face with the

sleeve of my jacket before taking it off and tossing it at the bench where Henry had left his after warming up. I added in little dance moves before the flip for fun, trying to get him to smile again.

Nope. Nothing. He was laser focused, watching me silently before he took his next turn, and I could practically see his brain working on what we were doing wrong and how to improve the technique.

I didn't really care about landing on one foot, so on my next pass I did that flossing dance move that used to be popular. I screwed up my timing and didn't even get into the air, instead plopping back on my ass, laughing as I slid toward center ice.

Without even the hint of a smile, Henry sped by and nailed the one-foot landing—because of course he did. I applauded and hollered, and he nodded. No smile, but he looked satisfied that his hard work had paid off. I hauled myself up.

Gaining speed with a few crossovers, I shot my arms back and used my right toe pick to propel me up and over—and fuck! I landed way short, pitching forward on my toes as gravity said, "*Merry Christmas, bitch!*"

Now splatted flat on my stomach, I wheezed through the pain in my chest. From the corner of my eye, I could see Henry blur toward me so fast I was afraid he'd run me over, but he stopped with a sharp, *whooshing* turn of his blades and was on his knees at my side. He squeezed my shoulder.

"Fuck, that hurt," I gritted out.

"Don't talk."

It was solid advice, so I followed it, my lungs expanding barely an inch. I sounded like my sister having an asthma attack. "'M fine," I mumbled.

Henry stayed put, his strong hand on my shoulder. One of the emergency lights high above buzzed faintly, but it was silent except for that and my pathetic gasping. It helped a lot when he stroked my hair, sending shivers down my spine.

"Are you hurt?" he finally asked.

I groaned, rolling onto my back. "Just knocked the wind out of me."

Lips pursed, he gently examined my ribs. I'd probably have some bruising, but nothing felt broken. He stood and offered a hand, and I took it, our damp palms clasping.

Want surged through me. I wanted to tug him down on top of me to feel more of his body. I wanted to strip him naked right there at center ice and kiss every inch of him. I wanted to hear his breathy little moan of release when he came. I wanted so much, everything tripping around in my head.

I let him pull me to sitting, but I moved onto my knees. I didn't let go of his hand. "Truth." My chest rose and fell, my body tingling as I looked up at him. "My truth, and a dare for you. Two for one."

He watched me warily, the lift of his eyebrow seeming to say, *Go on.*

"I want you to fuck my mouth."

Henry's eyes practically popped out of his pretty head. He looked so adorably scandalized that I *had* to kiss him, but he hadn't wanted to before, so I stayed on my knees. Honestly, if I tried to kiss him now and he turned away, it would hurt too much. I couldn't handle that rejection from him.

Which sent warning bells ringing in my head along with a voice too much like my mother's demanding to know what the hell I was doing with the biggest competition of my life looming. What I was doing with the one man who could beat me.

He was still holding my hand. Gripping it so hard I might have worried about bones snapping if I wasn't so turned on. And I silenced all the warnings because I'd deal with all that stuff later. Now was what mattered.

Henry wasn't just scandalized. Even in the dim light, I could see his pupils dilate, the pink tip of his tongue dart out to lick his lips. I could hear the sharp intake of breath as he whispered, "*Here?*"

Hell, why not here? We were alone on the rink, and I was already kneeling on the ice, cold through my pants, and I wanted his hot dick in my mouth. I ran my free hand up his inner thigh and bit my lip.

"I dare you."

He shuddered with his whole body, and—yep, he was rock hard already, the cutest little whimper escaping as I rubbed him through the stretchy, thick spandex.

He'd insisted he wasn't a virgin, but there was something so innocent in how easy it was to turn him on. Not that I could talk given my own massive hard-on.

"Come on. Fuck my mouth." I yanked at his waistband before stopping. "If you want to."

He was panting already. Nodding, he glanced around one more time before freeing himself. I was ready to be choking on his cock ASAP, but I waited as he watched me, his dick in his hand.

I wasn't much older than him, but I hadn't been with anyone so hesitant in a long time. The guys I hooked up with knew what they were doing, which should have been way hotter. But with Henry, my blood was on fire and my balls were going to explode without even being touched.

Tentatively, he circled my parted lips with the head of his cock. He'd let go of my hand, and I rubbed my palms up and down his legs and over his fine ass.

"I want it," I said, not able to take the quiet. "Please. Unless you don't?" Had I misread him?

"I'm not sure how… I don't want you to be in pain."

"You won't hurt me, I promise." I licked his tip and groaned. "You're already leaking. You're so hot. Do you need to come? I love it like this. You can go rough. I know you'd never really hurt me." I gripped his thighs, my words sounding like maybe too much of a confession. It was true, though.

Threading his fingers through my hair, Henry nudged his cock against my lips. I opened with a grateful moan, swallowing him deep. My cheeks hollowed as I sucked and slurped. He rocked into my mouth, slowly gaining confidence.

I mumbled praise he probably couldn't understand, wishing I could switch on the overhead fluorescents and see Henry lose control in stark light instead of shadows.

He had both hands on my head now, and I was sure he was about to come. I could taste bitter salt, my lips stretched, spit dribbling from my mouth as he took complete control.

The *thud* was followed by a rumble. I shot to my feet, Henry shoving his cock into his pants as we skated full out for the side of the rink. We leapt off and dove for the bleachers. There really wasn't anywhere to hide, and I ended up on the concrete floor behind the first row with Henry on top of me.

Panting, we waited. I realized our stuff was in plain view on the bench, but it was too late to grab it. So we waited.

And waited.

Annnd waited.

"I think it was the furnace or generator or something," I whispered. It was too dark between the bleachers to make out Henry's expression, but I saw the shadowy shape of his head nod.

Then the most amazing thing happened. His warm burst of laughter tickled my face, and I was laughing too. I hated that I couldn't see him, wishing again the overhead lights were on.

Though there was also something special about being tucked away with him in the dark, even if I was flat out on a floor that was perma-sticky from the soda and slushees and snacks they sold at the concession stand.

I'd roll around naked in crushed popcorn and dropped M&Ms for the rest of my life to feel Henry laughing against me, our bodies pressed tight in the narrow space between benches.

I rocked up with my hips, loving the little gasp he made. Loving how quickly he was fully hard again. And *really* loving that he rutted against me without any prompting.

His exhalations brushed my lips, and I barely resisted pulling his head down to taste his mouth. I did run my hands down his back and grab his ass, urging him on as I arched up. If I'd had the room, I would have spread my legs wide and begged him to fuck me.

I wanted him inside me. I wanted to be inside him if he was into it. I wanted to suck and fuck and be naked together—maybe in a bed rather than the arena floor—and I wanted to make him come harder than he ever had. I wanted to make it so good for him and see him smile and laugh and fall asleep in my arms until we woke and he kissed me.

My cry echoed in the empty rink as I shot my load, jerking and clinging to Henry, the pleasure running shockingly deep considering we weren't skin to skin. He dropped his forehead to my shoulder, his breath warm and moist on my neck as he fucked against me urgently.

"That's it." My voice was hoarse. "You want to come for me?"

He whimpered again, and it was still adorable. I wanted to give this man all the orgasms. He was so needy and desperate under his cool shell, and it made my heart twist in a way I couldn't understand. He was my fiercest competitor, and I shouldn't have wanted to give him anything but second place.

When he came, Henry gasped and quivered against me, and I held him with my hands spreading on his lower back. There wasn't enough room between the bleachers to get my arms around him. My tight shoulder blade did not appreciate our position one bit, but I'd have stayed squeezed together all night.

Of course we didn't. Henry climbed off me, and we went back to find our blade guards, both of us wet and sticky from coming in our pants. It felt very high school, and we were surely too old for this, but Henry had gotten under my skin and made me lose my mind.

Making sure we left no trace, we hurried out the back door. I reset the security code and turned the key, yanking on the door multiple times to ensure it was definitely locked.

Henry had wet wipes in his car—because of course he did—and we cleaned our junk as best we could, laughing at the absurdity and changing into spare practice pants in the back seat.

Snow fell thickly, and Henry drove carefully back to the condo in the waning afternoon. The seat warmer was amazing on my ass, and I held my fingers to the vents. Could I convince Henry to hit the Tim's drive-through?

"I didn't get you anything."

He seemed genuinely pained, and I rubbed his arm. "It's okay! You didn't have to. Besides, every orgasm is a gift."

"Mm." He didn't sound convinced.

"I mean, maybe I just did this to enable your workaholic perfectionism so your injury will flare up again and I'll beat you." I laughed like an idiot as Henry shot me a glare. I rubbed my face. "Oh my God, that was a terrible joke. I didn't mean it, I swear."

That elephant in the corner needed to be taken out and shot—no offense to actual elephants, who I didn't want to ever get shot. I added, "I really didn't mean that."

He sighed. "I believe you. But this is..." He drummed the steering wheel, shifting in his seat. "What are we doing?"

"I have no idea. But it's okay! We agreed—as soon as we leave for Calgary, it's all business and no more...*this*. Everything's fine. We're just... Hanging out."

He shot me a dubious look, which was fair.

"And in Calgary, we'll do our best, and it'll be up to the judges. We both have Nationals in January anyway. I'll be in Sacramento with Bill, and you'll be in Halifax with Manon. Oh, did you see that Ivan won Ukrainian Nationals? Not that he has much competition. And you saw Kuznetzov won the short program in Russia? I think the long is today. Their big holiday is New Year's. I'm sure you know that."

Henry's sweet, sexy mouth tugged into a smile that gave me a rush of joy. "I did."

We drove on in comfortable silence, the wipers thudding rhythmically, the wet snow falling fast and thick.

"What can I give you?"

I stopped myself from being a dumbass and joking: "*Olympic gold!*" What I did say was, "You don't have to give me anything. You've already done a ton for me."

The temptation to ask for a kiss was hard to ignore, but no. That wouldn't be cool. If Henry wanted to kiss me, that was up to him. I didn't want him to be guilted into it.

"Actually, there's one thing you can get me right now. Well, at the Tim Hortons if you'll make a detour."

He slowed at the light, turning on his blinker and carefully merging into the left-hand lane to make the turn down the block to Tim Hortons. He ordered us hot chocolate and maple donuts, knowing exactly what I wanted.

At the condo, he got out of the elevator first on his floor. We'd decided we'd shower, and I'd come down to his place later for a movie and dinner. The elevator continued up. Shouldering my bag, I took a step as the door slid open on my floor, jolting as I somehow came face to face with Henry.

"Wait, what?" I said.

We stared at each other, the door bouncing back since I was blocking it. Henry must have raced up the three flights, which was nothing for him with his cardio conditioning. But his lips were parted and cheeks flushed.

The elevator beeped, and Henry backed me up against the mirrored wall, one hand on my hip and the other cupping my neck as he kissed me like he wanted to swallow me whole.

He tasted like the forbidden cocoa and sugary donuts, and he made the softest, sweetest little whimper against my lips as I met his tongue, the elevator carrying us away.

Chapter Thirteen

Henry

"OH MY!"

It wasn't until the woman exclaimed behind us that I realized the elevator had stopped on another floor. I pressed Theo into the wall with my whole body, moaning into his mouth. I supposed our only saving grace was that he was clutching my waist and not lower.

We broke free. Theo's lips were shiny as he burst out laughing. I wheeled to face the woman, almost tripping over Theo's discarded duffel bag to find she was with three children and a laughing elderly couple. And that we were at the lobby, the concierge rising from his chair to inspect the commotion.

I stood frozen, but as the doors closed, Theo pressed the button for my floor and called, "Sorry! Merry Christmas!" Still laughing, he collapsed into me sideways. "Amazing."

I stood rigid, my face burning. My black pants didn't hide my arousal, and my instinct was to run and hide. But Theo was poking me.

"It's all right, baby. Don't freak out, okay?"

Baby. My stomach fluttered, and to my shock, I laughed. It could probably be more accurately described as a giggle, and it clearly delighted Theo, who grinned and kissed me, his arm around my back.

On my floor, I grabbed my abandoned bag, and we hurried to my door. I fumbled with the keys, Theo intoxicatingly close behind kissing my neck, his hands stealing under my jacket. We stumbled inside, barely getting the door closed before I pressed him against it in the faint red light from the kitchen.

Our tongues tangled as we gasped and moaned, my leg between his thighs. He was hard, but his lips were so soft. Hands everywhere at once, squeezing and exploring. I was probably a terrible kisser, but he didn't seem to mind.

Esmeralda's outraged meow broke through the haze of lust, and we laughed as she rubbed against our calves. Theo took my face in his hands and murmured, "Let me see you smile."

Suddenly self-conscious, I dropped my gaze. "You've seen me smile plenty of times."

"Not these smiles." He rubbed his thumb back and forth over my wet lower lip. "Kissing you is even better than I thought. Do you like it?"

I nodded, and Esmeralda meowed again. "I have to feed her."

"Right, okay." He dropped to a crouch. "Are you hungry, sweetheart? You're such a good girl. Yeah, you are."

After we took off our boots and coats, I dished out an extra teaspoon of her wet food, Theo still at my side touching me—a hand on my wrist, my neck, a kiss to my shoulder, my ear, a sweep of his tongue into my mouth for just a moment. My head rushed with blood, which was a miracle considering how much had been allocated to my groin.

"Is this okay?" Theo mumbled against my mouth. "Do you still want to kiss?"

In answer, I licked his lips, and he pushed me against the counter with his hips, rubbing our hard shafts through our practice pants. He pulled back, his eyes dark and searching.

"Do you want to go to bed? Can we get naked?"

A memory yanked through me with barbed hooks. I hesitated.

"We don't have to. It's okay. Whatever you want to do. Or not do." Theo peered at me carefully. "I know you said you've done stuff before, but—"

"I'm not a virgin."

"Okay, but if it's too much—"

"It's not."

I tugged him by the hand across the living room. I'd flipped on the kitchen light, but the rest of the condo was still in darkness, the distant lights from other buildings twinkling through the window, thick snow falling.

I paused again. Evaluating. Was it too much? Did I want to be naked with Theo? I inhaled deeply and blew it out slowly.

Yes.

I wanted this. I wanted to be with him. I was ready. Almost ripping my shirt, I grabbed the hem and tugged it off over my head. Theo grinned, and we stripped off everything. Standing naked under his avid gaze, my face burned, but I didn't give in to the persistent temptation to hide.

What exactly did I want to do? Feel Theo's naked body against mine? *Yes.* Heart pounding, I leaned back against my pillows, pulling him along with me. He straddled my hips and leaned low, but hesitated.

"Do you want me to fuck you? Or do you want to fuck me? Or we can just keep doing what we're doing."

"Why do we have to talk about it?"

I'd been fine a second ago, but my lungs seized, and all I could think about was *him.* What a fool I'd made of myself those years ago in Vancouver. I believed Theo was different, but suddenly the tender way he was looking at me was too much.

I said, "We can do whatever you want."

Theo straightened, still sitting over my hips. He smoothed a warm palm down my chest. "You're all tensed up. I know you don't like talking, and I know, I know, you said you're not a virgin. But I want to make sure this is good for you. I'm trying to understand what's going on in your head."

I forced a breath, trying not to think about what happened before. I knew I should have been over it by now. That most people would be able to move on after years. Had it really even been that bad?

I squeezed my eyes shut against the flashes of memory. I hated myself for being so gullible then, and now the doubt crept in. *Did Theo really want me?*

"You can tell me anything. I won't judge, I swear." He brushed back my hair, his face pinched in concern. "Did something…happen?"

"No." That was the one thing I'd never talk about. The one thing I never wanted Theo to learn. The idea of him knowing made acrid bile rise in my throat. I couldn't bear it. That humiliation should have been mine alone.

"It's okay if you don't want to tell me."

"I don't want to tell you." The words were barely a whisper. I inhaled and exhaled, feeling like a fist in my chest was relaxing. "I want to be here with you. Now."

"Okay." He nodded. "We're here. Just us. No one else. All elephants not even in the corner. Those bitches are outside in the snow. Sorry, elephants."

I let myself smile, and Theo bent to kiss me gently before straightening again. Then he leaned low and kissed me again as if he couldn't help himself, and I opened my mouth eagerly.

After we kissed and kissed, rubbing against each other until I was close to coming, I pulled free and asked, "What do you like to do?" I had to make sure he got what he needed.

He grinned. "What *don't* I like to do? Whatever you want."

I didn't smile, and I stopped him with a hand on his chest before he could lean down and kiss me again. Hair tickled my palm. "Tell me."

"Well... Earlier at the rink? I was thinking about how much I want you to fuck me." As my breath caught, he reached down to run his fingertips over my shaft. "If you're into it, I'd really love to have your cock inside me."

The thought of burying myself in Theo's body was almost too much. I didn't know whether to come at the idea or run away. I had to admit, "I've only done it the other way."

Something passed over his face—more concern?—but he nodded. "Okay. If you want me inside you, I'm game."

Part of me did, but it was too soon. Of course we shouldn't have even been doing this at all. What were we thinking? How had I gone from hating Theodore Sullivan to being naked in bed with him?

"Hey. No elephants allowed." Theo pointed to the window next to us. "Out in the snow."

I nodded. "Let's... If you want me to... I want to."

"Yeah?" He waggled his eyebrows. "Do you want to fuck me with your huge cock?"

I frowned. "Yes, but I'd say it's average-sized."

"Oh my God, only you would be pedantic about dirty talk!" He wriggled backward, nosing at the neat thatch of hair at my groin. "Do you like that word? Showed up in the easy crossword the other day." He licked a stripe up the back of my shaft. "And you have a perfect cock. It's going to feel amazing inside me. I've been dreaming about it."

"Really?" Excitement rippled through me.

"Hell, yeah. Now don't move a muscle." He clambered off the bed and was back near the front door in a heartbeat. "Sorry, sweet girl, you need to find a new perch."

I squinted across the condo, chuckling at the fact that Esmeralda had taken up residence on Theo's duffel bag, stretched out on it like a queen. She jumped off and disappeared into the bathroom, so I asked Theo to close the door after her. I knew she wouldn't like it, but the thought of her watching us made me nervous.

Which was silly, since there were far more important things to be nervous about. Theo returned with a small bottle of lube and an accordion strip of foil-wrapped condoms.

He said in a rush, "I packed these because I was being optimistic. Not because I'm having sex with anyone else. I'm not. I only want to have sex with you. If you still want to?"

"Yes." The care he took with all of this—with me—made my insides go soft. I'd once thought him so careless, but I hadn't known him at all.

"What?" His forehead creased as he unscrewed the bottle.

I pulled him down for a kiss, not able to find the right words. He sighed and moaned into my mouth, and I didn't know how I'd resisted kissing him for so long.

He knelt between my legs, leaning down to nuzzle my balls. "If I didn't want your cock so bad—" He lifted his head. "So *badly*, I should say, I'd eat your ass until you begged for mercy."

The thought of his tongue *there* was both intimidating and thrilling, and I groaned.

Naturally, he grinned. "Yeah, I bet you'll like that. You like it when I suck you, right? I'll lick you open and make you come so hard. Maybe later, hmm? We should go down to the hot tub first and recoup our strength. Do you like that word? 'Recoup'? Oh! How are your ribs?"

All flirting vanished as he tenderly slipped his right hand under my ribs. I said, "They don't hurt anymore."

"Yeah? Are you sure?"

"Positive." The strain had healed, and I ignored the odd, lingering twinge. "What about you? That was a hard fall earlier."

"I'm good!" With a grin, Theo squirted his fingers with lube and reached back to open himself. On his knees, he wriggled and moaned, mouth opening and head falling back. He was too beautiful not to touch, and I caressed his chest, teasing the scattered hair.

In the partial light from the kitchen, Theo's nipples looked dark and irresistible. I circled and pinched them, which Theo seemed to love.

"Oh, fuck," he gasped. "Harder. I like that." He strained, his hand working behind him. "That'll do." He ripped open a condom and rolled it down my cock. "Can I ride you at first?"

I'd barely had a chance to say yes when he clambered over me and sank down. The tight, hot sheath of his body was incredible. I gripped his hairy thighs, trying not to come immediately.

"Shit, Henry. You feel so good. Do I feel good?" He bared his throat as he tipped back his head.

I nodded, but his eyes were closed, so I rasped, "Yes."

His leaking cock bobbed, and I stroked it, but he grabbed my wrist. "Baby, stop, or I'll come all over you in a second. Not that I don't want to, but I want you to fuck me first."

"That's what I'm doing." I was buried all the way inside him, and I thrust up, squeezing my glutes. The tight pressure was incredible.

He smiled, leaning over for a messy kiss, his breath hot on my face. "Yeah, you feel amazing inside me. Are you still good with it?"

I thrust up. "Yes." My balls tingled and I was desperate for more.

"Will you just really give it to me? I still want to see your face, so if we..." He rose up, grasping the root of my cock and easing it out of his body. He lay down beside me, wriggling and pulling me atop him, spreading his legs wide and urging me back inside.

I pushed into his body past the grasping ring of muscle at his hole. He nodded enthusiastically, pulling at my hips. I thrust hard, and his cry of pleasure sent shivers down my spine.

"God, yeah. Like that. Will you fuck me hard? You won't hurt me."

A few beads of sweat formed at his hairline, glistening in the faint light from the kitchen. I pressed my lips to his skin, wanting to taste every part of him as I rocked into his body. I pinched one of his nipples, and he cried out.

It exhilarated me to give him pleasure, and I drove into him as he clutched at my arms and shoulders and back and face—whatever he could reach. He tugged at my hair before his eyes flew open.

"Is that okay?"

I nodded, remembering how he'd pushed his head into my hand the first time he'd sucked me. Keeping his gaze, both of our chests heaving, I threaded my fingers through his hair and tightened my grip.

"*Yesss*," he moaned. "Harder. I'm so close. Please. Make me come."

I wanted to give him anything in that moment. *Everything.* I took hold of his cock with my other hand, and it was clumsy and awkward, but he didn't seem to mind, squeezing his muscles around my shaft and drumming his heels on my lower back.

He gasped wordlessly—for once—and spurted between us, shaking and straining, his face red and eyes closed. He went limp, and I held myself steady on my arms. But he blinked and tightened his legs around me, words spilling from his lips.

"Don't stop. I want you to come inside me. I'm not letting go. That's it. You need this too, don't you? You're so hot, you know that? I don't think you do. Yeah. Fuck me. I want to see you let go. You feel so good. You're so good."

The words flowed from his tongue along with kisses to my face, and as my orgasm erupted and I spasmed against him—within him—I felt like I was flying across the ice. Flowing and gliding on deep edges, the wind on my face. Everything perfect.

When the stars cleared from my vision, I found Theo staring up at me, holding my cheeks in his hands. We breathed heavily, and I needed water. I was softening inside him, and now would everything become awkward and strange? I could imagine the elephants trumpeting.

Then Esmeralda meowed so forcefully from behind the closed bathroom door that we startled. Theo burst out laughing, but I knew he wasn't laughing at me. This wasn't like my first time. He wasn't like—

No. I refused to think about it. That belonged in the past. Theo was here with me now. I'd enjoyed the things we'd done together. That wasn't a powerful enough word. It was more than mere "enjoyment." Delight. Gratification. Euphoria.

Connection. Trust.

Tangled together in my bed with Theo's warm laughter filling the air, I knew he wouldn't hurt me. Too soon, we'd be leaving for Nationals and training every moment before Calgary. Even if the peace would be fleeting, tonight it was ours.

Theo grinned. "She probably thinks I murdered you. Can I give her treats?"

"In a minute." Right now I needed to kiss him again.

Chapter Fourteen

Henry

"THEO? YOUR MOM called my mom." Ga-young held out a cell phone.

I could only watch as Theo muttered under his breath and took the phone, breathing deeply before he said, "Hi, Mom! Oh, did you? Sorry, I've been too busy. Janice and the camera crew are here."

Mrs. Sullivan was extremely aware of this fact. She'd bombarded Theo's phone with texts and calls since dawn. The nerve of her to bother Ga-young's mother was astounding to me, but I'd witnessed it all from skating parents over the years.

"Aren't you glad your folks leave the skating to you?" Bill murmured.

I nodded. My parents had spent tens of thousands on my lessons, costumes, and ice time when I was young and had attended many competitions to cheer me on, but they'd always said I could quit anytime.

In some ways, I think they'd have preferred it if I had, but they never pressured me either way. I made a mental note to thank them explicitly for that as I watched Theo pacing at the side of the ice in his guards.

He was saying, "Yes. Uh-huh. Yes, Mom. *I know.* Okay."

"I wish he'd tell her to leave him alone," I said quietly, hating the tension in Theo's shoulders and the way he hunched as soon as he heard her voice.

Bill looked at me for so long that I shifted uncomfortably. I raised a quizzical brow.

He shrugged, but it was forced. "Just never thought I'd see the day you cared about Theo beyond resenting him for whatever new quad combo he'd mastered."

I didn't answer, forcing myself to look away. The camera crew from the American network were setting up to film footage of us practicing before the reporter interviewed Theo. I'd be doing my own interviews for the Canadian network soon.

In the two weeks since Christmas, he had all but moved into my condo. We trained hard every day before cooking healthy meals and treating all our aches and pains together. Theo often propped his twinging knee over my lap as we watched TV on my love seat. My freezer was full of our ice packs and portioned lunches.

A flare of desire twisted through me as I remembered waking him several hours ago in the darkness with sleepy kisses that quickly progressed to sucking him until he was shooting in my mouth and wide awake.

It was still surreal, to say the least. I'd never had a relationship. I'd never woken with another person in my arms or drooling on my chest or spooned behind me, warm and sometimes trapping my arm under us until I had pins and needles.

That it was *Theodore Sullivan* in my bed was almost beyond comprehension. My family hadn't pressed for details—aside from Sam, who teased me daily—but it was clear to them Theo and I were more than training mates and competitors. That we were...

What, exactly? The Olympics were in weeks. We were keeping the elephants sequestered, and there was no room for discussing labels or the future. We'd agreed to indulge in whatever this was until we left for Calgary. Then we would compete against each other.

After that, the world might as well have been flat and ended in a sheer drop. Right now, there was nothing but the time we had left and the Games. I couldn't allow myself to ponder any other future beyond.

Theo was still on the phone with his mother when the crew asked me to work on my jumps. As the cameras rolled, we took our positions, a crew member holding a boom mic over Bill and Manon where they stood by the side of the ice.

I gathered speed and performed my quad toe combo cleanly, returning to them so they could critique before I jumped again. We went on until Theo joined us, the cameraman focusing on him now.

He raced down the ice and reeled off a perfect quad Lutz— then turned and tacked on a triple Axel out of nowhere.

Everyone in the arena gasped and applauded. Even if the attention wasn't on me anymore, I focused in on my quad Lutz, though I was only able to add a double toe on the end. My consistency had improved greatly, though.

As I sped into my next attempt, I considered trying the triple Axel on the end like Theo had managed. It was very rarely done, and I'd be foolish to risk injuring myself. But I'd land a perfect quad Lutz-triple toe if it killed me.

Again and again, I jumped. Theo noticed, and he said, laughing, "Are we doing a jump off?"

I gave him a curt nod. He rarely missed any, and when he did, he laughed again. Even with the network cameras on him, he was filled with confidence, shaking off mistakes before nailing the jump a minute later.

On my next Lutz attempt, I slipped off the toe pick and fell out of the jump awkwardly, crashing onto my hip and sliding on my back. Before I could even push myself up, Theo was at my side.

"Shit, that was hard. You okay?" He reached for my shoulder.

Launching to my feet, I hissed, "*Stop!*" without looking back at him. The cameras were rolling! People were watching! Being friendly rivals was one thing. We didn't need any other speculation as grist for the rumor mill. I skated away, shaking off the fall and returning to Manon and Bill.

We discussed the aborted takeoff, and I tried again. Soon, Theo was off with Janice Harvey for an interview in Bill and Manon's basement office, the only suitable room in the old complex to set up lights and equipment and speak without background noise.

Most people were gone hours later when Theo followed me out to the car. He'd been unusually quiet the rest of the day, though we'd been on different sessions in the afternoon.

We settled in the Honda, and I waited for him to make a joke or start talking or playfully hit on me even though we'd agreed we should be careful outside the privacy of the condo.

He sat silently as I drove out of the Ice Chalet's lot, avoiding a pothole. Lots of snow had melted on a warm day around New Year's, but it was accumulating again now, fat flurries drifting down steadily. I flipped on both the seat warmers.

The elephants trumpeted. A strange tension twanged between us, and I regretted earlier. He'd only been worried about me. The problem was that even hours later, it pleased me too much that he cared.

Before I could apologize, he blurted, "Are you mad?"

"No."

He looked at me hopefully. "No?"

"No." I stopped at a red light. "I'm—"

My apology was swallowed quite literally by Theo as he lunged across the gearshift and kissed me, one hand gripping my face. He thrust his tongue into my mouth, my head spinning until the car behind honked. Dazed, I pulled free and stepped on the gas, clearing the intersection and continuing home.

Theo slumped into his seat with a dramatic sigh. "Okay, I'm glad you're not mad. God, I've been *dying* to kiss you all day. I thought it would never end! Of course Janice asked about training with you, and I tried not to say too much. I mean, I said nice stuff, obviously. About how you've inspired me to work harder, which is completely true. I didn't tell her we've been fucking like rabbits, which has been even more inspirational. I've consistently gotten up early more than ever in my whole life because getting off with you before practice is the best motivation."

I snorted. "Not the kind of fluff piece the network is looking for."

He laughed. "Oh, and did I tell you the federation is up my ass about sewing the V-neck in my red shirt another inch because someone at the network was clutching their pearls? I'm just too sexy in the free skate, I guess. Like it's nineteen fifty or something. I'm going to lower it instead."

I shook my head, hiding my smile. "You're your own worst enemy."

"I thought that was your job." He grinned, leaning over to playfully bite my earlobe.

Guilt washed through me, sticky and uncomfortable. I'd resented him so bitterly and unfairly for years. It was hard to believe how quickly he'd proven me wrong in so many ways.

"What?" His left hand caressed my thigh, coming to rest there comfortably.

I wasn't sure how to phrase it, and Theo opened his mouth to say something else but then waited. I slowed for another red light, the wipers thumping rhythmically, clearing the light snow that fell.

Finally, I said, "I don't want to be your enemy."

"I know!" He squeezed my leg. "It's only skating. It's not real life."

I could only stare at him. "Skating is everything. It's who we are."

"It's what we *do*. Green light." As I refocused on the road, he added, "Yes, we're skaters. We skate. It's our job. But there's a whole world out there that's not this crazy bubble. There's petty bullshit and kissing judges' asses and all the politics. And we're supposed to be enemies—sure, okay, whatever."

"Mm." Of course I knew there was more to life than skating—though it was difficult to imagine.

Theo leaned closer, dropping his voice. "If you want to get pissed off about how I've beaten you for the past two seasons, you should make me get on my hands and knees and fuck me so hard I'll barely be able to stand tomorrow, let alone skate."

I sucked in a breath, lust flaring. He shifted his hand to cup me as my cock swelled. "Driving," I mumbled.

"Uh-huh." He rubbed my shaft through my stretchy pants. "You're such a good driver too. So responsible. I shouldn't distract you." He stopped stroking and rested his hand lightly on my hard cock. "I'll stop talking about letting you punish me for all those gold medals I've taken from you. Those elephants are supposed to stay in the corner. I promise I'll be good."

I grunted, cursing as traffic slowed. We weren't far from the condo now, but it seemed an eternity. Especially since Theo kept talking because that's what he did.

"I really do try to be good, you know. But sometimes I can't help being bad. Even if I beg you to stop, you have to teach me a lesson."

I frowned. "If you tell me to stop, I will."

He chuckled before kissing my cheek. "I know, baby. Don't worry, I'll never beg you to stop because I love it when you fuck my brains out. We should have a safe word, though. Let's see." He idly traced the shape of my shaft with his fingertip. "How about

'Torino'?"

Memories of that rainy street, tiramisu, and falling asleep next to Theo for the first time unspooled. I nodded, affection threatening to choke me.

We managed to get into the condo without public indecency, although my erection had barely abated. I gave Esmeralda treats to tide her over until dinner and locked her in the bathroom, and when I turned back, Theo was already naked.

"Remember at NHK in Nagano last season when I beat you by, like, twenty points? My PCS were ridiculously high."

"Twenty-two-point-five-three." I stripped off my hoodie and shirt.

"It wasn't even close! You skated so well, but the judging was crazy. I could have gone out there and mopped the ice, and I probably still would've won." He dropped to his knees on the gray carpet, batting his eyelashes. "Can you forgive me?"

It was a silly game, and we shouldn't have been bringing up judges and scoring inequities I'd seethed over at the time. If you'd told me then I'd make light of being beaten by him, I'd never have believed it. But Theo was so gorgeous at my feet. His smile so seductive.

I'd never have believed any of this.

I stripped off the rest of my clothes and spread my fingers through his hair. Sighing, he leaned into my touch like Esmeralda might. Then I tightened my grip. "Turn over." As he eagerly flipped onto all fours, I grabbed a condom and lube.

"It's okay. I want it hard. I've been *bad*."

I knew he meant the lube, but I ignored him, slicking my fingers. I wouldn't risk actually hurting him. It was a line I refused to cross. Still, I didn't ease my fingers into him, instead pushing hard with no warning. Theo arched his back, crying out.

"Yes! *Please*."

After only rudimentary preparation, I drove into him. He

moaned and whined as I thrust in and out of the tight grip of his ass. With absolutely no shame, he begged to be used, and I reveled in giving him what he wanted. It felt wonderful to let go—to absolutely pound into him until we were sweaty and straining for release.

"I love your cock inside me," he moaned. He'd dropped down to his elbows on the carpet, pushing back against my thrusts. "Never stop fucking me."

Never.

I gasped for breath, my fingers tight in his hair. His shamelessness aroused me in ways I'd never imagined. I thought about what it would be like to have him inside me, and it was thrilling and frightening all at once.

I wasn't ready, but it didn't seem to matter since Theo was eager to give up control—though he was still demanding and in charge in many ways. I'd never imagined sex could be like this. Not after—

My motion stuttered, and I cursed myself for thinking of it for even a moment while I was with Theo. Squeezing my eyes shut, I clutched his hips, trying to find my rhythm again.

"Henry?"

I opened my eyes to find Theo craning his neck, looking back at me. I nodded. "Sorry."

Concern creased his face. "Do you want to stop?"

"No!" I was buried inside him, and my balls ached. It felt remarkable—not only the tight heat of his body, but the trust that had grown between us. I pulled back and slammed in, making him yelp and laugh delightedly.

"Feels so good. People think you're so uptight, but you fuck like a—a—I don't know, but it's amazing."

I had to laugh, and Theo gasped, looking back at me. Jerking his cock frantically, he rasped, "Smile! Keep smiling."

He tightened around me, coming as he watched me smile, the

pressure around my shaft white hot. After a few more pumps, I released too, filling the condom, stars filling my vision as I shook and spilled, my fingers digging into Theo's hips.

We collapsed in a sticky, slick heap on the carpet. Softening inside him, I nuzzled the back of Theo's neck, tasting salt as I pressed kisses to his damp skin. He mumbled about how good it had been and how amazing I was, the sound of his endless talking so familiar now, a comforting hum of sound.

After a time, he elbowed my ribs. "I know you're not listening."

"Hmm?" I had to smile as I kissed his shoulder.

He huffed. "You're lucky I—" Theo broke off, tensing beneath me.

My heart skipped. I held my breath, unsure what he would say. What I wanted him to say.

On cue, Esmeralda's demanding meow broke the silence, and we untangled, the moment passing. In a few days, we'd be apart for almost the rest of January attending our national championships before we traveled to Calgary.

Though part of me burned to know what Theo had almost confessed, it was best unsaid.

Chapter Fifteen

Theo

"**I**T REALLY IS the last thing I expected."

I tore my gaze from Henry where he dozed across the aisle, leaning on the cheap airline pillow stuffed against the window. Beside him, Bill snored open-mouthed, Giselle on the aisle watching a movie. I blinked at Manon in the middle seat to my left.

"What?" I murmured. Our flight to Calgary had left Toronto at the crack of dawn, and many people were napping.

Manon flipped through a fashion magazine. Beside her, an assistant coach restlessly tapped the screen in the seat back, scrolling through music. Manon said, "You and Henry."

Boom. My pulse zoomed. "What?"

"You think we can't see the way you look at each other? Henry is worse, I'll grant you. But you aren't as clever as you think." She turned another page. "You've been watching him sleep for an hour."

"I have not!" I shifted, resting one ankle on my other knee. My foot jiggled, my striped socks bright. I'd taken off my boots and shoved them under the seat in front with my Olympic team coat. There was hardly any legroom. Maybe if I got up to walk the aisle, Manon would drop it.

She shot me a look Henry would probably describe as "baleful." Or maybe "withering"? I wasn't sure. The point was that Manon was calling bullshit.

Sighing, I whispered, "Me either."

"Neither of you need this distraction. You know that."

"We know. That's why as of today, it's off. Well, on hold. We're all business from now on."

"Mmm." She pinned me with her assessing gaze, and I automatically sat up straighter and thought about the walnut between my shoulder blades. "As of today."

"Uh-huh. We made an agreement. A plan. We need to focus on the competition. You know we're both doing the short program in the team event later this week. It's time to concentrate a hundred percent on skating."

"And you think you'll be able to just—" She made a flicking motion with her finger. "Turn off your feelings? Like nothing?"

"We made a plan," I repeated.

Sure, the five hours and nineteen minutes since we'd last kissed felt like an eternity, but this was the plan. We'd had to get up in the middle of the night to get to the airport, so we'd barely slept.

There'd been kissing and having sex and then more kissing and more sex and cuddling with Esmeralda and dozing and then having sex one last time.

For now. One last time *for now*. Because the thought of that actually being the last time was unbearable.

Manon narrowed her gaze. "And you think it'll be so easy for Henry? Maybe you don't care, but Henry's different."

It shouldn't have hurt, but it did. I shrugged and smiled since that's what everyone expected. Actually? Screw that. I dropped the fake expression and whispered, "I care too. I *do*."

Her face softened, and she briefly squeezed my hand. "I know. I just worry."

"We're fine. We're great! We're focusing on doing our jobs. And then…" What? That was the question. "One thing at a time."

"All right. We expect your best. You've both worked too hard to throw away your shot for a fling."

I wanted to argue it was more than a fling, but… Was it? "Well, now that song's going to be stuck in my head."

"*Bon.*" Apparently satisfied, Manon returned to her magazine, and I pointedly did not watch Henry sleep. For a few minutes. He was beautiful, and this would be my last chance for a few weeks. And even though my ass twinged from riding him hard this morning, I imagined one more time.

Could I pass him a note and tell him to meet me in the bathroom? But surely someone would see us, and as fun as the mile-high club thing seemed on paper, airplane bathrooms were gross.

But once we got to the Athletes' Village, we would really officially be at the Olympics, and we'd be breaking our own rules.

Did I really give a shit? Yes and no. But Henry loved rules. I didn't want to tempt him and have him regret it. I never wanted him to regret anything we did together.

He'd gotten more comfortable and said he was into topping, which really worked for me. Most guys assumed I was a top since I was outgoing and loud and did my whole sexy, powerful routine on the ice.

And sure, I'd love to top Henry if he wanted it, but he clearly didn't at this point, so I hadn't pushed for it. I was happy doing anything, but with him, I could really relax and trust that he'd fuck me as hard as I wanted without going too far.

I was getting turned on thinking about it, which was extremely inconvenient crammed in economy with our coaches and Henry out of reach. *As of today, it's all business. Deal with it. Suck it up.*

No, don't think about sucking.

Was this only a fling? That word echoed in my head, nagging

and weirdly uncomfortable. This wasn't the time to worry about that. Whether it was a fling or more didn't matter until after the Olympics. This was go time. We'd had our last kiss in the back of the Lyft as we'd approached the terminal.

Leaning forward just enough, I watched Henry shifting in his seat, clearly trying to get comfortable, his eyes still closed. Until he opened them and looked right at me with that serious expression he wore so often.

My heart skipped, and we stared at each other, and all I could think about was the feel of his lips on my mine and how sleepy I'd been that morning. And that I needed one more kiss.

His chest rose with a deep breath, and he resolutely turned away, shifting to curl into the window.

I wanted to climb over Giselle and Bill onto Henry's lap and kiss him breathless. Feel him inside me one more time. Just once more, and then we'd be good the next few weeks. But ugh, that airplane bathroom really couldn't happen.

The rumor mill was probably already grinding away, although I'd know for sure if other people truly suspected about us when my mom lost her shit. Maybe her rink spy had taken pity on us.

Once more, once more, once more.

It was like a drumbeat, and I brainstormed ways we could be together before we got to the Olympic site. There was really only one option—the airport bathroom. There'd be one by baggage claim. But it would be busy, and we'd have no time. We'd have to be completely silent.

That thought had lust flaring bright and hot. Could we get away with it? Just one more time—then we'd be good.

Fidgeting, I rummaged through my backpack looking for gum. I should have dumped it out and reorganized it, but I'd packed in a hurry, eager to spend every minute with Henry. He surely had all his stuff zipped into neat compartments instead of floating around in the bottom of his bag.

My fingers brushed a foil packet. It was a stray condom, and a light bulb exploded in my head. I scrabbled around the bottom, hoping that maybe there would be—yes! A little packet of lube I'd gotten free at Pride in LA the summer before.

I knew exactly what to do.

Two hours later as I stood in the aisle waiting to deplane, my thumbs flew over my phone. I took casual glances toward Henry still in his seat, willing him to turn on his phone like everyone else. As the restless energy on board grew, he finally did.

His eyes widened as he read my message. He looked up at me, and for a horrible moment I thought he'd shake his head. But he gave me the barest nod before dropping his head.

Yes! I didn't lube my ass for nothing.

The plane bathroom had been such a tight squeeze that it had been awkward doing that, and I couldn't imagine actually fucking in there. Luckily, I'd remembered there were new bathrooms in the Calgary airport where the stalls were private and fully enclosed from floor to ceiling.

I grinned to myself.

This was probably stupid, and I should have let go of the idea of doing it one more time before our...hiatus. But I needed one more taste.

Speaking of which, I chewed a fresh piece of minty gum as we finally filed off the plane. I overtook several people on the walkway into the terminal, speeding to the bathroom, relieved we didn't have to deal with customs.

I waited in the last stall with the door unlocked. Only one other was occupied, most guys using the urinal. A minute later, someone tentatively opened the door. I shimmied back, leaning over the toilet so Henry could squeeze in and shut the door.

My text had just said to meet me in the last stall, and his brow was furrowed as he peered at me, waiting. We both wore our unzipped team jackets, which were full parkas. I thrust my arms around his waist, drawing him close to whisper right in his ear.

"I need you one more time." I felt a shudder run through him, but his arms still hung at his sides. I slowly licked the shell of his ear, making him shiver before I whispered again. "I know we said this morning was it. But I was too tired. One more time. I was rock hard half of that flight imagining it. Imagining you here with me. Our secret."

He exhaled a shaky breath, slipping his hands around my waist, his fingertips stealing under the hem of my tee to brush my lower back. He leaned away enough to see my face, his gaze flicking between my eyes and mouth. I bit my lower lip, slowly releasing it.

"Don't you want me?" I asked, barely a whisper.

After rolling his eyes—which was fair—he rubbed his erection against mine through our team track pants.

I couldn't hide my grin. "You can't resist me."

Henry kissed me roughly in response, pushing his tongue into my mouth and swallowing my groan as he shoved me against the door. My laugh was muffled by his lips.

"Be gentle with me!" I whispered.

It was definitely a joke, but he immediately paused inches from my mouth. We were panting, and I was about to drag his head close, but then he tenderly brushed our lips together. He drew back, staring at me with his typical seriousness. It made my heart flop like a dying fish on dry land.

We didn't have much time, so after more kissing and tasting, I broke away, a string of spit connecting our mouths for a second as I demanded, "Fuck me. Right here. *Hard.*"

I could see him about to argue, the concerned frown creasing his face. I reached back and guided his hand into my underwear so he could feel the waiting lube. His eyebrows shot up, and I grinned again.

Scandalizing Henry was my *favorite.*

I leaned close to his ear again. "I'm ready for you. Fuck me one more time, and I promise I'll be good."

He ran his finger around my hole before dipping in. I pulled the condom from my pocket, and his resistance evaporated. In record time, he had me turned to face the toilet, our pants around our knees as he slammed into me.

Even though I'd prepared for it, I couldn't contain my sharp, *loud* gasp. Henry slapped his hand over my mouth, and *hell yeah*. I nodded vigorously, reaching up to press my hand against his for a moment, letting him know I wanted it there. Then I braced myself on the mercifully clean and white tile wall.

There were still sounds of people in the bathroom, the odd flush and running water. With his left hand tight on my hip, Henry gave me the *hard-hot-fast* fuck I needed. I panted against his palm, staying as silent as possible, his breath warm on my neck.

We had to get our bags, and everyone would wonder where we were, but it felt too good. I jerked myself roughly, coming into my hand when Henry lightly bit the side of my neck. He thrust a few more times and emptied into me.

Kissing the spot where I'd probably have a slight bruise from his bite, he held me tightly, releasing his hand from my mouth. We quickly cleaned up before I squirmed around to face him. He was flushed and beautiful, and I brushed back the swoop of his bangs before gently kissing his cheek.

"Thank you, sweetheart," I murmured, even though now we were supposed to be all business. Maybe after one more kiss?

I didn't have to convince him since Henry was already taking my face in his hands and kissing me like there was no tomorrow. Which there wasn't. There was practice and concentration and competing at our very best.

And only one of us could win.

Reluctantly, we separated. "Okay," I whispered. "We're good, right? We've got this. It's fine. This was just—I don't know. Whatever. Starting now, it's all about the Olympics. We're good."

Henry nodded, then leaned in and pressed a tender kiss to my cheek. His lips lingered for a heartbeat. Then he squeezed out of the stall. I waited a few minutes until I could breathe again.

Luckily for us, the airport was busy, and suitcases were only starting to tumble out onto the conveyor belt. We'd be going to the Village on team buses, and I waved to a few people I knew at the next carousel who'd arrived on a flight from the States.

"Hi, Henry!" Hannah Kwan gave a cheery wave as she passed the carousel with her rolling carry-on suitcase. The bags from our flight were arriving on the first carousel in a line, and people filed by as other flights arrived.

Weirdly tense beside me all of a sudden, Henry nodded to her. Then Anton Orlov rounded the corner, and Henry's weird tension was dialed up to eleven as Bill always loved to say for some reason.

Anton had seemed about to say something to Hannah, but he skipped a beat as he saw Henry. He snapped his jaw shut, his gaze dropping to the ugly gray floor.

Whoa. What the fuck? Henry had never mentioned having beef with Anton, but his jaw was clenched so hard it was about to snap.

"Hey." Anton lifted his chin toward us, looking at me.

I put on a smile. "Hey!" I didn't really know Anton and Hannah, but we'd been at the same competitions before.

Henry disappeared from beside me, and I spun to see him powering back toward the bathroom. Maybe he actually did need to pee? I did, but was holding it since we'd already been in there.

Hannah watched Henry go with a pinched, sad expression as Anton tugged her hand, his gaze anywhere but on Henry. They continued on to get their bags, and I was left wondering what the hell just happened. Manon and Bill were deep in conversation and hadn't seemed to notice.

If I didn't know better, I'd think Henry and Anton had a history.

Did I know better? Despite his initial awkwardness, Henry had insisted it wasn't his first time. Had he and Anton hooked up in the past? I searched my memory for gossip about Anton playing for our team but came up blank. Weren't Hannah and Anton together off the ice too? Or maybe I assumed they were since so many ice dance and pairs teams dated.

"Theo, isn't that yours?" Bill asked.

I dodged around the clumps of people waiting and managed to grab my suitcase before it did another lap of the belt. Was I reading too much into it? It didn't matter if Henry and Anton had hooked up before. Or to be more accurate, it *shouldn't* have mattered.

But I found I didn't like the idea at all. Which was ridiculous! Henry and I were just…whatever. We'd been hanging out, and now we were at the Olympics and we weren't doing anything but skating.

Besides, he didn't owe me anything. Whatever had gone down between him and Anton had clearly not ended well. There was nothing to be jealous about. Since when did I do jealousy? I didn't. It was fine.

Yet I hated the look that had come over Henry's face when Anton had appeared. The expression had been…

Hunted. That was the word that popped into my head. Henry had a tense, hunted expression, and I didn't like it one bit. I shot glances to the bathroom, wondering if I should go after him.

Did he want me to follow and find out what was wrong? Maybe I should go. But before I could, he returned, talking to Etienne Allard, the Canadian ice dancer dating his brother. Well, nodding as Etienne talked.

Etienne's partner, Bree, appeared and gave me an excited hug, and I tried to focus. I said, "Congrats on making the team! You guys crushed it."

She beamed, tucking her blonde hair behind one ear and clearly trying to be humble. "Anita and Christopher did so well even to compete. If they'd had more time after Anita's injury…"

"That's the way it goes," I said. "Doesn't change the fact that you and Etienne *crushed* it." According to Henry, they really had improved significantly.

As Bree grinned, Etienne and Henry joined us. I gave Etienne a high five before hugging him, willing Henry to look at me and give me some kind of silent message that he was okay.

But Henry stood silently, his coat zipped up and his hands in his pockets. But not in a relaxed way. He was still…off.

Etienne gave me a grin. "I hear you and Henry have been getting along *way* better than anyone expected."

I winced internally. Etienne and Henry were rooming together in the Village, and Henry would smother him with a pillow if Etienne wasn't careful.

Henry didn't look angry at the insinuation, though. Just incredibly tense. I wanted to massage his shoulders and cuddle and kiss him until he relaxed in my arms.

"No more teasing," Bree said, pulling on Etienne's elbow. "We need to get our bags. See you guys later."

As they left, I stepped closer to Henry, but not too close. "Everything okay?"

Not looking at me, he nodded.

I wanted to huff in frustration and order him to spill it so I could make whatever the problem was better. But I tried to stay casual. "You're not a big fan of Anton?"

His gaze shot to mine, his mouth going tight. "It's nothing."

"Okay. Cool." This was the part where I was supposed to let it go. If he wanted to tell me he'd tell me, and he didn't, so that was fine. Cool, cool, cool. Yep. All good.

Except why didn't he want to tell me? What was the deal?

Why had they both acted so weird? Maybe there were a million things Henry didn't want to tell me, and this was just one more.

Although it made me think of when we'd talked about sex, and there was definitely something there in his past. A...shadow. Which he'd said he didn't want to tell me about. And I'd let it go! I respected that. It was his choice. I'd never want to pressure him.

But why won't he tellllll meeee?

"So, Anton—"

Henry's hand shot out to grip my arm through my parka. Then he shoved his fists into his pockets, dropping his gaze to the floor. "Please. Don't."

I nodded quickly. "Okay. I'm sorry. I won't mention it again." And I absolutely wouldn't.

But that didn't stop me from wondering.

Too soon, his suitcase appeared, and he had to join his teammates to get their bus. Henry glanced back at me. This was really it.

How was I going to sleep without him in my arms or spooned behind me, his breath tickling my neck and his lips brushing my cheek when he slipped out of bed way too early?

I reminded myself that it was only a couple of weeks, and there was no need to be so dramatic, Jesus. Henry half smiled at me—without teeth—nothing at all like one of his real smiles—and was gone.

Chapter Sixteen

Theo

*T*HE RICE AND *beans at the Mexican restaurant are very good.*

I reread Henry's text again. And again. I'd replied with a lame *"Cool, thx!"* I wanted to say so much more. Every time he tried one of the international restaurants in the Village's huge eating hall, he texted me a mini review.

The first time, I'd replied with a joke about him trying to make me fat, and he'd immediately responded:

Make sure you eat.

Waiting in the bowels of the practice arena, I scrolled back to that message. Henry was so good about eating healthy food and not junk, but he never seemed to feel deprived. It wasn't a big deal to him the way it was to me. I'd replied with a winky face and:

Don't worry, I love food way too much to starve myself.

Immediately, he'd responded again:

Make sure you eat.

It was weird how those four words made me stupidly happy.

I missed our dinners in his condo so much. I missed Henry's matching pajama sets and watching HGTV while we iced our aches. I missed Esmeralda and hoped she wasn't too lonely even though the cat sitter hung out for a bit every day. I mean, she wasn't my cat, so I shouldn't have really been worrying about her, but I did.

"Group B! Ready in five," a volunteer announced.

Manon and Bill were out with Henry now. The short program of the team event was tonight, and we were both competing. My teammate—and roommate in the Village—Justin Lee would be doing the free skate.

I didn't want to blow my wad in the team event, and it was unlikely we'd beat Russia for gold even if I did both programs. We were solidly going to take the silver medal unless we imploded, and this way Justin would get a medal too. But doing the short was a great warm-up for the real thing.

Not that a team event medal wasn't real. I had a bronze from the last Games, and it had been really fun. But it just wasn't the same as an individual medal. It would make more sense to have the team event after the individual events, but it all came down to what the TV networks wanted and their ratings.

The opening ceremony was tonight, and it was weird to be trying to focus on competing this afternoon, but whatever. I'd crush my short and then get to have fun and—

On cue, a text from my mom appeared:

I want you to rest tonight. You went to the opening ceremony four years ago. You don't need to go again. You have to focus. Sakaguchi probably isn't going. He's jumping well. Too well.

Actually, he *was* going, but I didn't tell her that. I asked:

How's his quad Lutz?

She replied insanely fast:

TOO GOOD. The best it's looked.

Luckily, she couldn't see my grin. I didn't reply, jogging around the concrete holding area. The other four guys in my group, including Kuznetsov, stretched and listened to their headphones, getting in the zone.

I know you ate pizza yesterday. Do you even care about winning???

I shut off my phone and shoved it in my bag. She probably had the workers at every restaurant in the Village on her spy payroll. So I'd had one piece of pizza! I'd eaten seared salmon and a big salad for lunch. I'd exercised for hours later, and the pizza had smelled *amazing*.

At least Dad and my sisters were coming next week for my event. Until then, Mom would be here on her own, and I could only avoid her so much. She was up in the stands now to watch practice with her pals from the federation.

It was our turn, and my heart leapt as I filed into line to take the ice. Henry was bent at the gate, putting on his guards, his hair falling over his forehead. I hadn't seen him in person since the airport, and I drank in the lean lines of his legs and narrow hips.

I remembered the secure pressure of his hand over my mouth in the stall, his cock inside me as he gave me what I needed…

The tension in my shoulders eased, and I wished we could escape together for a few minutes. A minute wouldn't hurt, would it? We could just check in. It made me grin just to look at him again. I'd gotten so used to being near him. I was antsy and scattered without his calm. I'd never missed another person this much.

But when Henry walked past me with the other skaters, his eyes didn't even flick to me for a second. Which was fine! This was the deal. He was focusing. I couldn't be mad about that. Now it was my turn.

Too bad I wasn't doing a good job of it after half the practice time. I was searching for my landings, and I popped my quad toe, which was fucking ridiculous.

I circled the rink, dodging out of Wang Zhan's way as he finished a killer quad Sal-Euler-triple toe combo. I launched into another quad toe, too impatient again but at least landing it this time and squeaking a decent enough triple on the end. I returned to Manon and Bill by the boards to gulp water.

"That was better," I said, taking a tissue and blowing my nose.

"Mmm." Manon didn't seem impressed.

Bill said, "Don't be satisfied."

That had been one of Mr. Webber's favorite motivational instructions, and a swell of emotion throat punched me. I could barely swallow my sip of water.

"That's what he told me," Bill added, giving my shoulder a squeeze-shake. "I didn't always listen, though."

"Me either." I managed a smile. "But I can pull it off when it counts." Since I was kid, I usually had.

Manon nodded. "Your turn for music. Full run-through."

Wang Zhan's short program music finished, and I took my spot. We each had a chance to do a run-through to our music, and some skaters only did bits and pieces of their programs. Kuznetzov never did the whole thing, but I dutifully skated through my program as Sinatra sang "Fly Me to the Moon."

The judges were here watching, and I put on my most charming smile, making sure to nail the quad combo so they'd forget all about that uncharacteristic pop earlier.

I tried to enjoy it. I'd worked my whole life to be here. I'd sacrificed a normal childhood. It should be fun, shouldn't it? What was the point if I was stressed and miserable?

If Henry, Kuznetzov, Wang Zhan, and the Japanese champion, Hayato Uchida, all did well in our short programs today, we'd see how the judges stacked us going into our event. The judging panels wouldn't have the same people on them, so it wasn't apples to apples, but it was obviously a good indicator.

The scattered people in the stands applauded when I hit my final pose, snapping my fingers with a wink. I visualized doing it again in a few hours in the competition arena with a full house. The Olympic rings decorated center ice below the surface, and I skated over them, trying to enjoy the moment.

And if I thought of Henry and how the arches of his feet were ticklish and when he really smiled his eyes lit up, that was okay too.

WELL, IT WASN'T perfect, but it was a trial run. I'd lost my concentration on my camel spin and wandered, losing speed and barely able to grind out the last two revolutions. But whatever—I hated spins. My jumps were bangers, and they were way more important.

In the team event, we got our scores in our country boxes with our teammates cheering and waving flags. I hugged them and smiled and made hearts with my hands at the camera. Henry was in first place from earlier, and though I hadn't seen him skate, I knew from his score that he'd done well. Maybe a little mistake?

They announced my score, and I zoomed ahead of him—but only by three points. The gap had narrowed significantly since he'd added the quad Lutz to his short program this season. The Canadian crowd still cheered for me, and I buzzed with excitement.

I'd been to Worlds plenty of times, but the Olympics really were massive in comparison. I passed under another set of iconic rings as I made my way into the maze of tunnels toward the dressing room.

The Canadian team members were clustered ahead in their red uniforms with white trim. They had to know they'd probably only get bronze, so they were having fun because why the hell not. My gaze immediately found Henry, but he wasn't laughing and chattering.

Was he upset that I'd beat him? Maybe it was dumb given it was literally my job to beat him and everyone else, but I wanted to apologize. I wanted to hug him. I just wanted to be near him.

You know who *was* near him?

Adrenaline spiked as I spotted Anton in the group. The group that Henry lingered on the edges of even though *he* was the one who'd just skated. Who the fuck did Anton think he was? He wasn't even part of Canada's top pair and wasn't competing in the team event. Sure, he and Hannah were allowed to sit with the team in the box and cheer, but Anton had to know his presence upset Henry.

It was almost an out-of-body experience as I followed at a distance as the group headed out, Henry walking quickly with his small, wheeled suitcase holding his costume and equipment.

I was still in my costume, and I couldn't exactly go clomping back to the Village in my skates, but I got lucky as Anton stopped to tap his phone. The rest of them disappeared around a bend in the concrete tunnel. There was no one else around for the moment.

I'd never been in a fight aside from a playground shoving match over who was next on the swings, but the urge to grab Anton's shirt and slam him into the wall exploded messily.

When he noticed me coming, he smiled for a second before a frown took over. "What's up. You okay?" I guessed I was projecting my fury, because he backed away a step even though he was bigger than me.

I resisted the wall slam, but barely. "What happened with you and Henry? What did you do?"

Anton seriously went a shade paler, and he was pretty white to begin with. He shook his head. "No, man. I'm not talking about that."

"What did you *do*?"

I gritted my teeth so hard they hurt. I wanted to shake the truth out of him. This felt like the missing piece to figuring out all of Henry. I'd learned so much these past few months, and I needed more. I needed to understand. He wouldn't tell me and, even if it was technically none of my business, if Anton had hurt him—and he *had*, there was no other explanation—I had to fix it.

Anton shook his head again. "I can't tell you. Like, no way. It's not my place. What do you care anyway?"

I ignored the question. "What the fuck did you do?"

"Did you ask him?"

"He won't tell me. When he sees you, he gets this look on his face. Like he's afraid. I swear to God, if you hurt him…"

Anton glanced around, but we were still alone. "I didn't—it's not what you think."

"What do I think?"

"I don't know! Look, man—you have to ask him. I'm really sorry for what happened." He backed up another step. "If I could change it, I would."

I hissed, "Stop! Tell me." I kept thinking about those little flashes of fear on Henry's face. How vulnerable he could be when everyone mistook it for coldness. I had to help, and I couldn't unless I knew what the fuck Anton did.

"You have to ask Henry!" Anton looked around guiltily again.

"He won't tell me. He wouldn't even let me kiss him at first." Shit, I hadn't meant to say that part out loud.

Anton's eyes widened. "It's true? *You* and Henry are banging? Wow." He ran a hand over his face, exhaling sharply. "Look, I know he can't stand to be around me, but I don't know what to do. It's been years."

"Since *what*?" I wished I could loom intimidatingly or something. "Did you guys hook up? What did you do to him?"

Shoulders slumping, Anton glanced around and whispered, "We didn't hook up. I'm not into guys. Hannah and I are together now, but we're not public because fans get so weird and nosy."

He wasn't wrong about that—fans could be freaky about skaters and who they dated. I nodded impatiently. "*And?*"

"It was when Henry still trained in Vancouver about three or four years ago. He was the way he is. You know, shy and quiet. Always so serious and particular. We had to share the locker room with a hockey team that practiced at our arena. Just a local league, nothing hardcore. They were mostly university age and more into partying than anything else. Henry couldn't stand those guys—although there was one he was hot for."

"How do you know?"

Anton scoffed. "People think he's a robot, but once you can read him, he's not. You must know that. I mean, he may not be telling you what's really going on, but it's pretty obvious when he's upset or mad or hot for someone. Like, we all guessed he was into you after Skate Canada in October but never figured you'd like him back."

"Why not?" I was indignant for Henry.

"Because you're *you*. You're fun. Everyone loves you. There's a reason you're in the Olympic Coke ad. Henry's an amazing skater, but he's…intense."

"You don't know him like I do. He's sweet and generous and he's actually really funny sometimes."

Anton held up his hands. "I'm not trying to bag on him. Look, I was seventeen and a moron, and I thought the hockey players were the coolest."

"Because you're so wise now?"

"Compared to then? Yeah. I wasn't taking training as seriously as I should have. I was hanging with these older guys and drinking way too much on weekends. My parents were pissed at me all the time and my dad threatened to stop coaching us. Hannah kept saying she'd find a new partner. She wouldn't have even considered dating me then. This one time—"

"I don't give a shit about you. Tell me about Henry."

He made an *ugh* sound as he exhaled. "So, Henry clearly had a crush on Mike, one of the hockey players. He'd sneak looks at his ass when he had the chance. Mike was gay and always going on about how he could score with any dude. Even though Henry was clearly hot for him, I figured there was no way he'd actually hook up with Mike. Mike was so loud and obnoxious. A nice ass can only go so far, you know?"

"Okay." I frowned, trying to guess where this was going.

Anton rubbed the back of his neck, looking anywhere but at me. "I bet Mike a case of beer he couldn't get Henry to sleep with him."

Rage flashed so molten I thought my head might actually pop off. "What the fuck?"

"I know. I *know*." He still wouldn't look at me. "I was an asshole. But I never thought it would happen! I figured Henry would blow him off in a heartbeat. He didn't party with anyone let alone hockey douches like Mike. It was supposed to be a joke. I forgot all about it until—" He broke off, swallowing hard.

Ice filled my veins, horrible, sick dread in my stomach. "Until what?" I should stop. Go talk to Henry. But I had to know. Possibilities tumbled through my mind, getting worse and worse.

"Mike texted me a picture." Anton was barely whispering now, glancing around again. "It was Henry. In bed. Like, naked."

"What the *fuck*?" My throat was raw.

"I guess Mike took it right after. You know. After they… The shocked look on Henry's face was just…" He shook his head. "He looked like he was going to cry. And the text from Mike just said '*Case of Bud*' with a bunch of eggplants and laughing emojis."

I felt like I did when I'd missed the back flip and had the wind knocked out of me. My spinning brain remembered Henry kneeling by me in the empty rink on Christmas Day, caressing my head instead of laughing his ass off the way most people would.

Anton's messy words fell all over each other. "I swear, I didn't think he'd actually go, like, *seduce* him or whatever! It was a joke! It wasn't supposed to be for real." He deflated. "I felt like shit. I still do."

"Good! You prick!" My fists were clenched, and I wanted to punch Anton before hunting down this Mike motherfucker.

"I know," Anton agreed miserably. "I hated myself. I didn't

know what to do. That picture was like having this little bomb on my phone."

"What did you do with it?" Jesus, the thought of that picture of Henry at his most vulnerable being passed around—being *laughed* at—was un-fucking-bearable.

"I told Hannah. She always knows what to do about…everything. We waited until Mike was practicing and cut open the padlock on his locker. Her cousin who can hack anything was waiting and got the phone open. Deleted the picture from everywhere and made sure he didn't send it to anyone else. Obviously I deleted it out of my cloud and everything too. Then Hannah threatened to report Mike to UBC and the arena and the hockey league. Henry was twenty, so he wasn't a minor, but those places all have a code of conduct."

I'd never liked Hannah Kwan more. "Did it work?"

"Hell yeah. Hannah's terrifying when she wants to be. She dumped me right after and looked for a new partner."

I vaguely recalled something about them breaking up and then getting back together. "She should have kept looking." Though Anton was probably too good a pairs partner, and they'd skated together since they were pretty young. Those years of gelling on the ice were hard to give up.

"Believe me, it took an epic amount of groveling to get her back. And two years before she'd even think about letting me kiss her. I was a stupid kid. I've worked really hard to get my shit together. To get to the Olympics. We're the second-best team in Canada now, and with retirements, we'll be fighting for number one next year. I'm not the dickhead I was back then."

"That's great for you. Doesn't do much for Henry."

He winced. "I know. I apologized, but he moved to train in Toronto after it happened. When I see him at competitions, he won't even look at me. Not that he doesn't have the right to be mad still. I wish I could go back and change it. You have no idea how much. I wish—oh *fuck*." He'd turned his head, eyes wide.

I followed his gaze, and somehow Henry was there at the bend of the tunnel. He gripped the handle of his wheeled suitcase. He was alone, and I had no idea why he'd returned. Maybe he'd forgotten something. Maybe he was coming back to see me—a thought that made my sad heart leap.

But in the next ragged breath, it was clear Henry knew exactly what Anton and I were talking about. I imagined the betrayed, wounded expression on his beautiful face must have been similar to the one in Mike's evil picture.

Anton backed away from me, his hands raised like Henry had pulled a gun. "I'm sorry, man. He made me tell." He ran back toward the rink even though it was the wrong way.

I practically lunged toward Henry, afraid he'd disappear before I could fix this fuck-up. "Please. Let me explain."

He stared at me with tears glistening in his eyes. His cheeks were flushed, and he shook his head decisively.

With jerky movements, he turned and disappeared, and as much as I wanted to chase him, this time I had to take no for an answer.

Chapter Seventeen

Henry

I SHOULD NEVER have stopped hating Theodore Sullivan.

I also should have blocked his number. Another pleading text from Theo joined the unbroken string from the past several days.

Turning off my phone, I tried to clear my mind as I listened to pop music on my headphones and aggressively worked my IT band on the side of my right thigh with the massage gun.

Manon was nearby, a silent support, and I knew Bill was with Theo in another corner of the warm-up area of the arena that was spread out through a few curtained-off blocks.

It had been terrible enough that Anton and Hannah knew my secret. The reminder each time I saw them was torturous. That shame had been seared into me on a molecular level when the flash on that phone had gone off.

Mike. I hated even thinking his name.

That night, it had been less than a minute since he'd been inside me when it had all crashed down. I'd still ached with it. He hadn't been rough, but I couldn't say he'd been particularly gentle.

He'd gotten up and peeled off the condom. Tossed it in the trash. When he'd turned back, I wondered if he'd squeeze into the bed again and kiss me. I'd hoped so.

The flash had blinded me.

I hummed along now to Lady Gaga to block out an echoed memory of his mocking laughter, but my brain didn't cooperate. He'd crowed about winning the bet, the words mystifying as I'd tried to process what was happening.

I'd fumbled for my clothes. Still unashamedly naked, he'd snatched them up from the floor, holding them high over his head like a playground game. I'd had to beg for my jeans and new sweater so I could escape his dorm room.

Enough!

This was the last thing I should have been thinking about. The men's short program was underway with the first couple of flights complete. We still had an hour before the final flight.

We. I shouldn't have been thinking of Theo and I as *we*. He shouldn't have been texting me. Even if I was speaking to him, which I most definitely was not, this was the time we had to be utterly focused on our job. *I* had to be utterly focused on my job.

He shouldn't have gone to Anton to find out what I had never wanted him to know. He'd promised. Not specifically about Anton, but I'd made myself clear. I had. Disappointment, anger, *hurt*—I vacillated from one emotion to the next.

I wasn't sure precisely what Anton had told him, but it was enough. Theo's pity was unbearable. How could I let go of the past when he *knew*? How would he want me again?

Enough!

I shouldn't care if Theodore Sullivan wanted me. The only thing I should care about was winning. I was at the Olympic Games. I was going to win. I was going to beat him. I was going to skate the very best I could. I'd trained years for this, and I wouldn't allow anyone to beat me.

Not even him.

Yes, it would be up to the judges in the end. His quad combination in the short was worth a few more points than mine. But I would execute every element to the very best of my ability and get as much bonus GOE as possible. And his skating skills score would be too high if he went clean, but I'd deserve every tenth of a point of mine.

I was going to win. I'd likely come second in the short program, but that was to be expected. I would beat him in the free skate. This was what I should have been focusing on all these months instead of letting myself be distracted. I'd let down my guard at the pivotal moment, but it wasn't too late.

I would achieve this goal. Nothing or no one else mattered.

Manon caught my eye with a little wave and raised eyebrow. She was wearing her stylish designer best. Her gold earrings were shimmering jeweled feathers, her black pantsuit was tailored perfectly, and rich red lipstick complemented her dark skin.

I realized I'd stopped using the massage gun, but it still vibrated in my grasp. I switched it off and nodded to Manon before I closed my eyes and visualized my perfect short program.

Exactly on schedule, I changed into my costume for the six-minute warm-up. We gathered at the entrance to the ice, bouncing and fidgeting and shaking like a pack of sequined racehorses in the starting gate.

I could sense Theo behind me, which sounded unnecessarily dramatic given that's where he obviously was since he wasn't one of the skaters in front.

I didn't let myself look.

I couldn't. I *wouldn't*. I refused to think about Theo and his beautiful, pleading eyes. This was the moment. *My* moment. My heart thudded as the attendant swung open the gate in the boards.

We surged, and I bent to remove my skate guards—left, then right, as always. I handed them to Manon and stroked across the ice over the Olympic rings, wind brushing my face, the audience chatter and pop music playing over the speakers blending into a buzz of background noise.

After precisely three laps of the rink, I performed an easy double Axel, ducking and weaving with the five other skaters as I did another lap. Theo's glittering gold shirt was easy to spot from the corner of my eye, but as we passed each other, it didn't matter who he was. This was go time. Even if he cared enough to understand me, even if he—

He's no one. He's not even here. He doesn't matter.

I launched into a quad toe with the lies filling my mind, much of the home crowd applauding my textbook landing. With a burst of adrenaline, I stroked around the corner and sped backward.

I registered the swell of audience noise just before I turned into my difficult one-foot transition to my triple Axel—

Massimo Musetti faced me in the same moment, a blur of orange as he lunged to the side. My stomach met his hip, and I flew, skates airborne as I sailed over him. My hands smacked the ice, shoulder impacting a moment later.

My cheek slid along the slick surface as momentum spun me before I pushed right to my feet. I was a few steps from Massimo, who blinked up at me, stunned, as I reached down to pull him up.

Through the haze of adrenaline and shock, I nodded to him, both of us apologizing. A hand settled on my lower back, wonderfully familiar and comforting. I caught a whiff of Theo's faintly vanilla body wash, which I hadn't realized I'd missed.

His pinched face hovered in my peripheral vision. Theo and Massimo were both speaking, but my ears buzzed loudly. Had I hit my head? I didn't think so—just the graze on my cheek. I circled my shoulder. Nothing broken. Joint still in place.

"I'm fine." My voice sounded distant.

Nodding, Massimo skated toward his coaches at the boards. I wasn't sure which of us was at fault, but it didn't matter. These collisions happened sometimes.

Theo's hand was still warm and grounding on my lower back,

and I allowed myself another heartbeat of that closeness before skating away even though Theo was talking to me. The warm-up was ticking down. I had to shake this off.

He's no one. He's not even here. He doesn't matter.

Still lies, but I repeated the mantra with each lap of the rink. Making doubly sure the path was clear, I launched into my quad Lutz. The audience thundered with applause now, all eyes apparently on me after the collision. I could do this. My shoulder throbbed, but it didn't matter. Nothing else mattered.

A strange calm shrouded me as the warm-up ended. I nodded to everyone who expressed concern, letting Manon whisk me to the medics. Bill appeared at one point, and I assured them not to worry.

They texted my mom in the stands to let them know I was okay, and I smiled to think of how Sam would likely tease me about being a drama queen after all. Obaachan would pinch me and say to watch where I was going. Then she'd yank me down for a hug.

In Toronto, Ojiichan was watching on TV. I asked Manon to remind my parents to call the facility and make sure he knew I was all right. Surely my parents already had, but just in case.

We'd had a family lunch yesterday downtown in Calgary, though I wouldn't see them again until after the free skate in two days. I had to stay focused. I was all right. This was my moment.

I was the fourth skater of six in the flight, so I had time to catch my breath after the collision, but not too much time that the adrenaline would wear off and pain would take over.

As the skater before me—who happened to be Massimo— finished, I waited by the gate with Manon. Normally, I'd analyze the response of the audience to determine how well a competitor had performed, but it was like my ears were stuffed with cotton.

While he exited to the Kiss and Cry, I took the ice, skating three laps and relaxing into my knees. Massimo's score and placement washed over me as I stood at the boards with Manon on the other side.

"This is your time, Henry. Stay in your center. Let your body do what it knows how to do. What you've trained it to do. Don't think. No doubts. Let the crowd love you." She grasped my hands and squeezed.

My name filled the arena along with a roar of applause. Of *love*. Unbidden, an image of Theo's beaming, generous smile expanded in my mind until it became too big.

I was left alone at center ice. A hush fell, thousands of people silent as I lowered my face in my starting position, arms at my sides.

Damien Rice's "The Blower's Daughter" played, calm and lyrical, the lilting melody emphasizing my soft, deep edges and glide that looked effortless but required strength, control, and power.

My first two jumping passes—the quad toe combo and triple Axel—felt like water flowing over timeworn stone. My quad Lutz out of footwork was in the second half of the program, garnering a ten percent bonus in the score. This would make or break me. A miss would knock me out of medal contention, and I tensed as I launched up.

I had to muscle out the landing, but it was on one foot and fully rotated. I extended my free leg, not getting the flow I would have liked on the running edge. It wasn't perfect, which I *hated*, but I'd done it. I glided into my step sequence, losing myself in the swelling music, one step closer to gold.

As the music ended and I took my final pose, a mirror of my starting position, the audience roared, leaping to their feet. In the last minute of my program, I'd almost forgotten they were there. I'd heard my music as though it was the first time. Their love washed over me, and I bowed gratefully.

Theo skated after me, and I was aware of him taking the ice as

I neared Manon waiting at the Kiss and Cry. The temptation to allow just one fleeting look at him stole my breath.

Flowers and stuffed animals littered the ice, and I bent to scoop up a moose wearing the Canadian uniform.

He's no one. He's not even here. He doesn't matter.

I only had to believe the lies for two more days.

"CAN I COME in?"

Hadn't I endured enough humiliation? Hannah Kwan stood outside my room at the Athletes' Village in her red and white team jacket, fiddling with her jangling bracelets.

It would be too rude to say no, and I knew she meant well. I stood back and closed the door after her. Crossing my arms, I waited for her to speak and get this over with.

"Congrats on the short! You were amazing. Only two points behind. It's so close! We're all really excited for you. Are you feeling okay?" She shook her head, black ponytail waving. "Sorry. That's probably a stupid question. Do you need more ice for your face or anything? The bruise isn't too bad today, actually."

"You're not here to talk about my face."

Hannah sighed. "Look, Anton feels like shit. Not that this is about Anton. But he really does feel awful."

I waited. I could believe his regret, but it wasn't my concern.

"The thing is—I heard a rumor the other day that you and Theo were hooking up in Toronto."

If that was a question, I wasn't answering it.

She paced a few steps. "It's none of my business, I know. I just… I thought you hated his guts? And Theo's always been so—" Flapping her hand, bracelets tinkling, she made a face. "Frivolous. It's so damn annoying how he can pull out wins when it counts, but I guess he was first in line when God was giving out jumping ability. And he's really friendly, don't get me wrong. He's just always seemed…surface-y. Like he never actually cared that much about anything."

"That's not true." The defense popped out before I could control myself.

She stopped pacing and peered up at me with a shrewd narrowing of her eyes. Like many pair girls, she was tiny but fierce. "You know, everyone's buzzing about how he flew to your side after the collision in warm-up."

My heart constricted. "They are?"

"Are you kidding? You really have been holed up in here since early practice, haven't you? He was like a speed skater out there. And the way Anton said he lost his shit the other day? He cares. Why would he be so protective of you of all people? You two are fighting for gold. But he was furious. *Jealous* even. With Anton I mean, not after the collision. I guess he thought you and Anton used to hook up?"

"Apparently." Had Theo really been jealous? The thought shouldn't have given me a thrill.

"And he thought Anton was an abusive boyfriend or something? I know Anton shouldn't have told him anything, but Theo was so worried about you. Honestly, I didn't think he had it in him."

Joy truly shouldn't have filled me at the idea that Theo worried about me, yet there it was warming my chest. I reminded myself he'd gone behind my back. He'd pressed on that bruise when I'd specifically told him not to.

It was intolerable that he *knew*. I'd worked so hard to lock away my humiliation and protect myself. Now I was vulnerable again. The joy evaporated. I wanted to vomit.

"Henry?" Hannah's face creased. "You look woozy."

"Is the picture really gone?"

She blinked in what seemed to be surprise. "What? You

mean…? Yes! My cousin scoured that bastard's phone and his outgoing messages in every app. To the best of my knowledge, he only sent it to Anton. We erased it from the cloud and factory reset his phone. Anton's too. It's been a few years now. I think you're safe."

Safe. I felt dangerously raw. I was an exposed nerve.

"If there's something between you and Theo—"

"Please leave me alone." My jaw clenched. My throat was too thick, and my eyes burned.

Face sorrowful, she backed away. "I'm sorry, Henry. We're rooting for you tomorrow. So many people are."

After the door closed, I stood frozen on the red and white throw rug. I couldn't move. I could barely breathe. I was going to shatter into a million pieces, and I couldn't allow it.

I *would not* allow it.

Tomorrow, I would skate the most important program of my life. I had to keep everything else locked away. I couldn't allow myself to think about Theo. I couldn't—

"Hey."

I blinked. Theo somehow stood in the now open doorway. Had he even knocked? I had to order him to get out, out, *out.* I should never have said yes to him training in Toronto.

Should never have offered him rides. Never have let him into my home. Cooked for him and cared for him. Let him smile and laugh. Let him make me feel everything I'd blocked out for so long. I should never have been fooled into thinking I could turn off my emotions again.

Loathing him had been so much easier. This *hurt,* and I couldn't stand it.

"Get. Out." Jaw aching, my teeth ground together.

"No!" He closed the door. "Please. We have to talk."

Fury boiled up, and I latched onto it desperately. "I believed you. You said you wouldn't ask. Are you happy now? You know how pathetic I am."

"What?" He shook his head, stepping toward me before stopping and fisting his hands at his sides. "I know that Anton and that Mike motherfucker were cruel assholes. That's what I know."

I scoffed. "I should have known better. It was all a joke. A bet. I should have realized no one would actually want to be with me."

"*They* were the pathetic ones! And hello, didn't the last month prove that I really want to be with you? Come on. Please."

"Maybe that was all a joke too." The words were like ground glass on my tongue.

Theo flinched as though I'd slapped him. "You don't really—" His voice broke, and he cleared his throat. "You can't really believe that."

"Why not? I should never have trusted you. You want to beat me. You want to win gold. Maybe it was all pretend."

His mouth tightened into a thin line. "Seriously? You don't believe that." He shook his head. "No way you actually believe that."

He was right, but I couldn't admit it.

Theo flung out his hands. "Was it pretend in Torino when I bawled my eyes out in your arms? What, you think I was faking being sad about Mr. Webber? Hey, maybe I arranged his death and it was all part of a long con to seduce you out of gold. Never mind the fact that I've beaten you every time we've competed head-to-head for the last two seasons! I don't need to fuck you to beat you, Henry. I have an extra quad, remember?"

"How could I forget?" I spat, desperate not to think about Torino or any of it. "This was a mistake. All of it."

His anger seemed to vanish. He swallowed hard, Adam's apple bobbing. "Please don't say that. I'm sorry I got the story out of Anton. I know I broke a promise, but I was dying to understand. To know you. Every part of you. I want to love every single part of you."

Love.

Blood rushed in my ears. That word seemed to hang in the air, growing huge along with the faithful elephants that had never left. I could only stare at him, my mouth dry and pulse pounding.

The door opened, Etienne jolting to a halt. He looked between me and Theo, his eyebrows lifting high. Glancing back into the corridor, he quickly closed the door behind him.

"Hey!" Theo smiled too brightly, even for him, on the edge of hysteria. "I was just checking on Henry. We're friends. We've been training together, so."

Etienne nodded, though he seemed decidedly dubious. "Theo, I think your mother is in the hall?"

Theo blanched. "My what?"

"Your mother?" Etienne looked to me with obvious concern.

I shouldn't care if Theo's mother was snooping. I shouldn't give a damn if she knew he was in my room. What had been between us was over.

Perhaps if I repeated that lie to myself a few thousand more times it would feel true.

Theo was still shaking his head, sputtering at Etienne. "What? How? She's not allowed in the Village. She can't barge in here." Nostrils flaring, his face went red.

"It's all right." I reached for him without thinking before snatching back my hand. I hated that his mother had no boundaries and upset him so much. I was surprised he hadn't quit skating as soon as he was eighteen.

She may never have hit him—to my knowledge, at least—but she was abusive. This was the biggest competition of Theo's life. She should only be supporting him.

And I wasn't supposed to care, but I marched to the door— and sure enough, Patricia Sullivan almost pitched inside when I opened it. The only thing missing was a stethoscope she could press to the wood to better eavesdrop.

She stumbled, catching herself and giving me a wide, insincere smile. "Oh hello, Henry. How are you after that nasty collision?"

"I'm calling security." I pushed the door shut.

Her foot shot out to stop it as she tried to peer around me. "Theo! I know you're in there. What do you think you're playing at? Enough of this nonsense. Do you even want to win?"

At my side, Theo snarled, "You know what, Mom? Screw you. What I do is none of your business. You have no right being here!"

Her gaze narrowed on me. "I thought you'd be a good influence on my son. But you've manipulated him, I know it."

Though my feet were planted in the doorway, Theo squirmed in front of me. "Don't you talk about Henry. Don't you dare! It's none of your business. God, just get out."

"How can you speak to your own mother like this?" Her voice wavered, tears filling her eyes on cue.

"*How?*" He practically shouted. "You want to know how? Fine. Buckle up."

Chapter Eighteen

Theo

I STORMED OUT of Henry's room. There were other athletes down the hall looking at us, but whatever. I was done. I was so fucking *done*.

"I'm twenty-five. I know being homeschooled and growing up in the skating world means I'm more like nineteen, but I'm an adult. You don't get a say in my life or my training. Obviously that hasn't stopped you from giving your opinions every single chance you get. But you're not in control. I am."

"I know that," she huffed with the nerve to act offended.

My fingers twitched at my sides, and my whole head felt boiling hot. I'd expected Henry to close the door after me, but he still stood watching. Maybe I should have been embarrassed for him to see me lose it like this, but I was grateful he was there.

I said to my mother, "When I first tried skating, it was so much fun. I loved going fast and spinning. Then I learned to jump, and it was even more fun. But sometimes I wish I'd never been good at it. As soon as I started winning and they told you I could be a champion, it all changed."

Steam practically coming out of her ears, she glared at Henry. Etienne stood behind him, a silent backup. Mom put on what I thought of as her "public supportive smile," which she'd perfected years ago.

She said, "And look where you are, darling. The Olympic Games! In first place about to win the gold medal! Of course it required discipline and hard work. I wanted the best for you. I won't apologize for that. And don't tell me you don't enjoy winning!"

"Yeah, Mom, I enjoy winning!" I threw up my hands. "Who doesn't? Winning's great! But I wanted to go to regular school and hang out at my friends' houses, and yeah, eat Doritos sometimes. You made my childhood so fucking miserable."

"You could have quit anytime."

"Bullshit! Are you kidding? I'd have never heard the end of it. And I do like skating! I just didn't want it to be the only thing in my life."

"Isn't that why you abandoned us and moved to LA? For your precious freedom?"

"How was that 'abandoning' you? Because I didn't want you to come with me? Dad has a career in Chicago, and the girls were in high school. And no, I didn't want you to come with me. I wanted to be in charge of my skating for once, and with Mr. Webber's help I did a pretty good job, didn't I? I've won two world titles!"

She sniffed. Here came the tears. "You know how proud I am. All I ever wanted was to help you succeed. But you shut me out. You make huge decisions without even asking for my opinion!" She glared at Henry again. "Now you're clearly letting emotions cloud your judgment. What were you thinking going to train with *him*?"

"Stop!" I hissed, aware that there were still people gathered down the hall watching this fight. "Don't talk about Henry. He's off-limits."

Her eyes widened, and she jerked her head from Henry to me. For a minute, I thought her head might actually explode right then and there.

She was still staring between us. "It can't be true. I discounted the rumors weeks ago because I didn't think it was possible you'd be so reckless." She gaped at me. "What on Earth are you thinking?" Then she whirled to Henry, who watched her warily. "I'd expect better of you!"

I had to laugh. Honestly, at this point, what else could I do? My shoulders shook, and I was on the edge of hysteria. "Sorry to disappoint you, Mom. He's not a machine after all. We're both trying our best. Unless I do everything the way you want, you're never happy. I'm afraid you're doomed to even more disappointment. Get used to it."

She swiped at her eyes. "I've only ever tried to help you. Now I'm the villain!"

I sighed, resignation settling in as her rage and hysteria faded. This was the martyrdom stage of her cycle, and I'd heard it all before. "Mom, I can't do this with you now. You need to go."

She nodded. "Fine. That's fine." She checked her watch. "You have an interview with Janice at the studio."

"*Fuck*," I muttered, pulling out my phone and checking the time. I'd have to run to make it. The federation would be pissed if I flaked, rightfully so.

Mom smiled thinly. "Go on. We can settle this later."

I wanted to argue that there was nothing to "settle." She wasn't going to change, and I wasn't going to put up with her crap. But whatever. "Okay. Let's go."

"Yes, you'd better hurry, dear."

Henry still watched us silently, and as much as he didn't actually have a poker face, I wasn't sure what he was feeling. Disgust, most likely? It might have been for me, my mom, or both.

"I'm sorry," I said to him again, even though I'd probably ruined everything permanently. I forced my feet to walk, but after a few steps, I realized my mother wasn't following.

Oh, hell no.

"*Mom.* Let's go."

"Yes, darling, you'd better hurry ahead." She took a step toward me. "You know how my lower back flares up with all the sitting in those arena seats cheering you on. Go ahead."

I stood my ground. "So you can grill Henry alone? I don't think so. Let's go. You're not supposed to be here." Not that Henry couldn't handle her, but nope. No way. If I had to drag her out screaming, I wasn't leaving her alone with him.

Again, she puffed up with outrage. "I'm not going to 'grill' anyone."

"I'm calling security," Henry said flatly.

"This is ridiculous." Mom lifted her chin and strode down the hall.

I glanced back at Henry, who watched us go. There was so much more I wanted to say, but I had to leave him alone. Tomorrow was the free skate, and we had jobs to do.

Right now, my job was to haul ass to the US network studio, a glass-walled temporary building with a view of the distant mountains. My mother was talking as I escorted her out of the Athletes' Village, but I mostly blocked her out. The shuttle bus was mercifully approaching on the horizon.

"If Janice asks about Sakaguchi—"

"Mom, stop. It's my interview."

"I should come along. I've spoken with the federation president in depth about messaging. We can go over some answers on the way."

It was like the fight had never happened. Like she hadn't registered a single word I'd said. But this was how it had always been. She wasn't going to change. For a second, my eyes burned, and I almost burst into tears, the frigid air searing my nose.

No matter how clearly I tried to explain or how angry I got, she'd still try and control me. And I'd still love her, but she'd never be the parent I wanted her to be.

I breathed through an emotion that felt a lot like grief. "Mom, please listen to me. I'm going to do this interview alone. You're not coming."

She opened her mouth, but then sighed. "Fine. Will you still be having dinner with us after the free skate?"

"No. We're going for breakfast the morning after. We went through this. Dad and the girls agree. If I win tomorrow, I'm going to be too busy and tired. If I don't win—"

"Of course you're going to win! Why would you even *say* that?" She wrung her hands. "You can't let Sakaguchi beat you. What have Manon and Bill been telling you? You know they favor him." Her breath puffed in clouds in the cold air like exclamation marks.

The shuttle pulled to a stop, the doors folding open with a whoosh. I stepped on and said to my mom, "I'll see you all for breakfast in two days."

The doors closed, cutting off her response. It didn't matter. I'd heard it all before, and I'd hear it again unless I entirely locked her out of my life. Maybe one day I would, but it was easier said than done.

At the studio, they got me right into hair and makeup, and soon I was settled by the big window across from Janice Harvey, the older reporter who did the fluff pieces and human-interest stories.

She dressed in pantsuits and kept her red hair in a practical bob. She was almost sixty now and had big nice-mom energy, like at any second she'd offer you home-baked brownies. I'd always liked her.

She softballed me questions about the dream of competing at the Olympics and the thrill of being here and all that stuff. Until she said, "Let's talk about your relationship with Henry Sakaguchi."

My heart skipped. Whoa. Was Janice ambushing me? That wasn't her style, and the network had never been overly keen on talking about my sexuality. "Um... Uh-huh?"

"It's not uncommon now for top competitors to train in close quarters. Would you say you've become friends over these months?"

Relief flooded me. Okay, this seemed to be the typical kind of questions. "Absolutely! It's such a family atmosphere at the rink."

Actually, that was more true of the Ice Chalet than anywhere else I'd ever trained, but talking about hugs and puppies and how everyone is so friendly in training and on teams was the bread and butter of figure skating bullshit PR.

Janice tilted her head sympathetically, and I knew what was coming before she said, "Your beloved coach, Walter Webber, sadly passed away in December. Did his loss hit you hard?"

I flashed on sobbing against Henry in the rain and breathed through a wave of feelings. "It did. Mr. Webber was such a legend, and he made me the skater I am today. But more than his coaching, he was an amazing person. Kind and patient, and he impacted so many people in the skating world over the years. I'm honored to have been his student."

"It must have affected your training?"

"Yes, but I can't say enough how wonderful Bill and Manon were to take me on. They're continuing Mr. Webber's legacy of empathy and expertise."

Janice smiled. "You know, many people have praised you for being a mentor to younger skaters in training and on the US team. Korean national medalist Ga-young Park told us: 'Theo will make the best coach one day.' Is that something you've considered?"

I blinked in genuine surprise. "Wow. First off, Ga-young is so sweet. I've loved training with her in Toronto. She's a future champion, mark my words. And... No, I haven't really thought about coaching."

Janice smiled. "Still focused on an Olympic gold medal first?"

"Yeah, my mind's here in Calgary." I laughed along with her. "One thing at a time. It was amazing to win silver with my incredible US teammates in the team event, and I'm hoping I can go out there and do my best in the individual competition."

"But have you thought at all about the future? You're twenty-five now. Will you continue competing after this season? Will it depend on the results here?"

"Yeah, I guess so."

I paused, trying to come up with the appropriate generic athlete answer. I could imagine my mother willing me to say that *of course* I was going to continue competing, and even if I'd be twenty-nine at the next Olympics it wasn't unheard of, and I loved skating so much, blah, blah, blah.

But in that moment, blinking under the bright studio lights as Janice waited for my response, the Olympic rings looming over us on the studio wall above the window, one word filled my mind. It filled my heart and soul if you wanted to get cheesy about it.

No.

I found myself saying, "Actually, win or lose here in Calgary, my competitive career is ending. I've won every other competition out there, including two world titles. It's been incredible. But I'm very excited about new challenges and the freedom of skating in shows without rules."

Her eyebrows flew up. "So this is your farewell to competition?"

"I guess I'm giving you the scoop. You heard it here first. Training at an elite level takes a ton of hard work and dedication, and I think I'm ready to move on to the next chapter of my life. Maybe I'll change my mind in a month or two, but we'll see."

Janice nodded. "You can always change your mind, and I know the skating world will welcome you back to competition with open arms." She joked, "Maybe not your top competitors so much, but you're beloved by fans everywhere."

We wrapped up the interview, and I headed back to the Village in a daze, walking the mile or so, my nose cold and my breath clouding in the crisp, dry air under a blue sky.

I honestly hadn't been thinking beyond the Olympics. Worlds would be a few weeks after the Games, but many of the top skaters here would skip it. Having to come down after the biggest competition of our lives and then ramp back up only a few weeks later was brutal.

Win or lose, I wasn't going. Was Henry? We hadn't even discussed it. The Olympics had been our line in the sand, and who knew what would happen after. But apparently I'd just announced my retirement?

Fuck, my mom was going to freak. At least the interview wouldn't air until tomorrow. Whatever. She could deal, because with each step I took, the instinct that this was right grew and grew.

I'd trained and competed my whole life, and I was *done*. I could still do shows and tours and hell, maybe I *could* try coaching. I loved kids.

And if Henry still wanted to compete—and undoubtedly he did since he loved training so much—great! I'd love to cheer him on. We could be a normal couple without all those elephants crowding us.

If he even wanted to be with me. God, had I really ruined everything between us?

Panicking, I dug out my phone and saw a text on the lock screen.

I'm proud of you.

My heart practically slammed right out of my chest. If I knew Henry—and I think I did now—he was talking about me standing up to my mom. I opened the phone with trembling, clumsy fingers. I wanted to say a million things in reply, but three words burned through me.

I love you.

I didn't type them. But they echoed through my head and heart—my actual soul if I was being incredibly cheesy again. I loved him. God, I loved him so much.

I missed him and I wanted to be with him and never go behind his back again. Never upset him at all—although I surely would at some point no matter how hard I tried.

"I love you," I said out loud to the sidewalk, a couple ahead glancing back with confusion. I said again, "I love you. I love you!"

But I couldn't lay that on him the night before the Olympic free skate. It wouldn't be fair. I knew he cared about me even after what I'd done. Did he *love* me though? I wasn't sure.

Even if he did… No. I wanted to say it to his face, not like this. So what I typed was:

Thank you.

I could have said so much more, and I did tap out another long-ass message before backspacing until only those two words remained. In twenty-four hours, one of us would have the gold— unless we fucked up and Kuznetzov or Zhan or even Musetti swooped in for the win.

Whatever happened, in twenty-four hours it would be over. Were Henry and I over too?

Guess I had to be patient for once and wait to find out.

Chapter Nineteen

Henry

THERE WAS NOTHING or no one else but me, the ice, and "Moonlight Sonata."

Taking my starting position with makeup concealing the mark on my cheek from the collision, a chorus of doubts clamored in my mind. I silenced them.

It didn't matter that I was bruised in multiple places from the collision. It didn't matter that this was the most important program of my life. This was simply another run-through like so many I'd done before. This was my moment. As Manon had instructed, I had to trust my training.

I was ready.

The piano might have been playing in my chest, I felt so connected to the melody. I had no doubt as I leapt into my quad toe. It was over in a blink, the landing perfect as I added the triple toe on the end.

Element after element, I flowed through the program, the music carrying me one moment and spurring me the next. Spread eagle into and out of my triple Axel, quad Sal, combination spin. More jumps. My feet barely felt like they touched the ice even as my deep edges carved a path.

Quad Lutz in the second half of the program.

I launched off my toe pick. Landed fully rotated, my free leg extending as adrenaline soared through me, soothing the lactic acid building in my legs. One more jumping pass—*no, listen to the music, don't skip ahead!*

Approaching my triple Axel combination, pressure intensified, everything on the line—forward into three and a half revolutions, reaching back to add the second jump—and a clean flow out on the running edge.

The crowd erupted. I felt even more than heard their cheers and applause. I could barely hear Beethoven, but the music filled my mind, every note etched in my memory.

I flew into my footwork sequence, the edited music building from meditative to the flourish of the third movement to finish my program. The arena was on its feet already as I hit the final pose down on one knee with my back arched and arm raised.

I'd done it. A haze muffled my mind as I took my bows, waving to the audience, not having to force my smile even a bit.

Theo skated by the rink's periphery as I made my way to the Kiss and Cry, his red shirt bright—V-neck still dipping low. My knees were jelly and my breath shallow. Flower girls and boys scrambled to clean the ice. Manon was crying.

She yanked me into a fierce hug, the Canadian skating federation president at her elbow. I couldn't understand what either of them were saying. It was all a buzzing blur as I put on my skate guards and took my seat on the bench. I remembered to wave to the camera after watching the replays of my performance.

I'd done it.

Already, my brain rewound to point out the tiny mistakes that most people wouldn't notice. Despite those imperfections, I'd done it. Now it was up to the judges.

"The scores please for Henry Sakaguchi." The arena announcer's calm voice cut through the buzzing as she read the scores.

The crowd *screamed.*

"He is currently in first place."

Manon hugged me from the side, practically shouting in my ear as she bounced up and down on the bench. I could only stare at the scoreboard. I was still breathing hard from the skate, the hair at the base of my skull wet with sweat and my forehead damp. I realized I was gaping and snapped my mouth shut.

"Enjoy this! Be proud of yourself!" Manon added something in French I didn't catch.

The audience was still cheering, and I stood, waving to them and bowing in thanks. I could barely feel my legs at all, and I walked from the Kiss and Cry as though I was levitating.

Theo was announced, and "Sympathy for the Devil" was soon playing. Part of me wanted to run back to the boards and watch him. The other part wanted to run into the bathroom and turn on all the taps.

In all likelihood, I'd have the silver. I'd done my best in the moment, though my sit spin had slowed down too much at the end, and I'd have to review the protocols for my second quad combination since I'd landed *slightly* off balance—

"Stop critiquing yourself! *Enjoy this!*" Manon gave me an affectionate shake before returning to the boards to stand with Bill to watch Theo's performance.

In a daze, I nodded to well-wishers and submitted to hugs before taking my spot in the middle chair in the contenders' waiting area. Kuznetsov gave me a half-hug before taking the chair to my right. Massimo moved over to my left, bumping the Japanese skater, who'd now likely finish fifth.

There were three cameras ready to cut to us for reactions after Theo's skate and a monitor showing his program. Mick Jagger's voice filled the arena. Now all I could do was sit and wait and be a good sport no matter what happened. Top rivals in skating had to put on fake smiles now more than ever with cameras in our faces constantly.

My top rival.

It didn't seem a remotely adequate way to describe Theodore Sullivan. Who was he now? A friend? My lover? Just thinking that word sent a thrill down my spine.

He *had* been my lover. And now he knew how gullible and foolish I'd been. That shame lingered. But how long could I let that poison stay in my system?

It was only when Theo put a hand down on his quad Sal that I realized I'd been watching him on the TV screen without truly paying attention.

The audience's gasping "oh!" of surprise was loud, followed by a flurry of applause to cheer him on for the next element, which was the quad Lutz combo in the second half of the program.

He rushed the takeoff.

Without enough height, he under-rotated the Lutz and could barely tack on a weak double toe. It was the kind of mistake he'd have made before going to Mr. Webber: lack of concentration. Sometimes we all slipped back into old habits under stress. I knew the feeling, and my heart hurt for him.

"Holy shit," Kuznetsov muttered. "Henry, you might have this."

The three of us watched the screen in tense silence. My gaze zeroed in on the technical score tracker on the top left corner. My score was there beside the word: *Leader.* Below it, Theo's score was being tallied as he skated. The GOE for the Lutz combination was highlighted in red with a -2.23.

As usual, Theo didn't let any mistakes detract from his performance aside from several seconds where I could tell he'd lost focus after the mistake. Then he turned on the charm and gave the audience everything he had. In return, they gave him a deserved standing ovation, and I clapped for him too.

I watched the replays, my pulse racing, the buzzing setting in again. The hand down on the Sal was a relatively minor mistake.

A point and a half lost on GOE.

But the quad Lutz would be examined by the technical specialist, who would surely deem it under-rotated, bringing down the base value. Theo was ahead after the short program, but would it be enough?

The scores rang out.

"And he is currently in second place."

Chaos erupted. Even though Massimo had just come in fourth, he was smiling and hugging me, and Kuznetzov was too. Flashes were going off, people crowding around, and on the monitor showing the Kiss and Cry, Theo was smiling and applauding.

For me.

I was going to actually pass out or vomit or cry.

I won. I'm the Olympic gold medalist.

"How does it feel?" someone asked. I'd have to talk to the media, but right now I couldn't speak. I was carried along by the tide of well-wishers.

"By less than one point, Henry Sakaguchi is the new Olympic champion!" Janice Harvey exclaimed.

I escaped to the locker room, which was blissfully empty for the moment. In the bathroom, I bent over the sink and splashed cold water on my face, not caring about the concealer. Straightening, I blinked at my blotchy reflection.

"I won," I said to myself.

As if I'd just been punched in the gut, I burst into tears.

I'd won, but Theo had lost, and I *ached* for him. He had to win too. I didn't want him to be disappointed or angry or sad. I didn't want him to hurt. Not ever.

Is this love?

It had to be, because if it wasn't, the only other explanation could be that I was losing my mind. I'd just achieved my lifelong goal, yet I staggered with sorrow. Gasping, I swiped at my face uselessly as footsteps approached. I lunged for a stall, but I was too late.

"Congratulations." Theo's voice was warm.

All I could do was face him. As I turned, Theo's genuinely beaming, beautiful smile transformed into concern. He was already moving, reaching for my hands.

"No! What is it? You won!"

"But you didn't." My voice was raspy. I couldn't stop crying, and *what was the matter with me?* If this was love, it was messy and uncomfortable. It *hurt.*

That perfect smile transformed Theo's face again. "Oh, baby. It's okay." He drew me into his arms, where I was safe again. "I'm okay. I didn't need to win. I really didn't."

"But..." I tried to comprehend it as I gulped against his neck, sagging into his embrace.

He stroked my hair and rubbed my back. "I'm disappointed in myself, but I'm so, so happy for you. You deserve this. I'm so glad you won. I wasn't bad today, but you were better. And this has been the greatest time of my life, and I wouldn't change anything. Not even this."

"How can you say that?"

He took my face between his warm hands, watching me intently. "Because I fell in love with you."

I couldn't breathe. Couldn't talk. My eyes filled with fresh tears, my throat painfully tight. "Why?" I croaked.

A little smile played on his lips. "You did my pukey laundry."

"I..." My brain attempted to process.

"You took care of me again and again. You listened to me even when I talked way too much. Most of the time, at least. You made me laugh and you never laughed *at* me. You were serious when I needed it. You're sweet and kind and strong, and I felt more at home with you and Esmeralda than I have anywhere else. And I'm so sorry I went behind your back to talk to Anton."

I squirmed, dropping my gaze, but he kept hold of my face, ghosting over my cheekbones with his thumbs, careful of the bruise.

Theo said, "You have nothing to be ashamed of. I understand if you don't want to be with me anymore. You're pure and good, and I wish I could keep you in bubble wrap so you're never hurt again. *I* never want to hurt you again. I'm so happy you won today. You deserve this, and I love you for caring about me when you should be celebrating. Coming to train with you was the best thing that ever happened to me. Not that it was good Mr. Webber died, obviously, but if there's a heaven he's watching and he's so proud of me because I tried my best today. Only one of us could win, and I want you to get up on that podium and sing your anthem—or maybe hum since you don't sing a lot—and you should enjoy every second of this victory and not worry about me. And I know I'm talking too much like always."

If not for Theo's hands grounding me, I would have floated away like a helium balloon. I captured his mouth gratefully, clinging to his now familiar body. Our kisses tasted like salt and surrender.

As Theo's young teammate exclaimed, "Holy shit, it's true!" behind us, I smiled.

Then I laughed. And I couldn't stop. I didn't want to.

On the podium, cheers and applause for me swelled like music filling the air, so thick I could almost touch it. The announcer's voice saying, *"From Canada, Olympic gold medalist Henry Sakaguchi!"* echoed in my head on a joyous loop as I waved to the loyal, wonderful audience.

Sam, our parents, and Obaachan were among the thousands, and I couldn't wait to find them afterward and hug them tightly. They'd supported me my whole life, but at the distance I needed—never smothering or controlling. Ojiichan and I rarely spoke about my skating, but I knew he was proud too.

I clapped for Theo as he was announced. He gave the crowd his beautiful, beaming smile. I couldn't comprehend how he wasn't devastated. Tears prickled my eyes again.

But as he hopped up onto the silver position on the podium, he opened his arms and hugged me fiercely. I leaned low, and we were probably embracing for too long. Tongues would wag.

Let them.

"Enjoy the hell out of this, baby!" he shouted in my ear as we held on, the crowd thundering in appreciation of what they might have thought was our good sportsmanship or Olympic spirit.

We finally had to let go of each other—but not for long.

"OKAY, MOM. I'M turning off my phone now. I'll see you all for breakfast in the morning." Theo hesitated. "Yeah. Love you too."

His cheeks puffing out as he exhaled, he switched off his phone as promised and tucked it away in the pocket of his coat hanging from the back of the door in my room in the Athletes' Village. Etienne was spending the night with Sam, so Theo and I were alone.

Theo and I were also in love.

We'd clearly established it now. I'd told him in a whisper while we waited in the corridor leading to the ice for the medal ceremony, and he'd squawked in outrage, motioning around us to the various people in the area.

True, perhaps I should have said "*I love you*" when we were still in the bathroom and he could respond, but I hadn't. Then I simply couldn't wait another moment.

"All right," Theo said. "She'll apply Valium and Chardonnay. Her dream of being the mother of an Olympic gold medalist is over, but she'll have to deal." He ran a hand through his still-damp hair. We'd both showered at the arena after the medal ceremony.

"Mm. What about you?"

"Well, it's a little soon to be talking about kids, don't you think? Though we could certainly raise a champion, I have no doubt."

"Ha, ha."

He grinned. "And we only just declared our undying love. You doing it when *I couldn't even say anything back*!" Theo playfully pushed my arm and kissed me. "The nerve. But now we're alone, and I can say all the things. Although I said them earlier, I guess. So, I could talk more, or we could get naked. Do you have a preference?"

I pretended to ponder, but he was already yanking off his clothes. He exclaimed "Oh, I have an idea!" and carefully picked up my medal from where I'd left it in its case, not wanting to remind Theo of it, no matter what he said.

He held out the medal. "Put it on."

Shirtless, I stopped folding my hoodie. "Pardon?"

"You heard me." He grinned devilishly. "Wear your gold medal." Motioning to my pants, he added, "Come on! Screw folding. I'll iron your stuff tomorrow."

"No you won't." Still, I did as he requested, disrobing completely and leaving my pants tossed over a chair. I put on the medal, feeling incredibly foolish. "This is silly."

Yet my protest faded as Theo eyed me lasciviously and beckoned me to bed, stretching out on his back. I leaned down to kiss him—and Theo winced and jerked back, rubbing his nose.

"Ow! That's heavy!"

I stilled the swaying medal. "You wanted me to wear it!"

It took a minute for us to stop laughing. I took it off and carefully left it on the side table before kissing his nose. Soon, the laughter faded as we moved together, mouths meeting, slow and then fast. We were hard, but I didn't think either of us wanted this to be over yet.

"Can I eat your ass?" Theo asked. "Would you like that?"

I made a helpless little whimper. He knew I liked it—he'd wrung all sorts of noises from me with his tongue. But I said, "Yes," because he wanted to hear it. As much as Theo wanted me to be aggressive with him sometimes and take control, he also loved giving me pleasure. And trying to shock me with his words.

His hot, rambling whispers in my ear did make my blood rush as he maneuvered me onto my stomach, shoving pillows under my hips.

"You have an amazing ass." He spread my cheeks and licked along the crease before dipping low to suck my balls. "You like this?"

"Yes," I answered, loving the sensation of his face at my most intimate places, the faint rasp of stubble perfect. He worked the tip of his tongue inside, and I drew up my knees under me, exposing myself further.

As I shuddered with waves of simmering pleasure, I wanted more. Theo wanted *me*, and even though I'd believed it before, that kernel of doubt and fear I'd stubbornly kept hold of had remained. It had felt seared into me like the memory of the camera flash.

I searched for it as he licked into me, but it truly was gone. I loved Theo, and he loved me. It was just the two of us. No skating, no competition, no *him*. Mike. No Mike. I'd denied myself far too much for far too long.

No more.

"Baby?" Theo kissed the swell of my buttock. "Still with me?"

"Yes." My voice sounded hoarse, and I swallowed hard. "Will you... Do you want to..." It was still difficult to say, which was foolish, I knew. Theo had just been licking me *there*, so I should be able to make this request aloud.

He stretched out on his side, facing me with our cheeks on the mattress, trailing his fingers up and down my spine. "What do you want to do?" An impish grin brightened his face. "Want me to put on my silver medal while I pleasure the champion?"

"No!" How he could joke about it was beyond me, but I had to laugh. He made everything so much easier, and what was love if not that?

I said, "I want you inside me this time," and my pulse raced, my head spinning.

And Theo made it easy.

He rolled me over and knelt between my legs, slowly working his fingers into me while he talked. "It won't hurt, I promise. I mean, maybe a little, but you know that's part of it. And you know what if feels like when you're fucking me. Anytime it's too much, just tell me. Duh, obviously. Right? Right. You're so hot. I feel like you don't believe me, but you're gorgeous. Maybe if I keep saying it you'll come around."

I had to smile. "Maybe."

Grinning, he kissed me, crooking his fingers. I gasped, and he did it again, murmuring against my lips. "Mmm. You like that? I'm going to make you come so hard."

"I didn't the first time."

For a moment, I wondered who'd said that. Somehow the words had slipped out, and I went rigid under him. Why had I said that? Why was I thinking about that terrible first time? I squeezed my eyes shut.

"Hey," Theo whispered, kissing my cheek. He eased out his fingers. "It's okay. Do you want to stop?"

I opened my eyes, shaking my head violently. "No. I want this. Want you." I clutched at his waist.

"Okay. I'm here. I'm not going anywhere. But we can talk first. You know how much I enjoy talking." He rubbed his nose against mine.

A breath whooshed out of me, tension releasing. I tried to

smile, and I was about to say that I didn't want to say anything else—I just wanted him to keep going. But... Perhaps I *did* want to speak.

"It was only that one time with him. Mike. I didn't come, and he took that picture. He was laughing."

Theo's jaw clenched. "I'm sorry. I hate him, and I hate that it happened like that. You deserve so much more. You believe that, don't you?" His eyes searched mine, his face creased. "You don't have to be perfect to deserve the best."

I nodded, but he was still frowning, so I said, "I deserve more."

"You do! Seriously, not just 'more.' You deserve the *best*! I'm going to give it to you. Not just fucking. I mean, I am absolutely going to do my best to fuck your brains out until you're begging to come all over me. A hundred percent. But you deserve everything."

"So do you." I drew him down for a kiss. "You have such a way with words."

Laughing, he sat back on his heels. "I'm eloquent as fuck, right? Articulate. Verbose? Or is that an insult. Hmm."

"Garrulous."

"Oh, that's a good one! I'll have to remember that." He grew serious, brushing a hand over my hair. "Thank you for telling me." He kissed my forehead. "You can always tell me anything."

I nodded. "Now about what you promised..."

"Fucking your brains out?" Grinning, he stroked my cock and squeezed a finger back into my entrance. "I'm on it."

Was he ever.

By the time he had my knees pressed to my chest and his cock buried inside me, I was sweating and moaning and desperate for release. The pain had subsided, and I urged him to move, tugging on him wherever I could reach.

"Prim and proper Henry Sakaguchi begging for it," he teased.

I huffed. "Not prim and proper when I fucked you at the airport."

Cheeks dimpling, Theo laughed. "Coarse language! And good point." He eased back, then thrust hard, making me jolt. "How's that?"

"*Yes.*"

He'd been so patient preparing me, and the fact that patience wasn't his strong suit made it all the better. I told him it felt wonderful, which was the truth. It was nothing like that awful first time, and with Theo, I knew it never would be again.

After we came, he flopped on his back beside me and said, "Let's do that a million more times." Tensing, he pretended to laugh, looking at the ceiling. "No pressure. It's not like we're married. I'm sure you want to fuck a bunch of guys and sow your wild oats and all that stuff."

I explored that idea for a moment in the silence. Then I asked, "Do my oats seem particularly wild?"

He turned his head to face me, his eyes hopeful. "Um, not especially? Well, you *can* be surprisingly wild—which is so hot— but I don't want to make assumptions or put my expectations on you. But really, if I had to say yes or no, I'd say no."

"Correct."

He bit his lip endearingly. "We're together, right? Exclusive?"

"Mm."

"Cool." His face flushed, and he grinned. "That's awesome. And I know we're still young, but I love you, and I love being with you. I don't want anyone else. I don't miss partying. I want to be with you and Esmeralda—and do you think we should move in together? I think so. I practically already live with you, and when you know, you know. But I'm probably jumping the gun. It's not like we're married."

Easing closer, I met his lips and said simply, "Not yet."

Epilogue

Theo

Seven Years Later

"THE CAMERA CREW'S here!"

Henry was across the ice, but I knew he was sighing in resignation at my announcement. He said something to our student, Grace, and she skated off to try her triple Axel again.

Henry watched her as he stroked over to me. The Axel was under-rotated, but she was off the harness now and getting closer. She looked to Henry eagerly, and he gave her an approving nod and a rolling hand motion to keep drilling it. Grace beamed.

Meanwhile, Jialiang gained speed and launched into his quad combo, but his shoulders were way too open on the landing of the Lutz, and he was off balance trying to squeak out the toe on the end. He barely managed a single.

I called, "Who's in charge? Are you just along for the ride? Don't let the jump control you."

Henry added, "Shoulders," as he passed Jialiang and joined me.

We changed into sneakers, both of us wearing our typical black practice pants and jackets. Henry slipped his gloves into his pockets, giving the ice a last longing glance.

Laughing, I tugged his hand. "Come on. I promise there will

238

still be hours of training left when we finish the interview."

He held my hand for a few moments as we made our way around the rink, squeezing my fingers before letting go. Henry didn't really do PDA, though I didn't mind. When we were alone? Hoo boy, did he make up for it.

I leaned in to whisper, "And I promise I'll reward you tonight for agreeing to film this fluff piece."

He didn't look at me, but a little smile tugged on his lips as we passed the snack bar. This arena complex was new, but still an ugly concrete monster like the Ice Chalet. Albeit not painted hideous colors.

Our first coaching jobs had been assisting Manon and Bill, and we still traveled across Toronto once a month to do guest clinics with them, and they returned the favor coming out here west of the city.

The crew was setting up in a small glass-walled conference room overlooking the main ice rink. There were three rinks in the complex, offering a lot of ice time for hockey, skating, and ringette. We often had to navigate the ice with other coaches and their skaters, and as we built our reputation, it was a perfect setup.

We sat side by side in chairs while they unpacked the big lights. Janice Harvey, still going strong, previewed the questions she wanted to ask. Of course she wanted to highlight our relationship—this was a fluff piece to air during the upcoming US Nationals, and the network always wanted personal hooks.

As much as I knew Henry didn't like these questions, he only objected to one. "I don't want to talk about my grandfather."

Mr. Sakaguchi had died recently at a truly freaking amazing hundred years old. It wasn't unexpected, but it still hadn't been easy. Honestly, I didn't want to talk about it either. Henry's family had welcomed me so wholeheartedly.

I missed those afternoons with Ojiichan while he and Henry did their crosswords and I played whatever game I was obsessed with at the moment on my laptop and tried not to shout too much.

"Of course," Janice said. "I'm very sorry for your loss." Her gaze flicked down, and she smiled.

I realized I'd unconsciously reached for Henry's thigh when he'd tensed, my hand still resting there. I squeezed before letting go and said, "Thanks for understanding."

"Of course," she said. "Hey, did you guys get a new house? How much over asking did you bid? My nephew lives in Toronto, and he's been trying for months."

"Yeah, we had to go two fifty over asking. It's insane, but we fell in love with the backyard. There's a nature preserve behind us, so it's really peaceful, but we're still in the burbs."

"Square footage? What's the commute? At least this arena's out of the city."

A makeup person powdered us for camera while Janice and I talked real estate and Henry surely wished he was back on the ice.

When they were ready to roll, Janice asked, "At this time last year, did you even dream you'd be coaching a national champion?"

I answered, "Honestly, we knew Grace was capable, but we didn't expect it for another season or two." I didn't add that the past US champion had choked—hard—and that luck had factored into Grace's win. "We're still learning and growing as coaches, and we're hitting that next level with Grace. She's improved so much this season. We think if she does her best, she can win again."

"And I'm sure you and Grace are looking to the next Olympic Games in two years. After all, you're both Olympic medalists, with Henry of course winning gold in Calgary and silver four years later in Norway. Theo, many were surprised when you retired after Calgary. Did you ever regret it or consider competing again?"

"Nope. I loved touring, and when I started coaching part time, I realized how much I loved helping other skaters. For me, it's more satisfying. It made me fall in love with skating in a new way."

Actually, it made me fall in love with skating full stop as opposed to doing it because I won and was good at it, and that it was what I'd always done.

"Speaking of falling in love, it was even more surprising when the two of you tied the knot a few years after Calgary! How did you keep your relationship a secret from the public for so long?"

Step one: I didn't tell my mother we were getting married until Henry and I eloped in Barbados, I thought wryly.

My sisters were thrilled for me, my dad was happy if I was, and my mom was...a work in progress. She was what she was. I didn't stress about it. Much.

I glanced at Henry and said, "It wasn't that hard, actually. He was still training, and I was touring a lot, so we were long distance for quite a while. But we made it work."

Janice looked to Henry expectantly. He said, "Being apart helped us know we were right together."

I elbowed him playfully. "Now he's stuck with me all day at work *and* at home."

"Not stuck," he said simply, and my heart swelled. Even after all these years, Henry's little declarations made me stupidly happy.

Janice beamed. "And what's the secret to your relationship?"

"If I answer, I'll probably get us in trouble." I winked playfully at Janice as Henry sighed.

She laughed on cue. "Henry, you'd better field this one!"

Most people would make their own joke, but not my Henry. He seemed to genuinely ponder it before he said, "We've always taken care of each other."

It was a miracle I resisted kissing him right then and there.

"As coaches, are you still competitive with each other?" Janice asked Henry.

"No. We have the same goal to make our students the best

they can be. We're still new coaches. We're learning together."

"Do you have a sort of yin and yang approach?"

I answered, "Yeah, I'd say so. Henry's more of the technician. He has such an eye for detail. He's the artist too—he has amazing musicality. I'm the cheerleader."

Janice smiled. "And an excellent one, I'm told. Speaking of music, Grace's long program this season is a piano piece composed by Etienne Allard, the former ice dancer who's your brother's long-time partner, Henry. What was that collaboration like?"

His lips curved into a smile. "Very rewarding. Etienne's quite talented."

Janice refocused on me. "Theo, what's your primary role with students?"

"My job's more about motivating and encouraging them. Especially when they're tired and don't want to do run-throughs. Henry will still do run-throughs all day if you let him."

Janice laughed. "Is it tough to juggle coaching with performing in shows?"

Henry shook his head, and I said, "Not really. The shows tend to be over the holidays or in spring and summer. We take turns performing so one of us is here with our kids."

Her eyes lit up, and she went off script. "Speaking of kids…"

Henry kept his poker face while I laughed and said, "We've got our hands full with our cats for now."

But in a few more years? Hell yeah.

When Henry cradled sweet old Esmeralda and lifted her up onto the top platform of her cat tree that she couldn't climb anymore, it made me love him even more. He'd wait patiently for her to want down and make sure she didn't topple off.

I knew he'd be an amazing dad one day. I was pretty sure I'd be good at it too, and sharing a kid with Henry was a life adventure we'd leap into when it was right.

We answered more questions and moved back to the rink so

they could shoot B-roll of us coaching, especially footage with Grace. With our skates back on, we watched her run through her short program, listening to "Moon River" again. We applauded when she landed her Lutz combination.

"That wasn't so bad, right?" I murmured.

"It was excellent. She has her timing back."

"I meant the interview, and you know it." I shouted, "Head up!" to Grace as she whizzed by. She gave a dazzling smile as though a crowd was watching.

"Mm." In Henry speak, that meant yes.

It ended up taking hours to do all the filming the network crew wanted. We had to get home to feed Esmeralda and her younger sisters Cosette and Eponine. We'd stuck with the Victor Hugo theme. The arena was closing, and I was so ready to get home to our girls, a nice big glass of red, and our favorite weeknight Bolognese.

But I said to Henry, "Want to do your new one before we go?"

His face lit up with one of his still-rare, teeth-exposing smiles. His fingers flew over the laces of his skates, and I went into the booth to start his music. He'd just set new choreography with Annabelle for a show program, and I knew he was dying to practice it.

Alone on the ice, he did run-through after run-through, lost in his own world of edges, spins, and jumps to Ravel's "Bolero." If anyone could do that classic justice, it was my warm, wonderful Henry.

We'd be home soon enough.

THE END

Find out how Sam and Etienne went from friends to lovers!

Will friends become lovers this Christmas?

Sam

People joke that Etienne and I are boyfriends, but whatever.

Sure, I think about him all the time—he's my best friend. If I've missed him way more than I expected when he left to train with a new skating coach, that's because he's so easy to hang with. And yeah, he's gay, but he's not into me. Why would he be? I'm straight.

We're not *boyfriends*.

But now Etienne needs me, so I'm rushing to the mountain village where he's skating in a holiday show. That's what best friends do.

Etienne

I know Sam will never like me the way I like him.

Never *love* me the way I love him.

But now that my competitive skating career might be suddenly ending, I need my best friend by my side. Thank god Sam's spending the holidays with me.

It's okay that he'll never love me back.

It's okay that there's only one bed in this cozy little cabin.

We're best friends. Nothing's going to happen.

Only One Bed is a gay Christmas story from Keira Andrews featuring friends to lovers, bisexual awakening, first times, snowy holiday vibes, and of course a happy ending.

Read Sam and Etienne's swoony romance now!

How did former pairs skater Dev fall in love with his Russian rival?

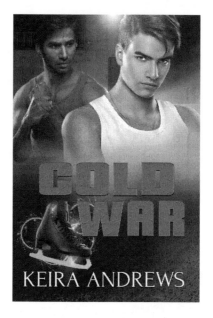

Enemies on the ice. Forbidden lovers in the locker room.

American figure skater Dev despises his Russian rival. Arrogant, aloof Mikhail is like a machine on the ice—barely ever making a mistake.

He's also sexy as hell, which makes him even more infuriating.

Dev and his pairs partner have been working their whole lives to become Olympic champions. He needs to keep his head in the game.

The very worst thing he could do is have explosive hate sex with Mikhail in the locker room after losing to him yet again before the Olympics.

But you know what would be even worse?

Discovering that under Mikhail's icy exterior, he's *Misha*. Passionate and pent-up, he eagerly drops to his knees. His sweet smile makes Dev's heart sing, and his forbidden kisses are unbearably tempting.

Dev must resist.

But he's falling in love.

Only one of them can stand atop the podium. To win gold, will they lose their hearts?

Cold War is a gay sports romance from Keira Andrews featuring enemies to lovers, forbidden hookups blooming into a secret romance, light D/s, alpha men in sequins, and of course a happy ending.

Read Dev and Misha's forbidden romance now!

Thank you so much for reading *Kiss and Cry*! I hope you enjoyed Theo and Henry's journey to their HEA. I'd be grateful if you could take a few minutes to leave a review on Amazon, Goodreads, BookBub, social media, or wherever you like. Just a couple of sentences can really help other readers discover the book. ☺

Wishing you many happily ever afters!

Keira
<3

Join the free gay romance newsletter!

My (mostly) monthly newsletter will keep you up to date on my latest releases and news from the world of LGBTQ romance. You'll also get access to exclusive giveaways, free reads, and much more. Join the mailing list today and you're automatically entered into my monthly giveaway. Go here to sign up: subscribepage.com/KAnewsletter

Here's where you can find me online:
Website
www.keiraandrews.com
Facebook
facebook.com/keira.andrews.author
Facebook Reader Group
bit.ly/2gpTQpc
Instagram
instagram.com/keiraandrewsauthor
Goodreads
bit.ly/2k7kMj0
Amazon Author Page
amzn.to/2jWUfCL
Twitter
twitter.com/keiraandrews
BookBub
bookbub.com/authors/keira-andrews
TikTok
tiktok.com/@keiraandrewsauthor

About the Author

After writing for years yet never really finding the right inspiration, Keira discovered her voice in gay romance, which has become a passion. She writes contemporary, historical, paranormal, and fantasy fiction, and—although she loves delicious angst along the way—Keira firmly believes in happy endings. For as Oscar Wilde once said, "The good ended happily, and the bad unhappily. That is what fiction means."

Made in the USA
Middletown, DE
24 August 2022

72061496R00154